The Imperiled Impostor

*Deception
without
Detection*

Charles E. Lake

BookLocker
Trenton, Georgia

Print ISBN: 978-1-958890-00-4
Ebook ISBN: 979-8-88531-517-3

Published by BookLocker.com, Inc., Trenton, Georgia.

The characters and events in all of the short stories in this book are fictitious. Any similarity to real persons, living or dead, is coincidental and not intended by the author. Events in the anecdotal articles are true but have been expressly described and written to protect the people involved.

Library of Congress Cataloging in Publication Data
Lake, Charles E.
*The Imperiled Impostor *Deception without Detection**
Library of Congress Control Number: 2023909004

Printed on acid-free paper.

Booklocker.com, Inc.
2023

Dedication

It is altogether fitting and appropriate that I dedicate this book to Joyce, my lovely wife, my best friend, and my companion for over 67 years.

There is no loneliness with a companion.

It is no secret that one seeking a happy life would do well in having a Christian companion who shares that life ... together ....

together

yesterday ...
i was
you were
we were
unknowingly

today ...
i am
you are
we be
happily

tomorrow ...
i will be
you will be
we will be
eternally

charles e lake

Preface

Reading fictional stories can be a form of magic. Reading can transport one to locales never visited and allow one to become safely and securely involved in situations never experienced. Reading not only provides entertainment but the magical means of being someone else and to be somewhere else for a short period of time. Louis L'Amour, one of the world's most popular writers, states it best, "*For one who reads, there is no limit to the number of lives that may be lived*". I hope you experience some of that magical transformation as you read *The Imperiled Impostor*.

The idea behind this story began in year 2016 while my wife and I were enjoying a two-month stay in Colorado. Nearly every summer since 1998 we had left the "warmth" of Texas to enjoy the wonderful summers in Summit County, Colorado, some 70 miles west of Denver. There, each summer, we leased a condo or townhouse where we devoted ourselves to hiking, playing duplicate bridge, relaxation, and fellowship with Texas A&M alumni and other friends. I used much of this relaxation time by writing short stories or gathering poems for an anthology.

During that summer of year 2016, I had two short stories well on the way to completion when I had this idea of a new short story regarding a look-alike person deceptively taking the place of an incapacitated CEO of a company being threatened by an unfriendly merger. I invested some 20,000 words toward that story before our summer months in Colorado were over. Even with 20,000 words, the story was far from being completed. I realized I had started a novel and not a short story.

Year 2016 was the last time Joyce and I were in Colorado. Family and health issues have precluded our summer visits in the following years. I did, however, continue writing short stories and gathering material for anthologies, but at a slower pace. I tinkered with the "novel" story line some, but I was not ready to take it on at the expense of completing several short stories I had underway. I wanted to complete and publish my second anthology of short stories which I did in the year 2020. It would be the spring of the year 2022 before I revisited the novel I had started some 6 years earlier. I completed the manuscript of *The Imperiled Impostor* later in the fall of that year.

Word count is the most measurable difference between a short story and a novel[1]. Word count is not the only difference to an author. Novels require much more dedication and focus than short story writing. A novel not only requires more time, but the time also has to be contiguous time. If I were away from writing or thinking about the story for several days, I had to spend considerable time immersing myself back into the world I had created before I could add anything meaningful. So, I found I had to make notes as to what I had previously written. It was helpful to me to have a one sentence note about each chapter with the chapter number, day, character(s), venue, and activity; these notes became part of a chronological spreadsheet where I could easily see the flow of the plot. And with more than 80 characters and over 50 venues, I had to list those proper names and note in what chapter they were first mentioned.

In my short story writing I almost always had the ending well in mind before I began writing the story. In *The Imperiled Impostor* I changed the plot flow and final scenes at least three times.

Perhaps unfairly but maybe with a sense of pride, I suggest writing a short story is like completing one elementary accounting course in college, whereas, writing a novel is like getting a BBA degree in accounting.

To me, the most enjoyable part of writing (besides just finishing it!) is the dialogue between characters.

---

[1] When asked, search engine *Google* surfaced with numerous "experts'" who provided their opinions as to what word count ranges constituted a typical short story and a typical fiction novel. After reviewing their comments, I think a reasonable word count range for short stories is 1,000 to 7,500 words and for fiction novels is 50,000 to 100,000 words. *The Imperiled Impostor* is 74,000+ words.

There is a pleasant surprise element in writing. Sometimes a trivial element written into the beginning of a story can later become the source of an unplanned interesting part of the story. In the *Imperiled Impostor*, for no particular reason, I added a surgical scar to the impostor's leg; that scar became helpful in saving his life later.

Some of you in the younger generation may not be familiar with the names Mutt and Jeff that I gave to the two bozo assassins who kept trying to kill the impostor. The names were from a long-running (1907-1983) syndicated daily newspaper comic strip created by cartoonist Bud Fisher and continued by Al Smith. They were two mismatched tinhorns: Mutt was very tall and lanky; Jeff was very short, bald, and a little overweight.

I am envious of the many people who are able to write or say many meaningful thoughts and stories with little or no editing; I have to shuffle my words, phrases, and even sentences to make my thoughts clear and comprehensible. As a writer without software such as *WORD* I would be like a homestead field worker equipped with a hoe instead of a tractor.

The Imperiled Impostor features two characters who are look-alikes; in fact, they can be classified as doppelgangers. Read the *Postscript* at the end of this book if you would like to read more about look-alikes and doppelgangers.

I hope you find the story of *The Imperiled Impostor* interesting and enjoyable.

Charles E. Lake

Prologue

The incessant ringing of the hotel phone woke Gordon up. He grudgingly answered the phone. *I wonder what great friend I have who wants to talk to me at 4:15 in the morning?*

"Yes?" He said irritably. *He wasn't going to give whoever a polite 'hello'.*

"Dr. Brewer," a quivering voice said, "this is the hotel telephone operator. I'm sorry we had to wake you. We don't allow anyone to call our guests directly at this hour in the morning, but you have a call from California from a person who says he must talk to you immediately. He says his name is Roland Turlington. He says he is the chief attorney of your company."

Gordon's attitude changed immediately. *Roland wouldn't call this way unless it was extremely important.* "Thank you operator for waking me. Yes, put the call through."

Gordon heard a couple of clicks, then Roland's voice asked, "Gordon, are you there? Can you hear me?"

"Yes, Roland. What's going on?"

"Gordon, I have some terrible news. It is really bad. There has been a helicopter crash about 20 miles from our villa. The local police called and advised me that all three occupants of the crash are deceased. They have tentatively identified that two of the passengers are Michael and Marley."

Gordon felt like he was the victim of a low blow. He lost his breath and composure for a few seconds. "How do they know who the victims are?"

"They traced the helicopter and established it was from a Los Angeles charter service. The helicopter's passenger manifest shows a Dr. Michael Langston, the CEO of Langston Industries, and his wife Marley. Michael put our villa's telephone number on the manifest to call if there was an emergency."

"Has there been a positive identification?"

"No. The police requested I make that identification. I'm waiting for them to pick me up and take me to the morgue. I asked Reginald to go with me. Reg has been employed by Michael a lot longer than me; so, together we will do that … I don't look forward to it."

"I completely understand."

"Gordon, what else needs to be done?"

"First, and foremost ... the identification must not be made public unless the victims are not Michael and Marley. Do absolutely nothing else until you make a positive identification. Then, call me. I will be making a to-do list of what our next steps will be."

"Yeah, that's fine; I understand."

"Oh, yes, Roland, by the way, I do have a question. What are you doing at the Langston villa?"

"I spent the night here. I was supposed to meet with Michael on something he'd put off for two years. He wanted me to work out the legalities of a new CEO secession plan."

"Yeah, he told me once he wanted to do that. I don't know anything about the current plan, much less about any new plan."

"Gordon, I don't suppose anyone will ever know what changes Michael had in mind. But, without going into the current plan's details, I'll just say this ... Your new boss is Earl, the Langston's 24-year-old son."

Gordon was glad that Roland could not see his negative reaction. Instead, he merely said, "Roland, get back to me as soon as you can. Goodbye."

"Right! Goodbye, Gordon!"

Gordon remained seated on the edge of the bed for several minutes thinking and grieving the loss of his former boss and friend.

Michael and I worked together for some 25 years making Langston Industries the robust company it is today. I'm really going to miss him and his wife. They were so nice. He was such a good friend as well as a great boss; I liked working for him as the Chief Operating Officer. I'm not looking forward to the days ahead. Earl, you've suddenly and unexpectedly become very important.

(There would not have been any need for *The Imperiled Impostor,* who came into being almost 3 years later, had the helicopter not crashed that night.)

The Imperiled Impostor

*Deception
without
Detection*

One

Nickolas, age 78, the oldest of the three septuagenarians in the room, fished the two beans out of his coat pocket. One bean was white; one bean was black. He turned his back on the other two men, hiding the color of the one bean he placed into the small, opaque dark blue jar on the coffee table the men were holding captive.

"Okay," Nickolas said, "You signori have voted and now so have I. I suggest we have a drink and relax by discussing what property values might be here in Florida the next year or two. Then we can see how the vote turned out."

"Good suggestion, Nick!" said Marcellus. "I'm ready for a little bourbon and investment talk. It takes my mind off of unpleasant things."

Dario nodded his head in agreement and headed toward the well-stocked liquor cabinet.

Each of the men got the drink of his choice and then settled back in their easy chairs and relaxed as they talked about Florida real estate, politics, and some of their other investments. Unlike many other men, they didn't discuss sports or the weather; they had little interest in things they could not financially manipulate or control.

They had these get togethers the third Thursday every month unless they had a called session, like today, because of something important that could affect each of them. They always met at the Indian River Ranch, a 2200-acre recreational property owned by Langston Industries, a company in which each of them was a shareholder and each was on the Board of Directors.

After an hour of conversation and another round of drinks, Dario said, "Signori, I believe the jury has reached a decision."

He fetched the blue jar and in one quick motion flipped it over and set it back on the coffee table upside-down. The three men gave their complete attention to the upside-down jar. Slowly Dario removed the jar, leaving behind its contents: three black beans.

Nickolas flipped his cigarro from side to side in his mouth.

It was Marcellus who announced the results.

"The vote is unanimous, as it has to be. Earl must die!"

The men nodded their consent; then rose and adjourned to the liquor cabinet.

Two

At the same time Earl's grim sentence and outlook were revealed, some 1100 miles to the north Carson Baker was amusing himself near his Uncle Leo's remote upstate New York cabin by target practice with his Glock22 .40 caliber pistol. Well, he was not exactly amusing himself, for he was shooting angrily at a man's image some 25 yards away. Carson wished he were shooting a real person not a target image that he was hitting with great accuracy. Yes, indeed … he wished he were shooting at Earl Langston, a billionaire kid who had great power and authority. Earl who had victimized his 23-year-old sister Isabel almost four years ago.

Yes, he wanted to shoot and kill Earl; but where was he? Despite being the CEO of the huge Langston Industries conglomerate, the scoundrel had not been seen in public since the police reported Isabel had overdosed on cocaine and died. *Isabel had never used drugs until she started attending Earl's parties. Without a doubt, some basic rules are in play: Earl was at fault, Earl must pay; Isabel had died, Earl must die. That's what prison taught me. This is driving me nuts. It's been two months since I had my 8 years in prison. Since I heard about Isabel all I can think about is killing that snotty big-shot kid Langston. I don't need no help, killing ain't new to me. But I got to find him first. Where is he?*

After his target practice was over, Carson began walking back through the heavily wooded trail to his Uncle Leo's cabin about a half mile away. Most people would have enjoyed this walk in these scenic woods that were part of the Adirondack Mountains, but Carson was not most people. And it was a nice day, but Carson didn't feel nice; he had never felt nice. All he could think of was finding and killing Earl. It didn't help his mood to be challenged by Leo's pet Rottweiler when he came within 30 yards of the cabin. Carson and Rottie had taken an instant dislike to each other when Carson had moved into the cabin two months ago. Time had only intensified their dislike. Rottie growled, bared his teeth, snarled, and moved slowly toward this invader to his home. Carson had seen all this before; he was fairly certain the dog wouldn't bite him; but he had had enough of that dog. He took his revolver out of its holster, aimed carefully, and shot Rottie once in the head. The dog yelped once and died immediately.

Carson waited a few minutes to see if Uncle Leo might come out of his cabin. He didn't. Carson went over to where the dog was, grabbed the dead dog by his back legs and dragged him to a part of the woods that was impassable, thick with brush. No need to bury him; Uncle Leo never got this far away from his cabin. Uncle Leo was confined to a wheelchair as the result of a bad accident over 15 years ago.

Carson felt better; one enemy, one distraction removed. He entered the cabin to find Uncle Leo dozing in front of his large TV screen. Uncle Leo woke up and asked, "How'd the target practice go today, Carson?"

"Just fine, Unc."

"Good. Oh, I've been dozin' but I thought I heard a shot close to the cabin about 15 or 20 minutes ago?"

"Yep! That was me. I saw that cougar that's been hanging around the cabin. I took a shot but missed him. Guess my practice ain't doin' much good."

"Well, you'll get him one of these days. Get me a beer, would you, boy?"

"Sure thing, Unc."

Carson retrieved two beers from the refrigerator, gave one to his uncle, then went outside. *I'm tired of waiting here. I'm going to make another attempt to find Earl. I'm going to Los Angeles one more time to see if Earl is at LI's Holmby Hills house. I staked out that house a month ago, but I never saw*

Earl. I'll try again. Once more won't hurt. He retrieved his cell phone and made reservations through United … he would fly to LA early the next day.

Three

California had not enjoyed the beautiful weather that the East Coast had enjoyed that day. For the last 10 hours a blinding torrential rain had blistered California's central coast, the Big Sur area all the way up to San Francisco. Now, just before midnight, there was nothing to be seen except rain and nothing to be heard except the roaring wind. With a storm like this one, residents of this desolate coastal area worried about the ever-present danger of mudslides.

Only a bull-headed, reckless fool would attempt to drive here, in this weather, through this cliff area with its narrow, winding road. The fool came, driving a Porsche. He was driving it recklessly, like there was no today, much less tomorrow. The result was only a matter of when and where. The Porsche skidded off the road and went over the cliff, into the abyss that waited greedily for its visitor, its guest.

Jose had witnessed it all. He and his wife were huddled in their beat-up van, parked on the opposite side of the road from the cliff and the ocean. Jose was wisely waiting for the heavy rain to let up so it would be safer for him to drive. The fool's car was the only one he had seen in the last hour. He was able to see the unforced accident even though it was raining steadily and heavily. Jose's first thought was to ignore what he had seen ... *there will be no reward and possibly even punishment for an illegal alien to get involved. They say I'm illegal, but I'm loyal, I love this country. I don't want my family to be sent back to Columbia.*

Conscience and his wife Maria, who also witnessed the accident, got the better of him ... she told him to go see if the driver had survived. He grudgingly put on his raincoat and trudged out into the bad weather to the edge of the cliff where the car had disappeared. The rain and wind were bad, bad, bad. He was getting wet, wet, wet and cold, cold, cold. Despite his discomfort he peered over the edge of the cliff. Down below he saw the wreckage of the car at the base of the cliff. It was burning despite the rain. He was also able to see the fool's body that had evidently been thrown clear of the car about 50 feet below on a ledge ... he couldn't reach the car or the driver, but he would call 911 and let the authorities know. He was sopping wet and cold when he got back in the car, but his wife was satisfied that they had done what was necessary. *Dare I tell her, next time we must investigate something in bad weather, it will be your turn? No, probably not.*

Four

Dr. Gordon T. Brewer was up early as usual. As was his business-based habit while in California, he had showered, shaved, and dressed by five in the morning. Five was early enough to be available to accommodate and address any business concerns his people on the East Coast might have. His people were the more than 43,000 employees of the medium-size conglomerate known as Langston Industries. Gordon was the Chief Operating Officer of Langston ... boss of all employees in the company except Earl J. Langston, the Chief Executive Officer, only son of the late founder: Dr. Michael X. Langston. Gordon had worked his way up and attained his COO position by hard work. Earl had attained his CEO position by inheritance. Therein was the problem. Gordon was experienced and very competent; Earl was smart but young, inexperienced, and stubborn. A bad combination of attributes for an executive. Gordon had thought about this problem for the last several years ... maybe it was time for him to move on.

Gordon walked out of the 5-bedroom seaside villa to have breakfast, seated beneath a sheltered patio that overlooked the Pacific Ocean and the California coastline. The ocean was always pleasant to view with its white caps and tidal waves that crashed relentlessly against the rock formations that jutted out from the cliffs and up through portions of the narrow sandy beach. The heavy rain from the night before was over; only the lack of a full morning sun, courtesy of a slight fog, caused the view to be merely attractive, not stunning. Such a beautiful view. He never tired of the view.

The seaside villa and 120-acre estate were situated on a singular oceanfront promontory, surrounded on three sides by cliffs and the ocean some 400 feet below. It was a gated estate with no neighbors. Magnificent! The villa was Dr. and Mrs.

Langston's residence when they were alive. Now, by inheritance it was Langston Industries' property with the stipulation that son Earl could live in it free of charge until he became 30 years old. Gordon regretted that he didn't come here more often. After all, Earl was here infrequently and it was owned by Langston Industries, serving as a guesthouse for Langston VIPs and special guests, but somehow Gordon only came when he had Earl in tow.

The year-round villa caretakers, an older couple named Reginald and Greta, were already up and about. Greta, who did all the cooking and interior housework, had a gourmet breakfast as usual. Gordon had no business calls, so he enjoyed a pleasurable trip through the meal and then settled back to relax in his chair with a second and third cup of coffee.

As he took in the scenic view and drank his coffee, Gordon's thoughts slipped back to the past. *What a great job I had when Earl's father, Dr. Michael Langston, hired me over 25 years ago. We were a great team. Michael had all the great ideas and I made them happen. We grew this company from almost nothing to the great, strong conglomerate it is today. It's just too bad that Michael and his wife had been killed in that helicopter crash. Hmm … that crash was almost three years ago.*

But, it is what it is. After Michael was killed, Earl took over through his inheritance. I guess Michael thought he would live forever; it's really his fault there was such a poor CEO succession plan. Bad … unbelievably bad. Earl is not only inexperienced; he does not listen nor take advice. After his dad was killed, he's become reclusive and introverted, probably hasn't been seen in public for two years or so. I'm not sure how long we can survive with him in charge. It's sure not working very well now. Maybe I should …

Martin came out on the patio, interrupting his nostalgic thoughts. Martin said, "How's everything going this morning, boss? Anything I need to be doing?"

Good ole Martin. Gordon's friend and working companion for the last seven years. Nothing seemed too difficult or too menial for Martin to handle in a cheerful and faultless, competent manner. Gordon's close friendship with Martin began in the Marines. After Gordon left the Marines, he had very little contact with Martin. But, then one Sunday afternoon some seven years ago he got a call from Martin who said, "Hey, Gordon, I got a request. I just completed my 25 years in the Marines and I'm sorta tired of the military; I'd like to do something else. You know me pretty well; I'd especially like to work for you if you have anything. I'll do anything you need done ... I just like to be kept busy."

Martin's request was a no-brainer. Gordon hired him immediately and made him his assistant. He needed an aide, a travel partner, a trustworthy, honest person who could help him with small, insignificant tasks as well as large, important projects. Martin was the ideal man for Gordon, and vice-versa. So, here Martin was, early in the morning, nudging Gordon for something to do.

Gordon replied, "Yeah, I've got somethin' for you to do! Sit down and have a cup of coffee and help me enjoy this view."

Martin said, "Okay, if you insist."

He plopped down alongside Gordon and they enjoyed their coffee, the view, and some 15 minutes of idle chatter.

Then Reginald brought them some more coffee and some bad news: "Sorry to bother you, Dr. Brewer, but I wanted you to be aware that Mr. Langston took a Porsche out last evening and hasn't come back."

Gordon shook his head ... "Well, isn't that just dandy! There goes this morning's 10 o'clock briefing and our 1 o'clock conference call.

"Martin, we both have something to do right now. We need to make some calls and a bunch of schedule changes today and maybe tomorrow if Earl doesn't get back soon. I just can't believe he went anywhere in weather like we had last night.

“Reginald, thanks for the heads-up. Please bring me my laptop. Martin and I will work out here this morning. I’m not giving up on this view and this nice day so easily.”

Five

Two mornings later Gordon wasn't entertaining any idyllic thoughts as he had the mornings before. Even having a mid-morning snack on the patio overlooking the beautiful view couldn't brighten his outlook and feelings. Earl didn't return yesterday. Not only had he not returned, but he also hadn't called, either. Unfortunately, all of Gordon's business plans and briefings were now on hold. *Well, it's not like this hadn't happened before. But this helps me make up my mind ... After the next board of directors meeting, I'm going to test the job market, I'm not going to spend the rest of my career being a warden or a mother-hen.*

It was Reginald who managed to interrupt his therapeutic thoughts of a new job.

"Dr. Brewer, there's a man from the sheriff's office at the front door. He asked me, 'if there is anyone here from Langston Industries, I'd like to see him.'"

"Sure, Reginald, bring him out here to the patio. And have Greta bring us some fresh coffee and rolls."

Reginald came back in a minute or so accompanied by a white, overweight, middle-aged man in a khaki uniform, sporting a sheriff's badge on his left shoulder pocket. He wore his uniform pants low, despite the presence of a protruding stomach.

"Howdy," he said. "My name is Fred Cochran. I'm the sheriff of this here county."

Gordon rose to his feet, gave the sheriff a hearty handshake and said, "Hi, sheriff. I understand you'd like to see someone from Langston Industries? I'm your man ... my name is Gordon Brewer. I'm Langston's Chief Operating Officer; I hope this isn't about my tax return!"

The sheriff laughed, "No, no, nothing like that."

Gordon said, "Well, maybe I can help you. Let's sit down by the table and help ourselves to some goodies that are coming our way."

At that moment Greta entered, bringing the coffee and rolls. Gordon courteously introduced both Greta and Reginald to the sheriff; then both of them left giving Gordon and the sheriff some privacy.

The two men helped themselves to Greta's offerings; then Gordon asked the question, "What brings the sheriff of Big Sur out to visit us this morning?"

"Mr. Brewer, there was an accident near Lucia Lodge a couple of nights ago. It looks like one of your vehicles was involved ... I came here to check that out. We ran the license number on the car and found it was a car registered to Langston Industries. Can you help me?"

Gordon managed not to change his facial expression, but his mind was racing full blast. *It must be our Porsche and it must be our Earl ... what kind of mess has he got us into now? I wonder if he's dead or if he's killed someone. This could be a lawsuit of gigantic proportions!*

He was able to produce a smile and then replied, "I probably can help ... Langston Industries owns this property as a perk for our management and their visitors. We keep several company cars out here for their use. We can check that out pretty quickly. Whatcha got?"

"It's a 2021 Porsche, California memorial plates MXL103."

"Well, I'm pretty sure that's one of ours. Those plates sound like our personalized plates that have our founder's initials on them. I'll double-check to make sure."

Gordon got his cell phone and selected Reginald's number. He leaned back away from the table and held the phone tightly against his ear so the sheriff couldn't hear Reginald's responses. When Reginald answered, Gordon said, "Reginald, do we have a 2021 Porsche, with license plates MXL103?"

Reginald stuttered, "Why, uh yes, sir. Uh, yes, sir. That ...That's the car I told you about yesterday."

"And you say it's not in the garage?"

"Oh, no, sir. No, sir. It's not there. I don't know where it is."

"Thank you, Reginald."

Gordon hung up. He nodded his head as he said, "Well, you found the owner, Sheriff. It's our car. Was anyone killed or injured? I sense there's a problem since the law's involved. Do I need to get in touch with our insurance company and a lawyer before we talk further?"

"Oh, I don't know about that ... let me give you some more info first. By the way, do you have a business card?"

"Yes, I do." Gordon fished a card out of his pocketbook and handed it to the sheriff.

The sheriff examined the card without comment and then said, "Well, here's the situation, Dr. Brewer. This was a one-car accident."

Gordon was beginning to feel better, but he didn't say anything.

The sheriff continued, "The driver of this car went off the road over a cliff in that terrible rain a couple of nights ago ... there was a witness who told us the car was just going too fast. Nothing we found seems to tell us anything different, although we do know the driver had been drinking some.

"Anyway, the driver was thrown from the car and landed on a ledge ... lucky for him because the car went all the way to the bottom of the cliff. And, even despite that night's monsoon, the car exploded and burned all the way down to its chassis. Couldn't tell it was a Porsche at first."

"Was there anyone else in the car or anyone else that was hurt?"

"Not that we know of."

"Good! How's the driver?"

"Not sure, really. He's on the critical list at the Community Hospital up in Carmel. That was the nearest hospital from the accident, but I know it's a good one. Course I'm a little prejudiced since my daughter is a RN and works there some 36 to 60 hours a week."

"Critical list? What's the problem?"

"Well, they can tell you more up there. All I know is that he's got a few broken bones and is unconscious ... hasn't come to since the accident."

"I'm glad he's alive. That's a big relief and him not hitting or hurting no one else is a huge relief!"

"Yep, I can see why your company would like that. I need to tell you, though, that the hospital wants to know who the fellow is and who's going to pay his hospital bill."

"They don't know who he is?"

"Nope, we went through his clothing. No ID on him ... no pocketbook, no credit cards, no ID, no nothin' ... just a wad of hundred-dollar bills. Any idea who he is? I assume since he's driving a car from here, he's probably a guest or employee here. Or, I guess he could be a thief."

Gordon thought fast. *It was time to put his CEO cover-up plan in effect; something he had prepared for but hoped he never had to use, sort of like his medical insurance policy.*

He shrugged his shoulders and said, "Oh, that's probably Carl Bergstrom ... he's a problem employee for us ... seems like he goes somewhere and always leaves a trail. He does this kind of thing occasionally and we have to go pick up the pieces and fix any problems that he might have caused."

"Carl Bergstrom, you say? Why didn't he have any ID on him?"

"You'd have to ask him ... probably for the reason as to what happened ... he caused a problem and didn't want anyone to know who he was.

"Tell you what ... I'll go over to the hospital to make sure this is who we're talking about and if so, take care of the bills. After I do that, I'll bring his ID over to you and take care of any police matters then. Sound okay to you?"

"Yep, sounds reasonable. I'll see you then. Let me give you my card; the directions to my office are on the back."

The sheriff handed Gordon a business card as the two men were leaving the patio and walking to where the sheriff had parked his pickup truck.

"Oh, one other question, sheriff. Did Carl do any property damage besides the car?"

"Nope. Haven't seen any and nothing has been reported."

They shook hands and Gordon said, "This matter is sort of sensitive to our company. I hope it won't receive a lot of publicity."

The sheriff replied, "Don't see why it would … just keep me informed."

"You bet … and thanks! Come back anytime!"

"Sure! See ya!"

Gordon turned back to enter the villa as the sheriff drove away.

Gordon thought, *I need to talk to the Florida guys, but I've got to get my stuff together first.*

Six

The next afternoon Gordon was ready to talk to the Florida guys. He was sitting alone in the seaside villa's office, located at the south end of the villa near the outdoor swimming pool. The office had been custom built; it was soundproof, had conference-like telephone, telecommunications and computer equipment and featured security measures that would make most government organizations proud. He had arranged this 1pm call yesterday, not knowing at that time what exactly he was going to do or say, but very necessary to keep those guys informed or they would be all over him. He certainly didn't want those guys to hear about Earl's accident from another source.

Those Florida guys: that would be Nickolas Fontano and the Bruno brothers Dario and Marcellus. All wealthy, all in their 70s, and all obstinate. Gordon was sure they were well-connected mob chiefs, probably semi-retired. How Michael got in with them he didn't know; all he knew was that they were the ones that provided Michael with the initial funding and whatever else that helped Michael and the company become wildly successful. If these guys had been providing funds for a theater production, they would have been called angels. However, these guys are no angels. And the problem is: once in bed with them, there's no way to say goodbye.

The Florida guys had a large ownership in the company and while Michael was alive, they seemed friendly and just a loosely formed, social group of investors who, as far as Gordon knew, had not interfered with Michael's decisions and management of the company. But that changed with Michael's death. Two months after he died, they formed what they called the FSC, the Florida Signore Council and they began their direct, hands-on management of the company. The FSC members could not be ignored. They were three of the eight members of the Langston Board of Directors.

The FSC met monthly at Langston Industries' Indian River Ranch in Florida. The 2200-acre ranch was used to host hunting and fishing groups year-round. In the center of the property was an impressive lodge surrounded by the caretaker's home and six other two-bedroom guest residences that remained unoccupied much of the time. One room in the 6100 square foot lodge was dedicated for business purposes: it was sealed off from all the rooms in the house including the beautiful leisure/assembly room that housed a massive stone fireplace. The business room had the same conference-like equipment and security features as the office Gordon was calling from in California.

From their monthly meetings the FSC made all their decisions, issued all their instructions, and made all their threats directly to Gordon. Only Gordon's aide Martin was aware of the council's existence and their interference and intimidation.

Promptly at one o'clock the call began. Gordon made his usual, cordial greeting and ensured that the telephones had their scramblers on. Dario's first comment was, "What's going on, Brewer? You know we don't like these kinds of calls where we have to get together at the last minute."

Gordon replied, "I don't like them either, but in my judgment, you needed to know what's going on.

"Earl has pulled another stunt. He was in an auto accident, totaled the car but fortunately hurt only himself. He broke some bones and was taken unconscious to a local hospital. Police tried to ID him, but he had no ID ... they traced the car to us here at the coastal villa. Fortunately, I knew that Earl had a fake driver's license that he used for his California escapades. I found the license and showed it to the police and the hospital; then smoothed everything over with dollars. They're satisfied. They believe he's a rogue Langston employee named Carl Bergstrom and leaving it up to us to administer punishment. They also agreed to minimize any publicity."

Nickolas interrupted, "Well, what happens when Earl wakes up or will he?"

Gordon replied, "The hospital folks don't know whether he will ever wake up or remain comatose ... some kind of trauma they said.

"I worry about him being and staying unconscious. So, if he remains comatose another week, I will move him to a more private setting... one that our company will set up and maintain. However, I've talked to his doctors, and they are very optimistic that he will be conscious within a week. I'm keeping everything quiet for now. If he doesn't awaken fairly soon, I'll have to release a statement to the media."

"Is that it? Anything else, Brewer?" Dario asked.

"No, that's it."

"Make sure there's no publicity and don't make a statement to the media until we tell you to. We'll talk this situation over and if there's anything we want you to do we'll call you."

"Right."

"One other question, Brewer. What's the name of the hospital where Earl is at?"

"It's the Community Hospital at Carmel."

The phone clicked; the line went dead; the phone conversation was over; the Florida guys had hung up. Gordon was used to their abrupt phone call endings. Actually, he was glad the conversation was over; the less time he spent on the phone with the council, the better. But he didn't like that last question. It didn't sound right. Why *would they want to know the exact hospital where Earl was? They never talk to him outside the board meetings ... something doesn't sound right. I need to get him out of there as soon as possible. But I have a 30-minute opening in my day right now. I'm going to go back to the patio, have a martini, and enjoy the scenic view. Why don't I come here more often?*

It was Nickolas who actually terminated the phone call from the council. Dario, Marcellus, and Nickolas were still sitting in their judgmental seats around the coffee table, toying with their drinks.

Nickolas opened the conversation, "So there was good news and bad news. Our boy Earl had a bad accident, but he survived."

Marcellus replied, "We almost got lucky … and, we still might."

Dario chimed in, "We can't take the chance that we would be, as you call it lucky. What's happening with our contract with Rico?"

Nickolas responded, "Rico called me yesterday. He's given the contract to Mutt and Jeff. You know those two: a tall guy and a short one. I didn't particularly like that; I don't think they're Rico's first team, but Rico and his boys haven't failed us before, and he knows the penalty for failure."

Dario angrily said, "So what are they doing? Just hanging around a beach somewhere hoping Earl will come by?"

Nickolas replied, "Of course not! I told him there was no particular rush right now. They found out Earl would be in Europe next month and thought it would be better to stage an accident over there. He realizes that our contract calls for Earl's death to look accidental."

Marcellus said, "Europe plan sounds okay to me, Nick. But why don't we take advantage of Earl's current situation? It's tailor-made for an accidental death. Let's call Rico and tell him where Earl is."

Dario said, "Wait! Wait! I don't trust Gordon! First, let's call the hospital to see if they have a patient named Carl Bergstrom. If so, get his room number."

Nickolas and Dario nodded their heads in agreement. Their decision made; Marcellus reached for the telephone.

Seven

After the long call to the Florida guys and a short visit with a martini, Gordon spent the next hour on the telephone. He had been concerned from the start that someone would discover Earl was in the Community Hospital under the name Carl Bergstrom. That was a worry in itself, but now he had very bad vibes emanating from Florida. Accordingly, he realized he had to get Earl out of that hospital asap. He had already decided if Earl was still incapacitated when he was moved from the hospital, he would be transported to Langston's vacation house in the 1000 Islands. Those arrangements had already been made; it was just a matter of giving the go-ahead signal. The move would now take place early tomorrow morning. Good judgement and quick, decisive actions were reasons Gordon had become the top executive at Langston.

Now it was time to take care of the really big problem. He asked Martin to join him on the patio.

Gordon asked, "Martin, I know you've got some Langston projects going. Is there anything that strictly requires you? Or can you off-load it to someone else?"

Martin responded, "I can reassign all my stuff in a couple of hours."

Gordon was pleased. He said, "Great! Do that! I need you full time on this situation we have with Earl."

Gordon continued, "Let me bring you up to date. Earl will be moved from the hospital tomorrow morning and transported by one of our planes to our place in 1000 Islands. He will be accompanied by a small medical staff. He will have round-the-clock, private and isolated medical help there ... the medical staff will only know him as Carl Bergstrom. It's going to cost a bundle, but it's a remote location away from media coverage. We can keep him there until we decide what's next. He's been out of public sight for over two years, so he won't be missed right away. However, he's scheduled to make the board meeting and some public appearances beginning in six weeks. That's a huge task if Earl remains incapacitated. I'll tell you how we're going to approach that task in a few minutes. First, do you have any questions about moving Earl?"

Martin thought for a few seconds and then asked, "Only one. Who's riding shotgun on the Earl move?"

Gordon replied, "Thanks, Martin. Missed that one. Do you remember Lincoln Smith? He was head of security two years ago before he took early retirement. I was able to recruit him for this task. He knows the whole deal, including Earl's fake identity. He said he could give me three months and I think that will be adequate ,,, we'll either be winners or losers by that time. Link knows Earl, he knows the importance of secrecy, and he knows the importance of security. As I mentioned before, everyone else thinks they are transporting and caring for Carl Bergstrom. Link will stay with Earl up to three months or when no longer needed."

"Great choice. Link is a good guy and a pro."

Gordon said, "I think that problem is under control. A much bigger problem remains. Earl hasn't made any public appearances in two years. Under our current circumstances I would like it to be for at least three years. He is scheduled to vote in a Board of Directors meeting, attend a movie premiere, attend a LI financial review in Europe, and last, but not least, the 80th birthday of his grandmother. The one that can't be missed is the Board of Director's meeting. The Board is meeting to vote on a tender offer that would result in a buyout and takeover by Kesterson Industries. We do not want that takeover. When I say we, I include Earl. If he's not there to vote, the tender offer will be accepted, the takeover will go through. The stakes are high. The jobs of all our employees will be negatively affected.

"I want to protect our company from this company raider called Kesterson Industries. I want to create a look-alike who will be Earl for the next two months or more. I want to give Earl time to heal so he will be able to veto the tender offer. My plan is risky and probably has a generous 20% chance of working. If this plan fails, I will probably face criminal charges. If Earl were to die before the board meeting, I would abort this plan and let the BOD vote without him. The bottom line is this: we need to hire and educate an Earl look-alike or double within the next four weeks. It is risky, but I will see it through. Martin, you've always been very loyal, but this one is so risky perhaps you should turn aside and not risk your career."

Martin laughed and said, "Whadda talking about, Boss? You trying to shut me out of the fun? Give me a break! How can I help?"

"We have to find a look-alike right away, so we have time to school him to be Earl."

After Martin left, Gordon took care of other company business for almost an hour. Then he happened to think about a social event where he and other LI managers got together. *That event was about six months ago. The southwest regional manager was talking and laughing about a stage show he saw in Los Angeles. I remember the guy said he thought Earl was one of the performers in the show. In fact, he even went backstage after the show to congratulate him and was really embarrassed to find out it wasn't Earl at all. What a lucky break this might be!*

Gordon had Martin rejoin him on the patio to brief him on a possible candidate to be Earl. He told him about the manager's conversation and asked him to follow up immediately. "Find the actor; see if he looks like Earl, but don't talk to him. If he looks okay, get his picture, complete history from birth and learn everything he ever did or aspired to do. Call me immediately if he's even close to being a good candidate. Of all the candidate's qualifications, looking like Earl is the most important."

In the meantime, Carson wasn't looking for a look-alike; he wanted to find the real one. If Carson had known his intended victim was lying helpless in some fairly nearby hospital, he would have been by his bedside immediately. But, thanks to Gordon's successful deceptions, Carson still had no idea where Earl was. Nor did anyone else except Gordon and Martin.

Carson had made his planned trip to California and was now in Los Angeles, staking out LI's Holmby Hills house. There had been no activity for two days until a middle-aged man arrived alone in a BMW. *He had been in the house since then; nobody had come in or out. Still no Earl. Where is he?*

Having lost a lot of unproductive time and grasping at yet another straw, Carson did some detective work on the internet. The only possibility that he could find was a reference regarding Earl's father. At the time of his death, Dr. Langston owned a seaside home in the Big Sur. *Maybe Earl is there. There's no address, but I know the Big Sur is sparsely populated; I can probably find it. People in the area would know where the home of a notable person like Dr. Langston was.* So, Carson decided to leave LA and go up to the Big Sur. He was frustrated but determined and resolute; Earl couldn't hide forever.

Eight

Sherry Miller sat in front of her computer monitor completing the requisite discharge papers for a patient named Carl Bergstrom. This was crazy, but she was complying with her instructions. Even with all the movie stars and notables who breezed their way through the hospital, she had never, ever discharged a patient at 2 o'clock in the morning. Not only the time was crazy, so was allowing a patient to be discharged early from a care standpoint. Consequently, there were extra papers and signatures involved so that the hospital would not have any liability once the patient left the hospital premises. Someone had pulled some powerful strings to make this happen. On top of that, her dad called her around 6 o'clock last night and said, 'Sherry, we talked before about that young man who had the terrible accident, and you knew as sheriff I am investigating the whole incident. Well, the company he works for wants him out of there asap and they're working with hospital admin to make that happen. Just so you know, it's okay for my sheriff's jurisdiction to allow that. Don't worry about that when it comes to his discharge. I know you're curious, but it's nothing to worry about. We'll talk about it at a later time when you make it up this way to visit.'

So, there it was and there it is. Grasping the clump of papers in her hand Sherry walked down to room 408 and started the paper signing regimen with a nice looking senior named Lincoln Smith who was accompanied by two younger, athletic-looking men. Sherry handed the paperwork to Mr. Smith; he scanned it quickly, signed a few documents, and initialed a lot of others. That chore done, the three men, along with the ex-patient in a gurney bed, moved down the hall to the elevator on their way to a waiting ambulance. There were some thank-yous and other pleasantries exchanged, then they left the hospital. Sherry went back to her desk and her normal 3rd shift duties.

Sherry thought she was through with the strange stuff, but she wasn't. A couple of hours later, a short, muscular man appeared at her desk seemingly out of nowhere. In a rather gruff voice, he said, "Lady, I'm a good friend of Carl Bergstrom. I went down to his room and there ain't nobody there. Where is Carl?"

Sherry didn't like his manners, tone of voice, and the fact he was on the floor outside of visiting hours. She decided she'd play dumb. She replied, "Oh, Mr. ....?" Pausing, waiting for a reply.

"What's my name have to do with anything? Where's Carl?"

"I'm not sure. Let's go see. I believe he's in room 410."

Impatiently, the visitor said, "No, he's in room 408. That's what I was told, that's where I've been, and that's where my partner is."

"Let me look that up." She fiddled with the computer monitor, then said, "You're right it's 408. Let's go see."

Sherry and the agitated visitor began their walk down the hall to 408.

Opening the door to 408, Sherry saw a very tall man, sitting in a chair with his feet propped on the bed. "Oh," she said, "I thought for a minute you were Mr. Bergstrom."

"Obviously, I'm not" came the sarcastic reply.

Sherry looked apologetic, shook her head and sweetly said, "I'm sorry gentlemen. Sometimes our records aren't updated quickly. I'll call registration and see if we can find him."

Ten minutes later Sherry returned to 408 where the two impatient, unhappy men were waiting. She said, "Well, gentlemen, it appears he has checked out of the hospital."

"When?"

"I forgot to ask. Would you like me to try to find out?"

"No, no! Who checked him out and where did they go?"

"Someone from his company signed him out. As to where, they didn't say. All we have is the company mailing address.

May I get that for you?" Sherry smiled very sweetly again as if she was doing them a terrific favor.

The two angry men left 408 and headed for the elevator. Sherry said to herself, *I enjoyed every minute of that. The next time I visit dad, I'll tell him; I'm sure he'll enjoy it.*

Nine

The black limo arrived and parked in front of the theatre at 11 pm sharp as scheduled. The informally dressed chauffeur moved from his driver's seat to open the passenger door for Trace. Trace asked, "Are you Martin?"

Martin replied, "Yes, I am, Mr. Reinhardt. Please get in. Our drive will take about 20 minutes."

Trace entered the limo and took his seat in the rear compartment. In a few seconds they were on their way. No words were exchanged between the two for the remainder of the ride. Trace settled back in his seat and enjoyed the solitude. They reached their destination in exactly 18 minutes; it was a large, nice-looking, but not extravagantly looking, two-story house in Holmby Hills. *Looks are deceiving. I know there's no poor or middle-class people living in this neighborhood.*

Martin escorted Trace through the front door of the house and into the library where Gordon was waiting. As Trace entered the library Gordon arose from his chair by the fireplace and greeted Trace, "Good evening, Mr. Reinhardt!" he said. "May I get you a drink before we begin our conversation?"

"Yes." was the reply. "Make mine black coffee with nothing added."

"Of course, an excellent choice." The host nodded to Martin, the chauffeur, now turned butler. "Please bring Mr. Reinhardt and me some black coffee and have plenty of refills available."

At this point Gordon shook hands with Trace and said, "Mr. Reinhardt, just for this conversation, please call me Victor ... not my real name, just a moniker we will use for now. If you don't mind, I will call you Trace."

Trace nodded his okay and his understanding.

Gordon continued, "I'm glad you came, Trace. I have a business proposition for you. If you decide to accept the deal I will be offering, I will share my real name and who I represent. My offer to you will not require anyone else's approval ... what I offer, I can produce."

Trace said, "Pardon me from interrupting, but maybe my agent should be here."

"Mr. Reinhardt, do not worry about your agent, Mr. Kenneth J Jones. He will be handsomely rewarded if you take my deal; we will either buy your contract from him or pay him a generous commission ... either way he will be taken care of and left with nothing but good thoughts of his relationship and parting of the ways with you. Along those lines we will also take care of your current contract with your theatre group as well as your understudy, who I'm sure will be happy to assume your role. Let me assure you that people affected by your leaving will be handsomely rewarded and will not feel jilted, shall we say. I tell you this so that you will consider my offer without worrying about hurting friends or business associates in any way."

"I do find that rather amazing, Victor. Why am I so desired?" Trace paused before continuing, "I know it's not my good looks."

Gordon aka Victor smiled, "Oh, I don't know, Trace ...perhaps it is, perhaps it is. Let's discuss my offer. I see that Martin has brought coffee for us ... let's sit and enjoy a cup."

At that point they both seated themselves in front of the fireplace. Trace had his first chance to really look around and see the beauty of the library and its furnishings. However, he saw nothing or had heard nothing that could help him identify who he was dealing with. *I don't know whether I'm in a good situation or a bad movie. Yikes! Maybe they're holding me for ransom? Boy, are they going to be disappointed!*

"Again, my question, Victor. What makes me so valuable that you would buy me out of my current situation if I accept your offer?"

"For now let's just say you are uniquely qualified. If you accept my offer, your question will be fully answered.

"Let me give you the ground rules of my offer. I will give you an overview of a job essentially made to order for you and your acting ability. I will tell you the job requirements, its pay, and its tenure. When I'm through I will give you 30 minutes to ask questions and another 30 minutes to think it over. If you find the job is unacceptable to you, our conversation will be over and Martin will take you back to your hotel, to your theatre contract, to your agent, and most notably, to your life. That's not a threat; it's just reality. What I offer will definitely be a life-changing experience. But if you do decline the job, you will sign a non-disclosure agreement about this conversation and for that I will pay you $5,000 in cash. There will absolutely be no fallout from your refusal; we will accept your decision and we will both go our separate ways as if this conversation never took place. You would not hear from us again unless we find out you broke the terms of the non-disclosure agreement. I suggest to you that breaking the non-disclosure agreement would be a very bad decision: it would probably damage or even ruin your acting career. Do you understand?"

"So far, yes."

"On the bright side, if you accept the offered job, you will sign a different, more binding non-disclosure agreement that will immediately make you an employee of mine and the beneficiary of a large sum of money. Your acceptance would also mean that I will take care of your current contracts as I mentioned before. With your acceptance of the job, I will tell you all the details about who I am, who I represent, and specific details about the job itself. Your "what makes me so valuable" question will be answered fully then."

"Interesting! Let's proceed ... I'm still puzzled ... do you want me to tell you about myself?"

"No, it's not necessary. I think we pretty well know your history, Trace. Highlights: Excelled as a High School athlete in all major sports; dropped out of college after one semester;

enlisted and served in the Marines for eight years; toured Europe by bike one year; toured the Pacific as a member of a yacht crew one year; graduated from NYC Film Academy with a major in drama; and had several acting jobs on live stage since, although nothing on TV or the movies. Married six years, widowed. Parents deceased, no siblings. Pals around primarily with his theatre group. Dates frequently, but no steady girlfriend."

"I'm impressed. What size shoes and shorts do I wear?"

"I might have that information, if you need help remembering."

"No! I think I had better be quiet and just stay impressed."

"Are you on good terms with your former in-laws?"

"Hardly any terms at all. Never close. Haven't seen or heard from them in over five years. They might not even recognize me."

"Good! So, Trace, why'd you turn to acting after being in the military? Isn't that unusual?"

"Probably, especially if you're a Shirley Temple or a Marilyn Monroe. But not unusual if you're a Steve McQueen, a Lee Marvin, a George C Scott or a Humphrey Bogart. I fall in that group. You'd have to ask those guys as to why they went from the military into acting."

"Ask 'em? Well, I would, but aren't those guys dead?'

"Yes! I suppose I need some better references. My answer and maybe theirs was I left the Marines with no marketable skills, nothing that could lead to a career or occupation. In the Marines I did learn how to kill a man with a bayonet or quietly with my bare hands. Maybe that's the skill you're looking for?"

"No! You don't need those qualifications for this job. However, that's an excellent reminder for me to be nicer to you. Maybe your Marine skills would be a second career for you after this one."

He pauses, then continues. "Actually, for this job, your acting experience will help you the most. I also understand you're a very good impressionist ... that too will be very helpful."

"Yes. I think I'm a good impressionist; I can usually study someone and pick up on his speech and mannerisms quickly and accurately. I don't think I'll have a problem with that. Can you be more specific about the job?"

"Yes. You will be an actor portraying the CEO of a large company. You will be subject to a very important Board of Directors meeting, some public appearances, and some media interviews. Your appearance will be slightly altered to match the person whom you will be temporarily replacing. If surgery is required, we will pay you extra. You must learn the person's mannerisms, his speech, his habits, his friends, and his business associates. In other words, I am asking you to forget being Trace Reinhardt and be this other person every hour of every day for the next two years. Not only that, but I'm also asking that you be able to convince other people, even close friends or business associates, that you are that person. There will be very few people who know otherwise; I will tell you who they are. In business matters you will be a figurehead ... I will make all the business decisions; you will give the orders and sign all the papers to carry out those decisions.

"You will be paid well for your acceptance and for your continued challenging portrayal of this CEO. You will receive a cash bonus of $250,000 immediately upon signing the acceptance, non-disclosure agreement. You will immediately go through an intense 4-week training and education period to learn the part you are playing. After those 4 weeks, if we jointly decide you can successfully portray the CEO, you will be given the CEO's on-going financial package, which right now amounts to over two million dollars a year. You must agree to serve two years; if you are not needed for the full two-year term we will still pay you for two years. Not only will you be paid handsomely for this acting job, but you will also get to live the life and have the perks of a billionaire. All the money you are paid will be deposited in a Swiss bank of your choice.

"The man you are portraying is divorced with no children. It's very possible that you might see his ex at some point. As a warning, they are not particularly neighborly with each other. His parents are deceased; the only blood relative is his grandmother. You will be visiting her on her 80th birthday; she was very close to him in his pre-teen years. She will be very difficult to deceive. He has a number of girlfriends, but no current or steady girlfriend at present. In fact, it will be necessary for you to have a female companion when you make any public appearances. We will hire an actress for that part. She will have only a platonic relationship with you. She will not be told you are an actor; she must always believe you are a CEO of a large company. None of these people will be told anything; you must play the part well.

"When we part ways, we ask that you take a 2-year hiatus in some agreed-upon foreign country away from the crowds and the paparazzi. If you agree, we will cover all expenses and pay you $100,000 per month. I know you will be bursting at the seams to tell the world about your successful portrayal, but your acceptance agreement requires your secrecy in this matter for another 25 years. You will have plenty of time to write your memoirs; but you will have a long wait to publish them.

"I need to emphasize the importance of secrecy in this venture. Some issues or problems may come up during this masquerade. Whatever happens, in fact, no matter what happens, no one must know.

"What questions do you have?"

"Why am I taking this man's place? Is he alive? Is this part of any criminal activity?"

"Good questions. Our current CEO is not in a position at this time to govern the company and make public appearances. There is no problem here; he will not be a factor as long as you are acting as the CEO. This is not part of any criminal activity. We see this as a deception for the good of the company, its employees, and its shareholders; there is no criminal intent. Any legal suit, frivolous or not, will be vigorously defended by our legal team at no expense to you."

"What's the downside?"

"I suppose you're asking if our deception fails. I don't plan for failure, but I suppose it's very real in this case. Failure could go either way for you. It would be great publicity for you as an actor, but I couldn't guess whether the publicity of our deception would work for you or against you. For me, it would probably be regarded as a criminal act, and I could probably face a prison term and lose all the financial benefits I have earned in this company.

My bet is not failure, but success."

Ten

Other questions and answers flowed to and fro between Trace and Gordon. After this Q&A period was over, Gordon gave Trace two non-disclosure documents, one accepting the job, the other rejecting the job.

Gordon said, "Here are the two contracts. I think you have a good appreciation of what we want you to do. We will pay you well, but we expect a lot. Let's call it deception without detection. Don't take your decision lightly. You asked for your agent or lawyer earlier. What do you think now?"

Trace replied, "I think I understand the terms and the choices. If there's a problem I won't go after a lawyer ... I'll come after you! Would you like to hear what I learned in the Marines again?"

"Trace, let me assure you, you'll have no reason to come after me. I hope you'll stay around for the next step and the biggest role an actor has ever been asked to take ... without any sort of recognition, of course."

Trace took both documents away from where Gordon was sitting to a table in the corner. He read both documents carefully and then signed one. He handed the rejecting document back to Gordon and said, "I guess this is it, Victor."

Gordon frowned but then saw it was unsigned. Trace grinned, then handed him the signed acceptance document.

"Victor, let's do it," he said.

Gordon responded, "You got me! I guess I've seen your first deceptive act."

Gordon smiled and clasped Trace's hand in a firm handshake. "Call me Gordon," he said. "My name is Gordon Brewer, Chief Operating Officer of Langston Industries. You are Earl Langston, Langston Industries' Chief Executive Officer. I'm sure we'll be able to work together just fine.

"This is Langston Industries' home for our employees and friends. It's a vacation perk we offer key employees: come to LA, do some sightseeing and use our membership to play golf at the nearby prestigious Bel-Air Country Club. So, Trace, make this your home for the night, but only one night ... don't build a nest. We'll be in Utah tomorrow night and spend the next several weeks there. There are five bedrooms available, but we've given you the CEO room ... just up the stairs, down the hall, and the last door on your right. There are plenty of clothes in the closet. Help yourself. You'll not be going back to your hotel. We'll check you out of your hotel and bring all of your belongings here.

"There is one important item that we must do before anyone else sees you. I am going to provide you with several bandage-looking caps. Let's call them accident caps. From this point forward for the next several weeks you must wear one of these accident caps at all times except when showering. That means even while you're sleeping! Only Martin, the man who drove you here, and I know your true identity. Martin is my right-hand man. Ask him for help if you need it. The staff does not know and it's important that they do not know. Consequently, you must be and must act like Earl from now on. No exceptions. I am telling our staff that you were in a car accident while at our California seaside villa and suffered some head wounds and a concussion. As a result of the concussion, you have experienced some loss of memory and you are under strict doctor's orders to rest and have solitude until you feel better. The concussion story will help provide a cover for you until you learn the names of our staff members and until you come up to speed on Earl's speech and mannerisms. The rest and solitude story will allow you time to privately study and learn all the information I have gathered for you to be Earl. The accident caps will give credence to those stories.

"Your watchwords for this role, this project is: 'Be calm, be cordial, and above all, be careful.

"The hour is late; save any questions you have now for our brunch together this morning at 11 am, about eight hours from now. We will talk again then; don't forget to wear your cap!

"Henceforth you are Earl, I will no longer address you as anyone other than Earl. Goodnight or is it good morning, uh, uh... Earl?"

Eleven

A visitor in a compact rental car pulled up near the gated entrance of Langston Industries' Seaside Villa. The driver reached out of the car and punched the admission entrance button. In a few seconds, a man's voice came over the gate speaker saying, "Good afternoon, sir. May I help you?"

Carson answered, "Yes ... yes, I think you can. My name is Brad Joiner. I'm from LA and a good friend of Earl's. He told me to drop by for a drink anytime I was in the area. He didn't know I was coming, and I'd like to surprise him."

"Sorry," the voice replied, "but Mr. Langston is not here at the moment, and he is not expected to be here any time soon."

"Oh, that's disappointing. Where is he? Maybe I can catch him at some other place."

"I don't know, he only tells us when he's coming here and never tells us where he is or where he's going."

"I'm sorry to hear that ... but let me come in and bring you a package for him ... it's part of the surprise."

"Just leave the package by the mail drop, I'll come and get it later."

"Nope ... can't do that ... what's in it is very valuable and it needs to be personally delivered."

"No. I can't ... "

"Excuse me for interrupting, but I know what you're going to say. I just need you to understand how disappointed Earl is gonna be. Look, I have to give this to someone directly. I can't mail it, I have to leave in an hour, and I just can't leave this material sitting around. What's your name anyway?"

"My name is Reginald. I'm the caretaker of this facility." He pauses. "Okay, I suppose it's all right. Please follow the drive to the front entrance; I'll have my wife meet you there."

"Thanks!"

The car gate opened, accompanied by the shrill ringing of a bell.

Carson was angry and he became angrier as he made the 400-yard drive to the front entrance of the manor. *What a creep! Earl has lots of money, owns a ritzy place like this and he takes advantage of a young, naïve woman like my sister. I can hardly wait to see him!*

Carson parked his car then made his way to the front entrance. The door opened before he rang the doorbell. The woman opening the front door, smiled and said, "Hello! I'm Greta, Reginald's wife. He told me that you had an important package for Earl. I'll be glad to take care of it."

"Look, I'm sorry, Greta ... I'll give you the package in a minute. Are you sure that Earl isn't here?"

"No, he's not. In fact, only Reginald and I are here."

"But I really need to know where Earl is ... I need to talk to him; it's really a matter of life and death." *Inwardly Carson smiled. Nothing like telling the truth!*

"I'm sorry. Mr. ...???" She paused.

"Joiner, Mr. Brad Joiner." replied Carson.

"Yes, Mr. Joiner ... I'm sorry ... we do not know his whereabouts. In fact, we never know his whereabouts until he comes here ... and that's on very short notice. We can't help you!"

Carson's impatience and anger were growing. *Why does everybody lie to me*?

"Well, you don't realize how important this is! Surely you can call someone and find out where he is."

"No, we can't do that ... we wouldn't have any idea who to call."

Carson drew his gun. "Now let's get serious," he said. "I mean to find out his whereabouts before I leave here! Now you get husband Reginald down here immediately ... don't tell him anything ... just get him here right now!"

Sobbing, Greta spoke into the intercom and said, "Reginald, we have an emergency situation at the front door ...please come right away."

Reginald's voice boomed back, "What's wrong; what's wrong?"

"I can't explain. Please come right now!"

"Okay! Give me a minute or so. I'm upstairs; I'll be there right away!"

When Reginald came down the stairs leading to the front door, he saw a stranger waving a gun around in front of his trembling, sobbing wife.

Reginald shouted, "What's going on, mister? What's the problem?"

Carson replied, "Okay, bud ... now you just take it easy and listen. I don't want to hurt you or your wife, although the idea is growing on me. Tell me where Earl is, and I'll be on my way."

"We don't know. He was here a few days ago, but he left in the middle of the night. We haven't seen or heard from him since."

"Let's say I believe you. So, **you** don't know where he is (pointing his finger at Reginald) well, **you better** call someone right now and find out!"

"I don't know who to call."

"Let's say I believe that. Well, I don't!" He pointed the pistol at Reginald and then at Greta, back-and-forth, several times.

Greta sobbingly said, "We're telling the truth, Mr. Joiner ... we don't know who to call."

"So, you don't know? Well, as they say on the quiz shows, 'Is that your final answer' and I do mean your **final** answer?"

He looked threateningly at both of them, still waving and pointing his gun back-and-forth between them.

"No, we don't know where he is, and we don't know who to call to find out."

"You just made my life more interesting and yours more painful. No more Mr. Nice Guy! Let's see what you know after this!"

That said, Carson turned and shot Greta in her left thigh. She screamed with pain. Reginald could not contain himself. He roared with anger and jumped on Carson to wrestle the gun away. He failed. Carson was able to shoot him twice. Reginald fell, mortally wounded. Carson turned back to Greta and shot her twice as well.

He looked at the mortally wounded couple on the floor and said, "Goodbye, you stupid idiots! You oughta know better than to mess with me."

Carson spent the next two hours rummaging through the villa. He found nothing to help him learn where Earl might be. He found several hundred dollars that he kept to help defray expenses but little else. Frustrated and angry he left the villa. He would have to return to his uncle's cabin in New York empty-handed.

As he left the front door to enter his car the caretaker's fawn-colored boxer dog came up the driveway to greet him. The boxer was curious, not aggressive. The boxer's motive or attitude made no difference to Carson. He shot and killed the dog with one shot to the dog's massive head. Carson wagged his head back and forth saying, "I hate dogs! Just hate 'em!"

He entered his car and headed back to LA to catch a plane to New York.

Meanwhile, the cause of all the consternation and activity rested quietly in the master bedroom of the Langston vacation home in the 1000 Islands area of the St. Lawrence River and the upper eastern shore of Lake Ontario. The vacation home was the only house on a small island, accessible only by boat.

Earl was there. He still had not regained consciousness, but his vitals were good, his broken bones had started their six-week mending process and there was no sign of further complications. The Indian doctor, Dr. Khatri, and his staff were taking care of their only patient and were enjoying their stay at the island home. The home was built for pleasure and with only a patient named Carl Bergstrom to take care of it was almost like a paid vacation. The doctor was bilingual and the only person there who spoke English; the Indian staff members did not. Gordon had Dr. Khatri put the group together in this manner, hoping they would not find out the true identity of the person they were caring for. Link liked this task, also. *This might be the best job I ever had while I worked for Langston Industries; I hope Gordon will let me stay more than my commitment of three months.*

Twelve

Things are moving pretty fast for Trace. Twelve hours ago he agreed to the biggest acting job of his career and probably one of the most important of any actor's career. Now, he was being whisked away from his comfortable acting job in LA to Langston Industries' Mountain Lodge in Utah. No suitcase, no extra clothes or even a toothbrush ... Gordon told him all that stuff is provided for him at every Langston Industries' house. "You'll get used to it very quickly," he said, "and when you do, you'll want it to be that way forever."

So, now at 3pm, Trace, Gordon, and Martin were going to board one of LI's private jets going to Salt Lake City where they would take a helicopter to LI's Mountain Lodge. The short time he has known Gordon helped him reduce any misgivings about taking this very bold step. *Gordon seems to be a straight shooter and I think I will be able to work with him very well.*

Gordon and he left the "interview" home in the same black limo he had arrived in last night. Like last night, Martin was driving. A short drive and they arrived on the edge of a private airstrip where the jet was waiting. He and Gordon left LI's limo, said goodbye to Martin, and walked briskly to the aircraft. A stewardess greeted them as they approached the jet. She cheerily said, "Good afternoon, Mr. Langston! Good afternoon, Dr. Brewer! It's a great day for flying. Come on in and make yourselves comfortable."

Trace said nothing ... just waved his hand in acknowledgement.

Gordon replied, "Thank you, Mary. After we get going, please bring Mr. Langston and me the usual."

Mary smiled and said, "Sure thing Dr. B! Please sit down and fasten your seat belt, we'll be leaving in ten minutes. After we get airborne, we have word that Lincoln Smith needs to talk to you."

Gordon went to his seat while acknowledging her comments with a nod of his head.

Then Mary turned her attention to Trace. “Mr. Langston,” she said, “I hope you’re feeling okay. We heard you were in a bad accident, and I see your head is all bandaged … anything I can get you besides the usual?”

Trace put his hand up to his mouth like he was clearing his throat, as he replied, “No, Mary, thanks.”

As Mary left to get the “usuals”, Gordon whispered to Trace, “You’re doing great. Just relax, I’m going to tell them not to disturb us; we have some important business to discuss.”

The rest of the crew was quickly informed about their cargo’s wish to be left alone and did so after their initial greetings, except for a few comfort visits by the staff while in flight.

Once they were airborne Gordon made his way to a small anteroom where he had some privacy while he had his telephone call with Lincoln.

“Hi, Link! What’s goin’ on. I understand you wanted to talk with me?”

“Right, Gordon. I know you’ve been getting my daily reports, but we’ve got some favorable reports about Carl’s status. If you remember my custom, give unfavorable reports by mail, favorable reports in person.”

“Yes, I do! That’s the only reason I called you back right away!”

“I’m going to put Dr. Khatri on the phone and let him talk about our patient.”

“Fine.”

Dr. Khatri was excited and pleased. He said, “Dr. Brewer, I have some good news! Carl has started to come out of his coma. He opened his eyes for a few minutes, went back to sleep for a while and then opened them again for almost 10 minutes. He did not say much, but he did ask where he was. I told him but I’m not sure he understood. He has repeated this cycle several times, but he has never stayed awake more than

15 minutes at a time. He is very weak, but I think he's getting better and his understanding is improving."

"Thank you, doctor. You must be taking good care of him. Now, I'm sure Carl is confused, and I want to help him understand his situation. He's not paralyzed, is he?"

"Oh, no, Dr. Brewer. He's weak, but not paralyzed. His broken bones are mending and when he becomes more conscious, we will start him on a physical therapy program, so he'll have full use of his limbs."

"Excellent! Look, if he starts asking a lot of questions don't try to answer them. Lincoln is there to answer any questions he might have. Lincoln speaks for me; but, if you have a problem, call me. As he begins to get well, I'm concerned he will rebel about his isolation and his situation. It's very important that Lincoln or I are the ones who explain everything to him. Do you understand?"

"Yes, I do. I will take good care of him."

" Thanks for the good report, Dr. Khatri. Goodbye."

After the call, Gordon gave himself a few minutes of quiet time before he went back to his seat to talk with Trace. Trace had some questions. "Gordon," he asked, "I'm still curious as to why you guys selected me to do this job. There must be hundreds of actors who have more experience than I ... why me?"

"Yeah, I did tell you I'd answer that question, didn't I? The reason is a very simple one. In fact, you've already experienced the answer. Mary saw you and immediately called you Mr. Langston. She has seen him many times; she thinks you are Earl.

"None of those hundreds of actors that you're talking about look as much like Earl as you do. When I first saw your photo, I thought I was looking at Earl; Earl before he went hippy on us, that is. I told you about his dad dying in a tragic helicopter accident and that's how Earl became the CEO. Well after that, either out of grief or freedom from his father's decrees, Earl let his hair grow long. He now has a beard, a moustache, and long hair halfway to his shoulders. Here's a photo of Earl taken a few months before his dad died; I want both of you to have that look going forward. My barber tells me it's sort of a messy Ivy League haircut with a mustache and short stubble facial hair. I'll see that Earl returns to that look and I want you to have that look also. Your acting and impressionist skills are very needed and important; but what will sell others that you are Earl will be your resemblance to him. Any problems?"

"No, that's okay. I'm used to those kinds of changes."

"Good. The first public look should resemble their last sighting of Earl. There'll be sometime in the future we will let you take the look you want."

"Gordon, you mentioned, though, that there would be some physical changes … I hope Earl has both arms and legs!"

"You're lucky … he's got 'em both! However, what we might have to do, and I will be relying on the advice of a plastic surgeon, is to make your ear lobes a little smaller and add two small moles: one near the end of your right jawbone and one on your neck. Nose work? I doubt it. I think that will be the extent of any surgical work. The surgeon will meet us tomorrow and will do any needed work right away. We want everything to heal up before your first public appearance. Doesn't sound too bad, does it?"

"Well, I'll go for the smaller ears, but I'm not keen on the moles."

"I understand, but what's a few moles for the money you're making. We'll see what the surgeon says about removing those moles once you finish your tour of duty."

"Fair enough!"

"Now let's talk about girlfriends."

Trace grinned and said, "Okay, yours or mine?"

Gordon laughed. "I like your sense of humor, but you'll probably have to tone it down a bit … Earl is not humorless, but he doesn't have the quick quips you have … and what funnies he says are more the hard-hitting, biting type."

"Thanks, I got it!"

"Now, back to girlfriends. We didn't identify any steady, but I thought I would check with you. Do you have a steady?"

"No!"

"That's good! We want Earl to have a steady; one who will make public appearances with you. One who is willing to sign up for your tour of duty. One who is trustworthy, friendly, and attractive. One who is relatively unknown and who is willing to change her appearance, so she won't be easily identified. Do you have any referrals?"

"Not really, ... no."

"How about actresses, preferably ones who don't really know you?"

"Let me think, Gordon. I can probably name or describe a few for you."

"Please do so asap. Other than start you on a training/education schedule, hiring a show piece for you is my highest priority."

"Will she know me as Earl or Trace?"

"Only as Earl. The less people who know otherwise the better."

"Having an attractive companion with me sounds great! How about letting me do the hiring? It sounds like a job for the CEO!"

"Sorry, Earl. It's not in your job description. And, all that aside, please remember; it's important you keep her convinced you're Earl. Earl always had a girl with him when he made public appearances. A steady girlfriend will help keep up appearances and help keep other ladies away."

Gordon and Trace didn't talk much after that. Trace spent his "free" time by reading and listening to music. Gordon took care of his backlog of business, both by telephone and email.

As the plane was landing in Salt Lake City, Trace gave Gordon the names of actresses in three different low profile shows who might fit the criteria that Gordon had established. He couldn't remember the actresses' last names, but he did have first names and in some cases the shows they were in. They were all relatively unknown. Gordon thanked him and told him they would be checked out.

The helicopter trip from the airstrip in Salt Lake City to the heliport at Langston Industries' Mountain Lodge was unexciting. Trace was ready; after the exhilaration of the past day, he was ready for nothing exciting.

Thirteen

Trace was tired when they arrived at the Mountain Lodge last night. He was tired and ready for a good night's rest. He got it. He arose the next morning refreshed and ready for the next step in this rather bizarre arrangement he had contracted for.

He got his first real look at the setting of the Mountain Lodge when he looked outside through his bedroom's picture window. The view was spectacular. The Mountain Lodge was a 19-room hotel-like mansion sitting on a mountainside overlooking a beautiful array of mountain peaks and interwoven ski slopes. His bedroom was extravagant in terms of space, furniture, paintings, and décor. His picture window provided the view that the lodge was built for. *So, this is how the rich live ... I'll attempt to handle it ... right now it seems like a dream ... it's a living definition of surreal.*

Breakfast was whenever he wanted it, wherever he wanted it, and whatever he wanted. He had met the cadre last night ... to his great comfort they all accepted him as Earl. Another test passed. So far, so good. He had a morning orange juice, roll, bacon, and coffee in his bedroom; then he dressed and made his way to a paneled room outfitted like a medium-size conference room that Gordon had shown him last night. Gordon told him: 'Consider this your headquarters: it will be your private study and meeting room from now on. It is soundproof and secure. The bookcase here has many shelves and can be locked to guard your personal papers. It has a private dressing room and full bath. Meet me here in the morning at 8 o'clock ... so here he was at his assigned HQ room at quarter till. Of course, Gordon was already there accompanied by his ever-present briefcase. He was seated at a small conference table near a bank of four monitors that provided separate access to the Internet.

Gordon greeted him and told him to close the door for privacy. Trace's detailed education and training were about to begin. Well, maybe not yet. Gordon told Trace that the facial surgeon would be there in an hour and discuss what surgeries would be done. He said if all was okay the surgeries would be done that afternoon which meant Trace would probably have to fast after the doctor briefed them. Trace immediately ordered some more rolls, coffee, and a fruit dish.

While Trace was enjoying his last meal of the day, Gordon briefed him on the layout of the Mountain Lodge, the nearby town, the ski slopes, and members of LI's local cadre. The time went rather quickly, and Trace was a fast learner who absorbed information well. Gordon was beginning to be more at ease with his student and the deception underway.

During Gordon's briefing, he told Trace: 'We will be issuing a short press release on your injury, but we will not respond to related questions or requests for interviews. The staff has been told that you need some immediate facial surgery as a result of the accident. In addition, you will not be taking any calls except from me, Martin, or the doctor."

The facial surgeon, Dr. Arnaud Janssen from Brussels, arrived promptly at 10. He was ushered into the HQ room and introduced to both Trace and Gordon. Dr. J got right down to business. He had a definite European accent as he said, "Dr. Brewer, I believe you were the one who sent me the photos of two men who you want to look alike. You requested only minor facial changes that would heal quickly. I'm prepared to do that this afternoon; I have two assistants waiting downstairs who will help me."

Trace asked, "What are the changes, Dr. Janssen?"

Dr. J replied, "Ah, it's the patient ... always the patient, who asks the questions. But wait ... the doctor needs to ask the patient something first ... there are fresh bandages on your head ... did someone beat me to you? Or as they say in your baseball, am I part of a double-header?" The doctor smiled as he engaged in a little wordplay.

Gordon jumped into the conversation. "Dr. Janssen," he said, "please ignore the bandage cap Mr. Langston is wearing. He wears it to avoid comments and questions from our staff about alleged injuries he suffered in a recent automobile accident. There are no injuries. The staff does not need to know. This is part of our confidential agreement on this matter."

"Oh, of course. Of course. No problem. So now I go back to Mr. Langston's question. I suspect he is concerned and really wants to know what I will do. Perhaps he's worried; but don't worry, sir. The changes are not significant ... a little eyelid and eyebrow work, a small amount of flesh removed from each ear lobe, and the insertion of two mole facsimiles: one on the end of your jawbone near your right ear and one just below that one on the lower part of your neck. The nose ... the mouth ... the jawbone ... they are okay. You are so fortunate, sir, because your facial features match the other person's features so closely. On the other hand, it's bad for me; I prefer major surgeries!"

Trace said, "I understand. I would suggest to the doctor we might have entirely different perspectives about this situation. Are any of the changes reversible?"

"Only the mole facsimiles ... a little plastic surgery will remove them and leave no trace that they were there."

"And what about recovery time?"

"Ten days at most ... the eyelid work is the biggest eyesore shall we say?" Again, the doctor smiled at his wordplay.

He continued, "The eyelid surgery will probably cause some swelling and give you a couple of black eyes for a week. None of these surgeries will affect your work schedule after 24 hours unless we have some unlikely infection."

"Not a pleasant thought."

"Agreed."

Now Gordon turned to Trace and asked him, "There is another thing I would like to have done with your permission. We haven't really talked about it."

Trace asked, "What is that, Gordon?"

"When our double was in high school, he had a skiing accident and injured his leg. The injury left a scar on the back of his right leg about 9 inches above his heel. I would really like to duplicate that scar, but it might be difficult to correct after this project is over. It's not a requirement, but I think it's a known scar and I would like you to accept it. What do you think?"

"How long is it and how ugly is it?"

"As scars go, it's not ugly. It's slightly curved and about two inches long."

"Doesn't sound like a big deal. I was afraid you were going to ask me to have a big tattoo on my forehead. It's okay, let's go ahead with the scar."

Gordon said, "Great! I'm sorry about the surprise."

Then Gordon looked at the doctor, "I believe you said the leg scar would not be a problem?"

"No, it's not a face, is it? It will be the easiest part of my work, but it probably will cause our patient here a little more pain for a longer length of time."

Trace said, "Thanks, gentlemen. I hope there's nothing else!"

The doctor asked if Earl had any further questions and if he was ready to proceed on what he had heard and what was planned.

Trace replied, "No further questions, let's get it over with."

Gordon said, "Fine. Dr. Janssen, it's my understanding that you have already made arrangements with the local clinic to perform the surgery at four o'clock this afternoon. If everything is okay from your side, please proceed with the surgeries you outlined today."

Dr. J looked at Trace and said, "I am ready. I will see you this afternoon. I need a list of your current medication and anything you are allergic to. Eat nothing else this morning. You may drink a little water or coffee, but that's all. Be at the clinic by two o'clock."

He grinned, then asked, "With or without my turban?"

"With!" was Gordon's quick response.

Then Dr. J said his goodbyes, shook hands with both men, and left the room.

After Dr. J left, Gordon asked, "That's not too bad, is it?"

Trace replied, "Ask me tomorrow!"

Trace continued, "No, it sounds okay. You told me there might be minor surgeries involved. I accept it as previously agreed."

Gordon said, "Yes, and I believe our agreement was a bonus of $20,000 for minor surgeries. The money will be put in your bank account tomorrow, the day after the surgeries."

Trace thought, *Acting never paid so well.*

Fourteen

Trace had a slight headache when he woke up the next morning following his surgeries. His neck, ears, and eyes felt sore; all the places where Dr. J said he was going to fix. However, when he started to get up from bed, he felt a sharp pain in his right leg. He looked down at the offending body part and saw a neat white bandage about two inches square covering the back of the fleshy part of his leg above his right ankle. *Wow, the doc was right …the leg scar is more painful than the facial stuff. I guess Gordon hobbled me so I wouldn't run off. Let's see what I look like.* He completed his exit from bed and looked at his face in the bathroom mirror. There were too many small, gauzed bandages to tell exactly the result of that work. Dr. J was right about one thing: he did have a couple of black eyes. He called the kitchen and had them send up some breakfast: orange juice, oatmeal, crisp bacon, toast and a small pot of coffee. After a shower and breakfast, he felt much better and ready to begin another day being Earl Langston.

Trace's training session began at 8:30 back in what they were calling the HQ room. Trace again arrived some 15 minutes early; Gordon again was already there working on his phone and computer. Trace wryly thought, *It was nice of Gordon to give me an extra 30 minutes this morning, no doubt in deference to the surgeries, especially the one on the leg.*

They said their good mornings to each other and then Gordon asked Trace if he felt okay. Trace assured him he was fine and ready to go. Gordon laughed and said, "Well, I sure couldn't tell by looking! How's the leg?"

Trace replied, "It's okay."

"Good!"

Gordon then put two small, laminated cards on the table. He said, "These are yours; protect them and don't lose them.

Each card is a duplicate of the other. They contain all the codes you need for internet access, telephone scramblers, combination locks for the bookcase here and for the safe in your bedroom. You can check out all those codes later. What we're going to do right now is look at some material that I've gathered together for you to master ... you must master it in order to be a good Earl Langston. Please unlock the bookcase, get all the material on the bottom shelf, and put it on the table."

Trace looked at one of the cards, got the bookcase code, and used it to open the bookcase. There were three large briefcases on the bottom shelf; he moved them from the bookcase to the table as requested. Now Gordon said, "Let's look thorough this material and I will explain what it is and how it is organized. As you can see there are three briefcases. Each of the briefcases is packed almost to capacity and is full of written material, photos, pictures, and DVDs."

So saying, Gordon opened the briefcase labeled "PERSONAL". Gordon continued, "I will open just this one this morning for you to get a feel of how much material is involved in your education process. The material in this one focuses on Earl's person: his voice, his mannerisms, his speech, his habits, hobbies, skills, strengths, weaknesses, personality, etc. Much of the material in this briefcase is on DVDs. As soon as you master this material you will truly become Earl.

"The second briefcase, labeled "FAMILY & FRIENDS" means just that. In it there are photos and information on Earl's childhood and growing up years, his parents, grandparents, girlfriends, close friends, and others.

"The third one, labeled "BUSINESS" contains an overview of Langston Industries, info on each of the businesses, key management and employees, the Board of Directors meetings, shareholders, public news releases and related business associates.

"The cadre come into this room only by permission. Regardless of that, this is sensitive information. Keep it locked up when not in use.

"There is a lot here, but you have a month, and I am satisfied you can learn it and master it. Any questions?"

"No. As long as I'm isolated here it looks like I should focus on the PERSONAL briefcase first."

"You are absolutely correct. And, there is one item I want you to master first as soon as possible. In that briefcase are copies of his handwriting, and, most importantly, his signature. Master his signature. We need it to sign important operational papers ... orders and material that have to be written and not e-mailed. I'll be frank with you. Some of Earl's business decisions and executive orders have been so bizarre and contradictory that most of the company's execs want written orders now to cover themselves. Don't worry about the orders ... I'll do those, but I will ask you to sign them."

Gordon paused, then he asked, "Any other questions?"

Trace replied, "No, I understand what you've shown me. What else do we need to do this morning?"

"Nothing together except have a cup of coffee and just chat for a few minutes. Take it easy today; one always needs more rest after surgery. You know what you have to do, and you have the freedom to master it on your own time schedule. As for me, I'll be leaving a little later this morning for LA to find you a girlfriend. One thing's for sure, I'm not showing any of 'em a picture of how you look right now because I wouldn't get any takers!"

"No compliments, please."

That was the start of Trace's first serious education of who he was to become.

Fifteen

It was mid-afternoon on the same day that Gordon had shown the three briefcases to Trace. And, just as he had told Trace, he was headed to LA on one of LI's private jets to hire a girlfriend for him. He was thinking about "his project" so far: *It's early in the game, but so far, I'm pleased with the way things are going. I'm especially pleased with Trace's cooperation and performance. However, he and I have a long way to go before we can relax and celebrate. One bobble and the game is over! Now I hope we can hire the right girlfriend for him.*

.Back to reality. Mary was bringing the telephone to him. "It's Lincoln Smith," she said.

"Hi, Link. I appreciate the call. How's our patient?"

"Not much change so far. The trip was rather tiring for him, but the doc said he is stable ... I notice they use that term a lot."

"Any problems?"

"No, everyone here accepts Mr. Bergstrom as a patient and there is no speculation on anything else."

"Great. Thanks, Link. Stay in touch!"

Martin met Gordon at the airport and drove him to LI's Holmby Hills house. While they were making the automobile trip, Martin brought him up to date on his assignment to prepare a list of candidate actresses. He had several folders containing 13 candidate names with pictures and a condensed background history of each person. None of the 13 had any legal, marital, or financial problem. Background checks revealed no flaws; all appeared to be good candidates. Gordon interrupted his report, "Martin, I'm not particularly superstitious, but you just had to wind up with 13, didn't you? You couldn't have 12 or 14? No, it just had to be 13! Right?"

"Sorry, boss! It's 13!"

"Okay, continue."

Martin then said he had eliminated 22 other actresses because for one reason or another they failed the criteria that Gordon had imposed. Two of the three actresses who Trace had given as referrals had been eliminated. All of Martin's work was done without the knowledge of any of the 35 women candidates. Martin had done a lot of good work in a short amount of time.

After they arrived at the Holmby Hills house, Gordon asked Martin to go get something for an evening meal while he began studying the list of candidates. He took almost two hours to make even a cursory scan of all the material that Martin had provided; but at the end of that time, he was able to set aside four names. He labeled those four candidates "Level 3 – Okay". One of these four was Trace's remaining referral. Gordon was concerned she might recognize Trace and not accept him as Earl.

Martin surfaced with some pizza and beer shortly thereafter and they took a short break to eat. Gordon used the mealtime to update Martin on Trace's surgery and progress. Gordon spent little time with the pizza and beer; he was ready to narrow the candidates down even further. This time he made a more careful and meticulous study of each actress's background information. Gordon spent almost three hours on this punctilious review. When he was finished, he labeled five of the candidates "Level 2 – Good" and the four other candidates "Level 1 – Excellent". He then called Martin away from the Laker basketball game on TV and told him he was ready for the next step in the process.

"Martin," he said, "I've made some judgments on these ladies. There are four of them I labeled Level 1 who I want to interview within the next two days. If they are uninterested after hearing just cursory information about our job, they will be purged from our list; if they are interested but cannot interview within the next two days, we will include them in the Level 2 Group and give them a chance later if we haven't hired anyone by that time. Work out a 4-hour time frame for those who will interview. I'd like to begin tomorrow. As soon as you know what these four will do, let me know. In the meantime, I've got a lot of LI work that I need to work through. Thanks for your help. You did a good job getting us to this point so quickly. Any questions?"

"No, boss. But, fyi, the Laker/Clipper game is probably in the fourth quarter ... I'd like to finish watching that first."

"Sure ... I'll have another beer and watch with you ... the LI work will just have to wait for another 30 minutes."

"Boss, I should have warned you. I'm a carrier! You are definitely catching my bad habits!"

By noon the next day, Martin was ready to report the status of the top four candidates. He told Gordon, "Only one will interview. Two are not interested and the other one cannot interview until the third day. I'll bring the lucky one here tomorrow morning at 9."

Gordon said, "Poorer response than I had expected. That's unfortunate. I may be rushing this too much. Hold off going to the Level 2 Group and set up an interview with the one who couldn't be here until the third day. I'd like to talk to at least two candidates before we go further down the list."

"Will do, boss."

"Also, Martin, I'm going to be plenty busy on LI operating problems for the next several days. However, let me know if you need anything."

Martin acknowledged with a nod of his head, then left.

Three days later there was good news and bad news. The good news was that Gordon had interviewed and hired an actress named Melody who agreed to play the part of Earl's girlfriend. Melody did have a near-term scheduling problem and could not join them in Utah for another two weeks, but that didn't matter because there was little for her to learn; she was basically window dressing and a diversion for the paparazzi.

Gordon wanted the actress to be a "mystery woman" as far as the paparazzi were concerned. Gordon had told her, "You're not Melody anymore, you are Dawn Young; only Martin and I will know your true identity. Earl will know you're an actress, but he will not know your real identity. It's also important that you change your appearance, so you won't be easily identifiable. You are a very attractive young woman; I want you to stay just as attractive but change your looks. I have nothing specific in mind, I feel sure you'll be able to do that, won't you, Dawn?"

Melody had replied, "Yes, I'm sure I can."

Melody looked forward to playing the part of an escort to Earl. She would be paid well, and she would enjoy all the trappings of a billionaire's lifestyle. She would be a public escort only; nothing else would be required of her.

The bad news was a surprise, a tragic surprise. Gordon received a call from LI's Public Relations VP. It seems that the caretakers of the LI California Seaside Villa had been brutally murdered several days ago. The bodies had just been discovered. The police were believed to have at least one suspect, but no motive had been established or announced. The police were currently tight-lipped and did not wish to release any further information until a formal announcement the next day. LI's Human Resource staff was engaged with the police in identifying the bodies and locating next of kin.

It was more than bad news for Gordon; it was terrible news. Gordon had known caretakers Reginald and Greta for over 15 years; they were wonderful people; dependable and efficient. There was just no excuse or justification for anyone to have taken their lives. Gordon dispatched Martin to the Seaside Villa area to take care of the unplanned funeral arrangements and any other circumstance that had to be dealt with from a LI perspective. He told Martin he would attend the funerals whenever they were scheduled.

Sixteen

Carson was sleeping soundly in his bedroom in Uncle Leo's cabin when a pounding on his bedroom door rudely awakened him. Uncle Leo was pounding and shouting, "Get up, Carson! Get up! We need to talk!"

Carson rolled over and grumpily said, "Okay, Unc. Okay. Give me a minute, will ya? I'll be right there."

Carson got up, put on his jeans, and came out of his bedroom to where a troubled Uncle Leo had parked his wheelchair. "What's goin' on, Unc? Can't you get your own beer?"

Uncle Leo replied, "No, Carson ... I don't need you to do nothin'. I just have a few questions for you ... just give me some answers and explanations ... and don't you lie to me, boy!"

"Sure, Unc! No need for me to lie. Why would I lie?"

"I've been watching *Fox News* ... they're reporting a double homicide in California. Evidently it happened a few days ago, but nobody was aware of it until yesterday. A man and woman and even their dog was murdered. They were shot to death. They were caretakers of a manor owned by Langston Industries. Do you know anything about that?"

"How would I, Unc? You said it was just on the news ... how would I know anything about it? Means nothin' to me."

"Maybe means nothin' to you, but to me it don't look good for you. I think you've got some explaining to do!"

"Why? How's that?"

"Well, you were in California at that time, and you've got it in for the CEO of Langston."

"Right, so what?"

"The murdered victims were caretakers at a Langston villa, and they were shot with the same caliber pistol as the one you have."

Carson laughed, "Is that it, Unc? You playing *Perry Mason* now? You gotta quit watching those murder mysteries and go back to *Howdy Doody* or maybe *Sponge Bob*."

"Don't use your fresh mouth with me, boy! Are you denying you're involved?"

"Yep! Is the interrogation over now? I'm hungry, I'm ready for some breakfast."

"Well, explain this to me then: How come *Fox News* showed a picture of you and ask viewers to identify that man in that picture? How come, big shot?"

Carson's eyebrows shot up and he was definitely blind-sided by Uncle Leo's question. He stuttered as he replied, "Wha ... Wha ... What are you talking about? What picture?"

Uncle Leo said, "Oh, I got your attention, did I? Yeah, your picture. It seems that the Langston place had some security videos. They got some shots of you at the entrance gate and at the front door. You tried to disguise yourself, but I knew that was you right away. You're in big trouble, boy."

"I didn't do nothin' and nobody can prove nothin'. I doubt anybody can ID me except you. And, nobody will know where I'm at now anyway."

"Now I want you to listen, big shot, and listen well. When I agreed to take you in after you got out of prison it was our agreement that you would behave yourself and not get into any trouble. Well, you've had some minor scrapes, but I've ignored them. And, you did something last week ... I know you did it. You shot and killed Rottie ... you knew I loved that dog, why'd you do that? Yeah, my friend Jamie was squirrel hunting up here last week and found the dog, dead, shot in the head. I know you did it ... don't deny it! That's bad, but it ain't as bad as what's goin' down in California. That's unforgivable! You need to turn yourself into the police immediately."

"Look, Unc. You know what will happen. The police would love to get their claws on me, an ex-con ... they'll string me up without giving me any benefit of the doubt. I ain't giving myself up to the police, and that's that!"

"Okay, nephew. I've always aggressively defended anyone in my bloodline, but I draw the line on murder or any suspicion of murder. I want you outa here before the sun goes down today. I don't care and I don't want to know where you're going. Tomorrow morning I'm calling the cops and identifying who you are. That's fair warning, boy. You'll have a good head start. You and I are different people ... I don't want to see you again."

"So, you're going to kick me out just like that? You're just too good for me ... is that it?"

"No, that ain't it. You don't get it! As I said, we're different people and I don't want you around. I want you to get out and never come back!"

The longer Uncle Leo's accusations and his lectures continued, the more irritated Carson became. He finally had enough. He whipped out the pistol from his back where he had tucked it under his belt and pointed it at his uncle. Without further comment he shot Uncle Leo twice ... each shot was a fatal wound. The force of the bullets knocked Uncle Leo out of his wheelchair onto the floor.

Carson looked at his uncle and said, "Well, dear uncle, I can't have you blabbing to the cops. Now you just lie there a while; I'll come and get you shortly. Right now I'm hungry and ready for breakfast. Sure makes cooking easier now ... I just have to cook for one."

Seventeen

The playing of *Taps* and the presentation of a folded American flag were the signature events of the burial ceremony at the Central Coast Veterans Cemetery in Seaside, California. The remains of Reginald and Greta Fredrickson were laid to rest there, attended by less than 60 people. Three of the attendees were Gordon, Martin, and Trace.

Gordon had flown back to Utah two days before and was pleasantly surprised at seeing Trace's portrayal of Earl. It was remarkable; no wonder the cadre accepted Trace as Earl and did not question anything as being different … except they did comment how much friendlier and easy-going Earl was after his accident. Nevertheless, Trace's progress and his current portrayal exceeded Gordon's expectations. His surgeries had healed, his facial hair had come out in the mustache and stubble effect that Gordon wanted, and Trace had Earls' mannerisms down pat. He wasn't wearing his "accident" cap either; Gordon had told him to discard it. Everything was going great.

Gordon had returned to Utah to check on Trace's progress before leaving the next day to meet Martin at the caretakers' interment at the veteran cemetery. Their murder was still unsolved, and it was still a TV newsworthy item; viewers would much rather watch this kind of story than politics or international news. Gordon knew there would be some news coverage at the cemetery, and he felt LI should be represented there. More importantly, they were not just his employees but his friends. He would have attended regardless of the circumstances.

Gordon had planned that only he and Martin would attend, but with Trace's favorable progress, he saw the caretakers' interment as a wonderful opportunity for Trace to make a public appearance as Earl. How better to honor these LI employees than to have the CEO of LI attend; a CEO who hadn't made a public appearance of any kind in a couple of years? He talked to Trace about it and Trace was enthusiastic; he was more than ready to be out and about again.

They timed their arrival at the cemetery to be just a few minutes before the short graveside ceremony began. Gordon did not wish to cause any hubbub to precede or take away from the honor and tribute of the ceremony itself. And, actually no one, except a local newsman named Fred Parker, seemed to even take notice of the three strangers who arrived at the last minute in a limo. Fred had met one of the men; he knew he was a LI person because he had interviewed him several times regarding LI and the murders. Then, suddenly, he had an adrenaline rush like he had only once before, when he scored the winning basket against his high school's rivals, the Monterey Wildcats. *The young unshaven guy wearing the suit coat and no tie is Earl Langston; the guy that no one has seen in several years! I know it's him! Ole Fred has a scoop! I'm going to handle this one carefully and perhaps the other two networks represented here won't identify him; at least not until after I've interviewed him!*

After the burial service was over, the three LI men did not linger, but walked back to their limo. Fred gratefully and happily saw that the other two networks were paying little if any attention. He had already primed his TV cameraman to stand near the limo and be in position for his interview with the bearded guy. Fred caught the three just as they reached the limo.

Fred nodded to the cameraman to turn on the camera as he looked at Trace and said, "Excuse me, Mr. Langston. Would you mind saying a few words about this terrible tragedy?"

Fred aggressively stuck a mike in front of Trace's face; the camera was grinding away. Gordon quickly moved in to intervene. To his surprise and concern, Trace grabbed his elbow and held him back. Trace spoke into the mike: "Sure, I'll be glad to."

"Were these personal friends of yours, sir?"

"They were friends of everyone who stayed at our Seaside Villa here in California. They were nice, honest hard-working people."

Now the other two networks saw the interplay between a rival network and this fairly young, unshaven man. They belatedly scurried over to get their cameras and mikes in place.

Fred asked, "What is Langston Industries doing to get to the bottom of this crime?"

Trace answered, "We are cooperating fully with local, state, and national law officials. We have offered a $100,000 reward for the arrest and conviction of the killer or killers."

"Are you implying there were more than one person involved?"

"I'm implying nothing of the sort. That's a question that should be directed to law officials."

"The police have released the photo of a man taken by security cameras at your villa's front gate and front door. Do you recognize that man?"

"No, I've never seen that man before."

Gordon had been extremely concerned when Trace stepped before the camera and began answering questions. He didn't think Trace was ready for that kind of pressure. He was wrong; Trace was performing admirably.

Fred continued, "Speculation is that the murders were a reprisal against your company. What do you think, Mr. Langston?"

"Speculations are just bad guesses. Speculations are by people who have little else to do; I do not have time for speculations!"

"What do you plan to do with your Seaside Villa? Will you sell it?"

"We will not use the villa until law officials are satisfied it will yield no more clues to the murders. After law officials release it, we will staff it as before and use it as before. Langston Industries has always had a high regard for Big Sur and the

Seaside Villa area. We like the people there and we wish to maintain a presence there."

"Do you have any further comments?"

"Yes, I do! I'd like to thank those law officials who are working diligently every day to solve this horrific crime. And, I'd also like to thank those of you in the media with your coverage. I applaud your efforts and I hope those efforts will continue until the person or persons who did this cowardly and unwarranted act is brought to justice."

Then Trace turned toward the car and said, "Now, if you'll excuse me, we must go."

Fred asked, "One last question, sir! You have not made any public appearances in two years. Any particular reason, sir?"

Trace stopped and looked first at Fred and then directly at the camera. He made an emphatic, Clintonesque response, "Sir, I work for the shareholders and employees of Langston Industries. They pay me for the work I do; they do not pay me to make public appearances."

The interview was over. Fred had his scoop. Gordon had his CEO.

When the interview played on *Fox News* for the first of several times that night, a man named Carson in New York who saw it became violently angry. He could not contain himself. He leaped to his feet and overturned a table that had a lamp on it, causing the lamp to be smashed and ruined. He shouted out to the unhearing television set, "Damn you, Earl!" Damn you ... damn you ... damn you! You're a damn liar! You know me! You know who I am! Quit hiding from me! You're a dead man!"

And, in Florida, Dario Bruno saw the interview. He raised his fist in a people-less room and shouted, "Rico, Rico, where are you? How come that kid ain't dead?"

Eighteen

Gordon was very pleased at Trace's performance in front of TV cameras that was sure to be played and replayed over the next couple of days. On the plane as they traveled back to Utah, he told Trace how pleased he was but also told him to be careful and to coordinate with him any further interviews. He told him: "Remember, we're in this together. One misstep and we're both cooked."

After their arrival back in Utah at the Mountain Lodge, the next two days were spent entirely by Gordon testing Trace's knowledge and command of the information contained in the three briefcases. They isolated themselves in the HQ room away from the rest of the household while they went through the material carefully and thoroughly.

At the end of the second day, Gordon said, "Great! You've done a good job mastering the material I gave you. I couldn't ask for anything better. I know nothing of Earl's personal nature that you haven't mastered. All his mannerisms are yours now. Sometimes I think I'm talking to and dealing with the real Earl. I believe we're ready to honor all public appearances just on that basis alone. And, let me add this: we've not heard anyone say anything or even show any suspicion that it wasn't the real Earl giving that TV interview the other day.

"There are a few holes in your knowledge of Langston's businesses; but I've never been too worried about that because Earl has never taken a strong interest in our business ... actually you probably know more about it than Earl himself does. We're in good shape there.

"The only place I see that could still be a problem is with family, friends, and acquaintances. You certainly know the material I've given you. But, even though we tried to cover all the bases, I doubt that the material is complete; we may get blind-sided by someone or something we don't know about.

There's nothing more we can do; we'll just have to play it by ear.

"Now I need to tell you something about our BOD that isn't in the material I gave you. There were 9 original members of the board: the CEO, COO, CFO, our Chief Corporate Attorney, two technical associates of Dr. Langston he classified as co-founders, and three founding investors who all presently live in Florida. Dr. Langston was the chair of the board. This is a private corporation; Dr. Langston as the owner could make all binding decisions with or without the approval of the board. His position was the only position that could and can be inherited; thus, Earl is now CEO and chair. However, Earl, unlike his father, cannot make unilateral decisions until he reaches the age of 30 years old. Thus, the board members currently have the decision-making authority. Now, it gets more interesting. One of Dr. Langston's co-founder friends passed away about five or six years ago. Dr. Langston could have replaced him or just absorbed his voting right. He exercised his right to obtain that vote, giving him two votes on the board; two votes that Earl has inherited. So, now we have 8 members and 9 votes. But, there are no proxies. A board member must be present to vote.

"So, let me put this in a simpler perspective regarding the tender offer Kesterson has made. If Earl is at the BOD meeting, the offer will be rejected 5 to 4. If he is absent, it will be accepted, 4 to 3. The three Florida investors and our Corporate Attorney favor the offer; they feel the company has lost value and leadership with Dr. Langston's death. Their shares are not marketable otherwise; this is their opportunity to cash in.

"There's one thing I'll add. The three Florida guys are almost impossible to deal with since Dr. Langston died. Be careful with them; they hate Earl and don't disguise it. They would like to take over the company and I think they have undisclosed ties with Kesterson. Please keep my opinion of that to yourself.

"So, Earl, let's adjourn for the day. Great review! Let's use our half-filled beer glasses to toast the end of your formal education and training!"

Melody renamed Dawn, arrived at the Mountain Lodge the next afternoon. Her entry into the charade dovetailed very nicely with the end of Trace's training and education. Martin had escorted her from LA, and he delighted in showing her around the lodge and introducing her to the cadre. As he had been instructed, he brought her into the HQ room last where Gordon and Trace were waiting.

Gordon had not seen Dawn since he had hired her in LA. When he saw her now, he blinked his eyes in amazement; she had totally transformed herself from one attractive woman with long blonde hair to a different-looking attractive woman with short brown hair. She now looked like the girl next door instead of the Hollywood-looking actress type. She had listened to him; and like Trace, she was making his choice of people look good.

The first meeting between Dawn and Trace was warm and cordial. She was told what she had been informed about before; she was to be an escort for Earl on all his public appearances. She was to be like a charming hostess, courteous and polite to everyone. The relationship between Earl and her was to be strictly as platonic friends, nothing more. She was not to contact any of her family or friends for a month; afterwards, that restriction would probably be removed or relaxed. She was not told the secret that Gordon and Martin shared; that Earl was not really Earl, but an actor named Trace.

Gordon was feeling pretty good until he got the phone call. It was Sheriff Cochran from Big Sur in California. After polite greetings between the two, the sheriff said, "Dr. Brewer, I thought it might be appropriate to warn you about an incident at the hospital shortly after your Mr. Bergstrom was discharged. I remember telling you my daughter works there. It just so happens that she was the one who discharged him. Well, a couple of hours later these two tough guys came to her floor looking for him. Said they were his friends. With what my daughter told me it sounds more like they were there to harm him."

Gordon asked, "Who were they?"

"Don't know. They never gave their names. The only thing she mentioned is one was fairly tall; the other was fairly short."

"What did your daughter tell them?"

"I think she recognized that they weren't buddies with your guy. She sort of frustrated them. Didn't really tell them anything; acted dumb, just told them someone from your company checked them out and gave them your company's address."

"Sheriff, I don't know anyone from the descriptions you gave me. Thank your daughter for the way she handled them."

"Oh, she really enjoyed it. But because they were so threatening, I thought I would let you know."

"Thanks for the heads-up. I really appreciate it."

"Sure ... and how is the patient anyway?"

"Oh, he's doing okay."

"Great! Good-bye, Dr. Brewer"

"Wait a sec, Sheriff. Any news on the caretaker murders?"

"Well, I guess they got a picture of the perp from the villa's security videos from your folks. I really don't know anything else."

"Thanks for your call, Sheriff."

"You betcha!"

Gordon hung up the phone. *I knew everything had gone too well today. Now I have something else to worry about.*

Nineteen

Trace looked out the window of the Gulfstream G650, Langston Industries private jet. The view from 31,000 feet was beautiful; it was a clear day with few intervening clouds. Gordon, Martin, and Dawn were the only other passengers on the plane. Trace was glad to be out of the lodge again, although it would have been much simpler and less stressful to stay home.

They were headed to Hot Springs Village, a very large retirement/resort area near Little Rock, Arkansas to visit with Earl's grandmother. Trace was as well prepared as he could be for this visit. He knew Earl had visited his Grandma Martha many times during the summer months in his pre-teen years, but as he grew older, he visited her only occasionally. He had last seen her on the occasion of his parents' funeral following their tragic helicopter crash. Trace had seen some family photos of her but had little else to go on except what Gordon could tell him. The cover story with her would be the same one they had been using with the staff: *'Earl was in an auto accident, suffered a concussion and head wounds. He has suffered some loss of memory.'* Hopefully, he could sell that story.

Martha and husband James had retired to this scenic area over 20 years ago. Martha and James both loved to play golf and there were plenty of golf courses around to support their habit. The residents in the village were like-minded; they fit in well with those other residents.

Unfortunately, James died suddenly of a massive heart attack only six years after they became residents. Martha grieved but she was determined not to let her life die with James. She became busier than ever; she still played golf, she took up bridge and oil painting, and she continued to spend many hours a week in support of her church's various ministries.

Before Trace's performance at the caretaker's funeral, Gordon had thought about canceling this visit. It would be difficult to fool Grandma. But, Earl had promised her he would come visit her on her 80th birthday ... and here they were. There was one big plus. Grandma treated Gordon like her own son. She loved him. She trusted him. Gordon had been an important part and friend of her real son in his life; she treated him like family. That trust would play in Gordon's favor.

Grandma Martha was outside her home in her front flower garden when the foursome's limo drove up and parked near her front entrance. The setting of her modest 3-bedroom home was beautiful, high on the hills with a great view, and not a neighbor within a quarter mile. She greeted her visitors warmly and graciously as her southern upbringing had taught her. She gave Trace a huge hug even as she berated him for being out of touch with her for such a long time. Gordon received a Grandma hug and he was also gently berated for being too busy to see her. She smiled pleasantly at Martin who she had met from previous visits to her son's office. However, Dawn was a new face, a new person, so when Dawn was introduced Grandma Martha clasped Dawn's hand warmly, looked in her eyes and smiled ... after all, she was her grandson's girlfriend. She invited them inside. After they entered and refreshed themselves, they all were seated in her den around the dining table. Of course, Grandma had a large chocolate cake with the number 80 inscribed on it, courtesy of her church Sunday School class. First things first. No cake until they sang "*Happy Birthday*". Grandma was really pleased. Sandwiches, chocolate cake, and ice cream followed.

While they were eating, Gordon thought he should provide their cover story.

"Grandmother," he said, "I'm so glad to be here. I miss seeing you very much. I'm glad we were able to come and celebrate your 80th. I do need to mention this to you about Earl.

He was recently in an auto accident and physically he has fully recovered. However, he has experienced some memory loss. Nothing severe and the doctors say it will just take a little more time before he's fully recovered. That's one reason I came with him, and I'm glad my schedule was open. Martin and I thought it would be best if we accompanied him for the next several weeks until we are assured that he is 100%. Please don't worry; we're just taking some extra and probably unneeded cautionary steps. After all, he is the CEO of a large conglomerate and if we didn't keep up with him the shareholders would be very unhappy."

Grandma replied, "Yes, Martin had called me and told me about his accident; but told me not to worry, he was recovering fine. I hope no one else was hurt."

"No ma'am, only Earl."

"Well, he sure looks good. Y'all must be taking good care of him."

"Yes, ma'am."

From that point on, Grandma devoted her time almost exclusively to grandson Earl and his girlfriend, Dawn. She had been told that her visitors would only be there two or three hours, so she wanted to make the most of that time. She was ready. She had Trace and Dawn sit on each side of her by a table that had two old photo albums on it. Grandma loved to make those journeys through her photo albums.

The first photo album contained pictures of her marriage and the rearing of her only son Michael. As they went through the first album, Trace and Dawn did not have to say too much; Grandma was the tour guide, and she relished the telling of her remembrances and recollections.

Traveling through the second photo album was different. This album focused on Michael's family and there were many pictures of Earl as a baby all the way up to his early twenties. Now and then Grandma would ask Trace if he remembered that photo, that location, that vacation, that friend, etc. Trace did the best he could. Grandma seemed satisfied with Trace's answers, so she plowed right along through the book. Something great happened for Trace, however, when Grandma got to Earl's school year pictures. Dawn became very interested ... she started asking the questions and Grandma was doing the answering ... Trace was off the hook and it became sort of an advanced training and education time for Trace! Grandma and Dawn hit it off well; their bonding and her visit couldn't have been any better for them and for Trace.

They were there a full three hours. Gordon told Grandma that they absolutely couldn't stay any longer. Grandma teared up a little, but she nodded her head in understanding. She put her arms around Trace and asked for a favor.

"Sure." he replied, "What is it?"

I need your personal e-mail, telephone number, and mailing address ... I don't like going through those telephone menus and such. And, I never know how to send any thing I write to you."

"Sure, Grandma." he said. He started to hand her a business card and she said, "No! No! I need it in this little address book I have."

She handed him a small notebook and asked him to write it under the E's.

He did so. Then she hugged him again and gave him a motherly kiss.

Grandma then said goodbye to Trace and Dawn; she chided "Earl" for being away such a long time and for him to make sure he and Dawn would come back soon.

As they began leaving out the front door, Grandma grasped Gordon gently by his arm, pulled him aside, and asked him to tarry just for a minute. Gordon began telling her what a nice visit he had had and how much he enjoyed it.

Grandma thanked him and then said, "Oh, I enjoyed it, too, dear. I miss you and all the good times we had when James was alive. You need to come here more often too.

"I do need to mention something to you before you leave. You know I'm an old lady and sometimes things happen that just don't seem quite right to me. I've had these feelings before and I'd have to say, I'm right most of the time. You know I haven't seen Earl very much since he grew up. He had trouble growing up and I've heard he's had more trouble later on. But you know somethin', I've never seen that boy listen as well and be as respectful as he was today ... maybe he's just more mature ...maybe it's the girlfriend ... maybe it's because of you ... maybe it's because of his injuries from his auto accident. Maybe, maybe, maybe ... I just don't know. I do know one thing, however, there's no girlfriend and no head injury from an automobile accident can make a man be right-handed after he's been left-handed all his life.

"Love you, Gordon! I hope **he's** okay?"

Gordon was caught completely off guard. After a few seconds he looked Grandma directly in her questioning eyes. He simply said, "Yes, ma'am, **he** is fine. Everything is fine. Happy Birthday! We love you! Bye-bye!"

Twenty

It was 8 o'clock on Sunday morning. Normal people had the day off. Gordon concluded he was not normal people; it was a workday for him just like the other six. Today he was in the HQ room in LI's Mountain Lodge looking at a lengthy "to-do" list and several days of correspondence that had piled up while he was shepherding Trace and Dawn around.

Before he tackled his LI backlog, he reflected on what a nice lady Grandma was. *She knew something was going on, but she trusted me enough to not ask questions and to conclude that it was an okay thing. How in the world did we miss the fact that Earl was left-handed? I'm glad that flaw was noticed at Grandma's, not in public. I'll warn Trace and we need to make sure he doesn't write anything in public. The good news was that the visit to Grandma's had not really been a failure; so, that makes the work in front of me a little more palatable. Our difficult preparation job is over; now comes the more difficult job of selling our prepared product to friends, business associates, and the public.*

These thoughts reminded him to check on Earl. He put in a call to Link.

Link answered promptly with the standard hello.

"Good morning, Link," Gordon said. "How are you and our boy doing?"

Link replied, "Good! I would give us a seven right now. Our boy seems to be recovering nicely. He's up; walks a little bit each day; his injured parts are healing with only a modest amount of pain. I suspect he'll be good as new in a few weeks."

"How's the attitude?"

"Surprisingly good; that's what scares me. I never remembered him like this before."

Gordon laughed. "That's wonderful, you must be a good nurse."

"Undoubtedly, undoubtedly! But, there's one unresolved issue right now. Earl has fainting spells. He feels them coming on, so he is able to prevent hurting himself, but it still causes an unplanned break in his normal activity. The doctor hasn't diagnosed it yet."

"Sorry to hear that but keep me informed. Now let me change subjects." (pause) "I need to pass on a 'watch-out' to you. After you checked out of the hospital, two thugs came looking for our boy. Doesn't sound good to me. Be careful!"

"Sure. Any descriptions?"

"All we were told is that one is really tall and the other really short."

"Twins, huh? Okay, boss, we'll be careful. Thanks!"

"Also, I hope to visit there in about seven to ten days. See you then, Link!"

"Great! Bye!"

Gordon then turned his complete attention to his job as Chief Operating Officer of LI. He worked non-stop for a couple of hours on LI business matters and generated quite a few letters for Trace to sign as the CEO. After he finished the majority of that work, he sent for Trace and discovered Trace was not normal people either. Trace had been working on the patio, trudging his way through public correspondence addressed to the CEO of Langston Industries. Most of the letters were fluff, easily answered. But he brought with him a stack of correspondence containing telephone calls and mail wanting the privilege of interviewing Earl either on television or the radio. The caretaker murders plus Trace's interview at the cemetery had evidently made "Earl" into a short-term celebrity; he was newsworthy; he was hot.

After Trace took care of his *right*-handed signature duties, he asked Gordon, "Lots of folks want to talk with me. I counted 47 requests. What do you think?"

Gordon paused for a few seconds before answering. "I can see that there are definitely some advantages in doing so, but there are also some risks. At this stage, I'll leave it up to you."

"I'm okay with it," replied Trace. "I've already thought it over. If I do anything near-term, I'd prefer an appearance on a late-night talk show rather than a radio or TV news show. That would be more fun for me, and I think I can make a better impression."

"Fine. I assume there were requests from some of those shows?"

"Yes, four of the late-night shows contacted us."

"Do you have a preference?"

"No, not really. I haven't followed any of them very closely or consistently."

"How about Arlo Tuffin? Did his show contact us?"

"Yes."

"Okay, I do have a preference if you don't. Let's go with Arlo Tuffin. He's the new guy on the block, the least political of the four and, in my opinion, he has more fun with his guests than the others. I met and briefly talked with Arlo several years ago when Fox had a reception party for him trumpeting Fox's return to the Late Show business. He's a good guy. Have Martin set it up and ride shotgun. Leave Dawn out. Do it this upcoming week or early next week. I feel sure if Arlo wants you, he will bump somebody and schedule you in. Do it as early as you can because I'm afraid we might get tied up on other matters any day now. I'll explain later."

"Sounds good! I'll go talk to Martin right now."

"Before you go, two things. First, your visit to Grandma really went well ... until you wrote your signature. In our prep work, we forgot Earl was left-handed."

"Oh, no!"

"Yep, but she's okay with knowing you as a sub. There's no problem with her. I'm not asking you to be ambidextrous, just be careful with others around. Don't sign anything in front of others."

"Right!"

"The second thing: some thugs came to the hospital looking for Earl. Fortunately, we had already checked him out. The only description we have is one is really tall; the other is really short. Be careful! I'm not sure what they were up to."

"Got it! See ya later!"

"Okay!"

Gordon allowed himself a few minutes to think about this mess he was in.

I remember a cartoon showing a poor, tired and sweating little guy pushing a huge boulder up a steep hill, afraid to stop pushing because the boulder might roll back and crush him. That poor guy is me!

Twenty-one

This was going to be fun. Trace was pumped, just like he always was before his initial performance in a new stage play. He was looking forward to his time with Arlo Tuffin just a few hours away. He and Martin had flown into LA and now were in a cab headed for Fox's TV studio located on the 6th floor of the fairly new Hudson Building. It was late afternoon. They were a little ahead of schedule, so Trace had asked the driver to go by the theater where he had last performed for a brief nostalgic look. His old play was still being performed and his understudy's name had replaced his on the marquee. *Good for him!* The nostalgic moment satisfied him, but he quickly reminded himself of the task before him. Having a short interview in a cemetery was one thing; having an ad lib "performance" before an audience of millions expecting instant entertainment was another. He was pumped!

Two gentlemen who were not pumped were dawdling with their second cup of coffee, nursing it, in the small café tucked away in a corner of the ground floor of the Hudson Building. They looked grim; they were grim. Each had a copy of today's *LA Times*. One appeared to be reading; the other was "working" the crossword puzzle; *he had two words filled in.* They didn't talk to each other; they kept looking up and over their newspapers frequently to scan people as they came into the main entrance of the building. They were not there for the coffee; they were looking for someone; waiting for someone.

A rather athletic, handsome someone arrived in the company of an older, slightly bearded person. The coffee drinkers nodded to each other as if they recognized the someone. The taller of the two coffee drinkers said nothing, threw some dollar bills at their coffee cups and hurriedly followed the target up the wide slow-moving escalator to an upstairs lobby that the Hudson Building called the first floor.

The short coffee drinker quickly followed his taller friend. The two men followed the target to a bank of elevators and even managed to squeeze into the same elevator going up. However, they didn't get off the elevator on the 6th floor as the target and his older friend did; they seemingly showed no interest in anyone. They continued to ride the elevator all the way up to the top, the 22nd floor, where there was a fancy and classy restaurant. They got off the elevator but didn't go into the restaurant; instead, they entered a door by the restaurant that was plainly marked "Maintenance – Employees Only".

When Trace left the cab and entered the Hudson Building, he was totally focused on his upcoming performance. He paid no attention to the people around him as he made his way to the elevators. However, Martin was paying attention. He had noticed the two men who suddenly left the café and seemingly shadowed them all the way up the escalator and into the elevator. He didn't like their looks and he was suspicious of their actions. He remembered what Gordon had told him about the two guys looking for Earl at the hospital. These guys fit the only description they had: one tall and one short. He was sorry he hadn't worked out some cautionary signal with Trace that would alert him to a potentially dangerous situation. Kidnappers love rich persons. The 6th floor came, and nothing happened. When Trace and he got off the elevator on the 6th, Martin turned to confront the two suspicious guys. There was no one to confront. The two stayed on the elevator, completely ignoring everyone. The two would-be bad guys didn't get off with them. Martin's worries were for naught. Martin guessed he was just getting paranoid in his old age.

There was a third person having coffee that afternoon. He watched his target enter the Hudson Building as well. He chose not to follow the target, but he was pleased the target had arrived. Carson was in a good mood. He had traveled to LA the day before. Earl's appearance on the *Arlo Tuffin Late Show* had been advertised for three days. He knew he wouldn't be able to get in the *Late Show* audience, so he'd let Earl have his fun on the show, then he'd just take care of business afterwards. He had cased the Hudson Building last night and he had chosen to kill Earl as he came down the escalator from the lobby to the ground floor.

Carson suddenly became very hungry. He signaled a waiter and ordered a BLT. While he sat there, munching his BLT, waiting on the show to be over, he had visions of how the shooting would look on TV. He envisioned himself as Jack Ruby waiting for the appearance of Lee Harvey Oswald. His Glock22 was just gonna blow Earl away. It was gonna be great. He could hardly wait!

Twenty-two

The *Arlo Tuffin Late Show* started with their theme song and some hype for their guests of the evening. After the theme song Arlo came out and did his pre-guest monologue as usual; it was good. The audience was receptive and in good humor. Then it was time for the guests, right after a commercial, of course.

Following the commercial, Arlo introduced his first guest: "Tonight we have a special guest. He is the young Chief Executive Officer of Langston Industries. The company has been headline news the past several weeks because of the brutal slaying of a married couple who were employees of Langston Industries and who took care of Langston Industries Seaside Villa in the Big Sur area. Please welcome Mr. Earl Langston."

(applause)

Trace stepped through the back curtain onto the stage in front of an audience he couldn't see because of the glaring stage lights. He briskly walked over to Arlo; they shook hands and then were seated facing each other at an oblique angle.

Arlo said, "We're sorry to hear about the caretakers. They were an older couple, weren't they?"

Trace replied, "Yes. Reginald was 68 and Greta was 63. They loved what they were doing, they were in good health, and planned to continue for another ten years. They were excellent employees. It was a senseless killing."

"I understand that even their dog was killed … is that right?"

"Yes, the dog was a pet boxer, a non-aggressive dog. The police think he was killed after the two caretakers were killed. Again, it doesn't make any sense."

"Was anything taken from the villa?"

"Maybe some cash … nothing else appears to be missing."

"Well, if nothing was missing … what was the motive?"

"As far as I know, no motive has been established yet."

"What about the suspect?"

"The police wish to talk to an unidentified man caught on video cameras at the front gate and front door of the villa. Police said I could share his picture with your audience. I believe you're showing his picture now. This man is a prime suspect in the murders but remains at large. The police are asking that he be identified so they can interview him."

"And, I hear there's a reward?"

"Yes, we're offering a reward of $100,000 for the arrest and conviction of the person or people who committed this crime."

"Great! Well, speaking of money ... We'll have a commercial break and then we'll switch to some more pleasant topics ... okay?"

"Fine!"

The commercials played; the studio lights came on; Arlo and Trace had some private small talk, as did members of the audience.

The commercials ended; the audience quieted as the studio lights turned off; the TV cameras focused on Arlo and Trace again.

"Welcome back!" Arlo said to the studio and TV audiences.

(cheers and applause)

After the applause died down, Arlo said, "I'm talking to Mr. Earl Langston, the CEO of Langston Industries. Langston Industries is a pretty large company. Aren't you a little young to be a CEO?"

Trace replied, "You know I was thinking the same thing about you being a TV Show Host!"

(laughter)

"Okay, Okay ... I get the point ... how's the company doing?"

"Fine! We're growing steadily and surely. We have a great company and I'm proud to be a part of it."

"Slowly and surely, huh? What do you predict your earnings will be next year?"

"I rarely make predictions. I remember what Yogi Berra said: 'It's hard to make predictions, especially about the future!'"

(laughter)

"Well, would you recommend that I buy your company's stock?"

"Sorry, our stock is not public. And, I really can't say too much about our company right now. There's the possibility our company might be taken over by another company."

"Ahhh! It sounds like you might be out of a job!"

(laughter)

"Well, that's one of the reasons I'm here tonight. Do you have any openings?"

(laughter)

"Maybe a doorman ... that's sorta like a chairman isn't it?"

(laughter)

"I'm not sure ... I'll look it up on the internet."

(laughter)

"Well, let's talk about careers and professions. When you were younger what did you want to be when you grew up?"

Trace made his first error of the night. Without thinking, he answered truthfully, "I liked to do impressions. I thought about doing something along that line."

He immediately regretted his answer; Gordon was going to kill him. He knew what was coming next and now he was afraid his deception as Earl was in peril. Someone might recognize him from impressions he had done in the past when he was entertaining people as Trace, the actor. He had forgotten Gordon's watchwords: calm, cordial, and careful.

Sure enough, Arlo said, "Oh, really! Do you have a couple you could show us?"

Seeking to do something safe, Trace did not do his favorite ones, but the ones he did, he did well, and the audience applauded each one.

Then he said, “Now this fellow wasn’t around when I was young but see if you recognize him. Trace stood up and proceeded to do a perfect imitation of Arlo’s walk, mannerisms, and stand-up comic routine.

The audience went wild with laughter and applause. Arlo shook his head and laughed the hardest of them all. Then he said, “Sorry, Earl ... we don’t have any openings here at all!”

(laughter)

“Earl, one more question. We haven’t seen you in a couple of years. You didn’t go off somewhere and get secretly married, did you?”

“No, but I do have a girlfriend, she’s real nice and we enjoy each other’s company, but it hasn’t gotten to the serious stage yet.”

“What’s her name?”

“I’ll tell you, but I want to hear about your love life first. I’d like to make sure we’re not dating the same girl.”

(cheers and laughter; then the audience starts chanting: “Yes, Arlo, yes. Yes, Arlo, yes. Yes, Arlo, yes ...”)

“Okay, okay ... my girl’s name is Helen ... but not the one from Troy. She’s beautiful and very nice. Er ... uh ..., she’s not the same one, is she?”

“No, no ... thank goodness. My friend’s name is Dawn.”

“That’s a lovely name.”

“She’s a lovely girl.”

“Earl, it’s been great talking to you. Give Dawn a hug for us! Come back and visit us again.”

“Thanks, Arlo! I’d like that!”

The crowd applauded. The interview was over. Trace left the stage. Trace hoped he had covered his error; he had never imitated Arlo before.

Twenty-three

Backstage, after the show was over, Arlo greeted Trace and Martin cheerfully. He laughed about Trace's mimicking him; he said, "I thought my guest was me for a minute." He was pleased; he thought everything had gone well; ratings would be up tonight. He then apologized; something unexpectedly had come up; he had to leave in a few minutes and could not join them for the customary post-show get together in the producer's suite on the 21st floor.

Trace said, "No problem, Arlo. I enjoyed meeting you and the conversation we had on the show. I look forward to seeing you again ... perhaps you will come to our movie premiere we're having in a few weeks? I'd like to visit with you when I have the home field advantage."

Arlo replied. "That sounds great! Schedule permitting, I'll be there! Look, again, I'm sorry about bailing out early. One of our hostesses, Jane Munson, will take you and tonight's other guests up to Harold's suite for some drinks and stuff. I do look forward to next time! Give my regards to Gordon!"

"Will do. 'Bye."

Jane was right by Arlo's elbow, ready to do his bidding. She knew the drill; she had done this many times before. She herded Trace and Martin along with the show's other guests: a comic, a female singer and the singer's friend, into one of a bank of elevators marked private. She put a key into one of the elevator's control panels to activate its mechanism, then she pressed the UP button. The elevator ascended swiftly to the 21st floor where Harold Perkins, the producer of the show awaited them. On the 21st floor they exited the elevator and entered a reception area leading into the producer's suite. As they exited the elevator Jane removed her elevator key, which essentially disabled it and held it on that floor until they were ready to leave.

The get-together was a mini-social event; the producer had it just as a matter of courtesy and etiquette; the show's guests attended it as a matter of courtesy and etiquette as well. They all had a little typical cocktail party small talk with each other, had a drink and some finger food, and then said their gracious farewells in less than an hour.

Jane performed her herding function again; she walked them back into the elevator, ready to escort her band of five to the Hudson Building lobby.

As they entered the elevator, Martin noticed a maintenance man leaving the reception area by way of the stairwell exit. He just saw the back of his head, but something about him looked familiar ... hmmm. He was mulling this over when he heard Harold call out to them just before Jane closed the elevator door: "Wait! Wait! Earl, could you and Martin hold up a few minutes? I have an item I'd like to discuss with you?"

Trace replied, "Sure!"

He and Martin left the elevator to join Harold by the receptionist's desk.

Jane nodded and said, "Fine. I'll come back for you after I make this run to the lobby." So saying she closed the elevator door, put her key in the elevator, and pressed the DOWN button on the control panel. Besides screaming, her words about coming back were the last thing she would ever say. The elevator plunged over 20 floors and crashed into the lower part of the underground car parking area of the building. There were no survivors.

Twenty-four

Two days after the horrific elevator catastrophe, Gordon and Martin were in the Mountain Lodge HQ Room reviewing the events in LA following the talk show. Trace was not present during this discussion. The mood was tense.

Martin said, "I appreciate your telephone calls yesterday. It was frustrating to Earl and me to have all the interviews, questions and delays we had to put up with after the elevator disaster; but it's hard to complain, we're lucky to be alive. If Harold hadn't called us out of that elevator ...

"Anyway, things were in a panic mode all night after the crash. Emergency crews were there, police were there, curiosity seekers, and, of course, the media. We were two of the many people who were interrogated by the police that night and most of the next day. It certainly wasn't our choosing to spend an extra day in LA."

Gordon asked, "So, what's the police's verdict at this point: accidental or intentional? They're not telling the media anything right now."

"Sorry, Gordon, the police didn't give me a clue as to what they're thinking."

"What do you think?"

"It's hard for me to believe it was accidental. Elevators have several safety devices to prevent a freefall like what occurred."

"You mentioned on the phone yesterday about two suspicious looking guys who you said followed you onto the elevator. Do you have any further thoughts about those guys?"

"Not really, just what I told the police. I told them that earlier in the day when we were on the elevator going to the TV studio, these two guys joined us in the elevator at the last minute. I didn't like their looks. Later that night I was pretty sure I saw one of them leave Harold's reception area just before the incident. That's the main reason we had to hang around LA.

The police wanted me to identify them from the building's video recordings. I did so. They looked even more suspicious on the videos. Also, I told them about the incident at Community Hospital; perhaps the nurse there might recognize them. I hope the police are following up."

"How's Earl taking all this?"

"Very well, actually. I didn't mention I saw those two weirdoes and I didn't tell him about identifying them on the videos either; I didn't want him to worry."

"I agree; it's probably the best thing to do right now. However, I'm worried. We have the incident at the hospital, the murders at our California villa and now this. Looks too coincidental to me. We need to increase our security around Earl. Take care of that, will you, Martin?"

"Sure! Anything else?"

"Yes. I'd like to meet with you and Earl right after lunch about Kesterson's tender offer. I want both of you to be aware of our position regarding their tender offer. We need to be unified on this. On the surface their offer looks good, but we know their history of buyouts. They're good at dismantling a company, selling the assets, and downsizing the employee population. There are several board members who are strongly in favor of the tender offer; I think it's only to enrich themselves at the detriment of our employees. I want both of you to be aware of who they are. I want you to be well-informed in case you get questions from others. So, if you'll tell Earl, I'll see both of you here after lunch."

"Okay, see you then."

In Florida, the three members of the Florida Signore Council were angrily discussing the elevator incident and asking questions that required immediate answers. They read the papers; they heard the news and commentary on TV; the elevator incident didn't look accidental to them.

Marcellus, who had made the contract with Rico, called him. Without any preliminaries he irately asked, "Rico, what's going on?"

Rico replied, "What's going on with **what**? What are you talking about?"

"I'm talking about that elevator crash in California that killed four people without killing our boy."

"I don't know nothin' about it. What's the problem?"

"Let's not play dumb. We know it's your guys who caused the so-called accident. Now we got the LA cops alerted and if we're not careful they'll be all over us."

"Well. I don't know nothin' about it. Who in the hell did you think you're hiring ... some rookies? You shoulda known that wasn't my guys' work ... the target is still alive, ain't he? Now you just cool down; stop your worrying. We know who the target is, and we will take care of him. Okay?"

"No! It's not okay! No screwups! None! No excuses! None! Understood?"

"Yeah, Marcellus, yeah. I'll make you happy! Goodbye for now."

Meanwhile, in a hotel room in Las Vegas, two surly-looking individuals were having an argument. It was the same argument they had yesterday, and it was starting again today. The participants were not polite.

Jeff, the taller of the two, said, "You blew it! You gave me the thumbs up! You said he was in the elevator, and he wasn't. Is he a magician: now you see him ... now you don't? Or maybe he just flew out like a bird as the elevator went down?"

Mutt, whose real name was Elmer when he didn't work with Jeff, angrily replied, "Stuff it, Jeff. I ain't gonna go through this again. I saw him get on the elevator. I ain't blind; I wasn't drugged up; I seen him with my own eyes ... and, that's that. The TV said he got called outa the elevator at the last moment. Now you just forget what happened; we can't do nothin' about it now. We better use our energy talking about our next try ... our client is pretty angry and I suspect we have only one more shot or it'll be us on the hit list."

"I know all that, Shorty! I ain't ignorant! You just never accept blame when it's your fault!"

"Keep talking, Lurch, and I'll be betting you won't see the outside of this hotel room."

"Yeah, yeah, I'm getting scared! Hand me the phone so I can call 911!"

"Okay, let's cool it! Let's enjoy Las Vegas until we hear from our client again. Right now we don't know where to find our target."

"Hell, I don't believe you knew where he was last time!"

" Why you ... Mutt's cell phone interrupted his more than likely ugly remark. "Yeah, what is it?" he barked.

Mutt listened for a minute, then cut off his telephone call without saying a word. He looked at Jeff and said, "Okay, get your long johns; our guy is in the snowy mountains of Utah now. Let's go get him!"

Twenty-five

Jamie Buford put on his ball cap that sported the NY Yankees insignia and got into his beat-up pick-up Ford truck. He was worried. Two nights ago he thought he recognized someone on the *Arlo Tuffin Late Night Show*. It sure looked like Leo's nephew Carson. They said the police wanted to talk to that guy about some murders in California. Jamie was always behind on the news; he guessed he was just gonna have to watch more TV ... right now he just watched sports and the late-night talk shows. He was a little ashamed; he should have gone to Leo's yesterday, but he can't change that now; it'll have to be today. He cranked up his pick-up and started the 12-mile drive up the twisting mountain road to Leo's cabin.

The morning was cool and clear, so Carson was practicing his target shooting early. He was only about 20 yards from the cabin; he hadn't had to walk that half-mile to shoot his pistol since Unc was gone. After he finished shooting, he went back inside, tossed his pistol on the couch, and went over to the stove and got some coffee.

He began thinking about Earl again. *I can't believe my bad luck and Earl's good luck. I had to leave the Hudson Building right away after I heard the crash although I didn't know it was the elevator .That noise was going to cause a lot of panic and commotion. I knew the police would be coming and I didn't want to be caught carrying a gun. I saw the news the next day and I saw how lucky Earl was by stepping out of that elevator just before it crashed. How lucky can you get?*

Carson was taking this bit of misfortunate philosophically ... *Earl, you were very lucky this time, but there will be a next time. Count on it!*

Carson had almost finished his coffee when Jamie arrived. Jamie drove right up to the cabin entrance and parked. He got out of his pick-up and cautiously walked up to the open cabin entrance.

"Leo! Leo!" he called. "Are you home? It's Jamie!"

Carson used his body to fill and block the empty entrance way. "Mornin', Jamie." he said. "Leo ain't here. Whatcha need?"

"Mornin', Carson. Don't need nothin' in particular. Just dropped by to see your uncle. Where is he?"

"Well. He had a bad case of somethin', so I took him to the hospital, and I suppose they're taking care of him right now. I'm plannin' on goin' there in about an hour or so. They told me not to worry."

"When did this happen?"

"Yesterday afternoon."

"Tell me again ... what's he got?"

"Jamie, do I look like a doctor? I don't know."

"I see his wheelchair over there by the table ... he don't need it?"

"No, sir, he don't!"

"Why, why ... that looks like there's some blood on it."

"Yeah, he was bleeding some when I took him in."

"Carson, that don't sound good. I don't believe you're telling me everything. What's wrong with him? What hospital is he in?"

"I don't need to be talkin' to you. Now you just run along and leave me be!"

"Just tell me what hospital he's in ... then, I'll go."

"I ain't sayin' nothin' else to you, except goodbye."

With that flare-up, Carson turned away from the door and started walking toward his kitchen table.

Jamie was no coward, but he could tell by Carson's attitude and evasive answers it was time to leave. But, he was angry, and he just couldn't help himself; he just had to have the last word: "Okay, Carson, I'm leavin' ... maybe you'll be a little more polite and helpful after the police get here."

That lit Carson's fuse. He turned around, glared at Jamie, and then walked briskly toward his couch.

That's when Jamie saw the pistol. *Oh, my*, thought Jamie, *I've done it now.* Although Jamie was thinking, he wasn't standing still; he turned and ran to the sanctuary of his pick-up. He had his truck almost turned around before he saw Carson nearby, holding his pistol and aiming it at him.

Jamie had no choice but to duck down and keep the pick-up moving toward the road that led back down the mountain. He just had to hope that Carson was a bad shot. The pickup plowed its way through some shrubs and saplings beside the road, but it did make it onto the road with only minor dents.

Jamie didn't have to worry about getting shot. Shots were attempted, but no shots were fired. Carson's pistol was not loaded; it hadn't been reloaded since his early morning target practice. Jamie didn't know what happened; all he knew was that he got away and the police had to be notified. Not only was Carson being wanted in California; it looked like he had something to do with Leo's absence.

That damn Jamie! Carson knew he had to leave his hideout as soon as he could. He figured that Jamie had seen his photo on TV and that he'd sic the police on him. He hadn't planned to move away from the cabin this early, but he had no choice.

He packed a couple of suitcases and then did something he had planned to do after Leo was gone. He knew Leo kept a small safe-like cabinet under the floorboards of his bedroom. He got a crowbar and tore through the floor where the cabinet was. He savagely beat on the cabinet until the door came off revealing several stacks of money and three uncashed checks. He took it all. It looked like Leo had over $35,000 in cash and $5,400 in checks.

"I always did like Uncle Leo!" he said as he stuffed the loot in a satchel.

He loaded his suitcases, the satchel, and the newly loaded pistol into his car.

"I won't be back!" he promised. Carson always kept his promises.

Twenty-six

Trace and Dawn were having breakfast together for only the third time since they had met. There was nothing scheduled for today; Gordon told them to take the day off and enjoy themselves. After discussing some things they might do, Trace asked her, "Dawn, have you ever been snowmobiling?"

Dawn shook her head and replied, "No, I never have. I've skied a number of times, but I've never been snowmobiling. Have you?"

"Yes! Not frequently, but a couple of times. I really liked it! Why don't we do that today? You have nothing going do you?"

Dawn hesitated, "No, nothing special. But I'm a little leery of driving one without some kind of lessons or training."

Trace countered her doubt by saying, "Well, have I got a deal for you! We have two snowmobiles in the garage. They're gassed up and ready to go. I do have something to do this morning, but why don't we take them out this afternoon? I'm sure you'll enjoy it."

"It does sound like fun, but I'm not ready to take one out until I know more about what I'm doing."

"Okay, I understand. But, what about this? The snowmobiles we have will seat two. What about riding with me, as a passenger? You'll sit right behind me. I'll do the driving; you can be the navigator."

"Oh, yes, I'll do that...and maybe you can give me a few lessons so I can solo sometime."

"Deal! Let's lunch together at noon, then go snowmobiling for a few hours."

"Earl, that's sound like fun! I'll meet you back here at the lunch table at noon."

"Great!"

Dawn left to go to her room; Trace headed for his "headquarters" room that Gordon had provided for him. In the hallway on the way there, he was stopped by Martin.

Martin said, "Earl, I have a problem! I need your help!"

"Sure, Martin! Lay it on me!"

"I have a very, very unhappy major shareholder on the phone. It's Nickolas Fontano. He's one of those three guys in Florida who call themselves the Florida Signore Council. He specifically wants to talk to you. If Gordon were here, he'd take the call and keep you out of the verbal barrage. I'm not as skilled as Gordon. This guy's a bigshot; he's irate and he won't take no for an answer."

"Understood! I'll take the call."

"Yes, I was sure you would, but Gordon didn't really want you talking to any of those three guys. Is there another way out of this?"

"Martin, I can't think of any. I'll assume the blame if I screw up. Let me go to my office and I'll talk to him."

"Okay, Earl, you're on your own. Remember, he's a vociferous voice in favor of the tender offer."

The call was waiting for Trace when he got to his office. Before Trace took the call, he took a deep breath and repeated Gordon's watch words: 'Be calm, cordial, and careful'. Then, Trace switched on his telephone recorder as he picked up the phone and said, "Good morning, Mr. Fontano. I understand you wanted to talk to me. I apologize, I'm sorry you had to wait; the staff had a difficult time finding me."

"Earl, you are certainly not your father's boy. Every time I called him; he took my call promptly because he was at his desk working. His staff didn't have to hunt him down. He was working."

Trace grimaced and thought: *My first response was terrible. Gave him an opening and he took it. Careful. Be Careful.* Trace replied, "Yes, my dad was the best man I ever knew. He was very dedicated, and our resulting company is a product of his dedication."

"Well, that's what I'm calling you about. You, Gordon, and the other board members are stupid for not accepting this tender offer from Kesterson. They are a good company, they've made a fair offer, and it will be very positive for all concerned."

"Mr. Fontano, I don't accept your favorable characterization of Kesterson. They are well-known as a company raider. This is not a buyout or merger. It's a takeover. If they get control of our company, they will drastically change it. They will chop up our businesses and sell some of them. Many of our employees will be downsized; jobs will be lost."

"Sonny boy, you are not only wrong, you are stupid. This is a money-making deal for all the shareholders. Kesterson has a lot more expertise in the financial world. You know nothing. You are a figurehead. You couldn't manage a boy scout troop."

"I'm sorry, Mr. Fontano. In recent years, my lack of experience did hurt my leadership. I feel quite confident now that I can manage the company and continue its upward growth and profits."

"Earl, the only thing you've added to the company is expense. If you're a fair-minded person you will see that and you will also see that this is probably your only opportunity to cash in on your father's efforts before our assets become a fire sale. Think of your shareholders for once. We shareholders want the buyout deal with Kesterson."

"Mr. Fontano, I respectfully disagree. I appreciate what you and the Brunos did for my father in getting our company going. But, the facts are this: Both economically and morally this tender offer is a bad deal for our employees and the company."

"Earl, you remind me of an aquarium fish. You just swim along in your little environment, not thinking, bumping into glass walls, just letting others take care of you."

"Mr. Fontano. The tender offer is a bad deal. I am not in favor of it!"

"Well, you don't think right, son ... and what you think means absolutely nothing to me! I've been around a lot longer than you and I'm telling you that we need to accept Kesterson's offer."

"Mr. Fontano, again, I respectfully disagree. My vote is to reject the offer and continue along the strategic paths my father established."

"Earl, I've watched you get older since you were a little kid, but you haven't got any smarter. If this deal was about driving fast cars and chasing women, I would rely on your vast experience. But this deal is about business, and you have the business sense of a turkey on Thanksgiving Day. You're where you are and have what you have because of your dad-dee ... not because of anything else!"

"Mr. Fontano, what you said is very inappropriate. Our conversation just ended. I'll be hanging up now."

"Earl, I'm warning you ... accept Kesterson's offer off or else!"

"Or else, what, Mr. Fontano? Or else, what? Is that a threat?"

"Take it anyway you like. You may not have another chance to call it off!"

"I'm glad it's my last chance ... I don't want to talk about it with you again until our board meeting! Good day, sir!"

After hanging up the phone, Trace sat back in his office chair and thought about what had just transpired. *No major mistakes I hope, but regardless I will get the recording tape for Gordon to review. I sure didn't like Fontano's threat at the end. I'll cover that with Gordon after he reviews the conversation. Wow! And this was supposed to be my day off!*

Twenty-seven

After a light lunch and a nice conversation with Dawn, his lunch mate, the two headed for LI's garage where a snowmobile was gassed up and ready to go. The trauma of the morning telephone call was over. The fun of some outdoor recreation beckoned. Trace had told Martin and several of LI's maintenance staff he was going to travel to Hotel Wilderness about six miles away. There were several snowmobile trails near the hotel and even a frozen lake where they could glide across. The first mile was on a narrow trail leading through a large patch of trees. Martin told him that if he went that route to be careful of the sharp hairpin curve near the center of the thick patch of trees.

Riding on the snow to Hotel Wilderness on such a nice day was exhilarating. They rode a short trail there and took the ride across the small lake. There were not many people there, so they were fairly unrestricted as to their travel. After a couple of hours, they decided to take a break and have some hot apple cider at the hotel's outdoor café.

As they enjoyed the outdoor atmosphere and their cups of cider, Dawn talked about her early childhood and growing up with her parents and two brothers in a small town in East Texas. After studying journalism and drama at North Texas University, she decided she would like to be a performer: either in dramas or musicals. She had done both for the past seven years, but nothing major had developed and she was seriously thinking about getting into the communication arena either on TV or journalism. She was pleased to have this job, acting as Dawn; this job would help her decide what she would do next.

Of course, Trace could not share his real past; he had to draw on Earl's background as his own. He felt guilty about that. Dawn seemed so nice and trusting that he hated to deceive her, but he had no choice. Also, how would she feel if she knew he wasn't the billionaire she thought he was?

Trace really liked Dawn and the feeling was mutual. They were no longer actors pretending to like each other; what they felt was real. Trace said. "I appreciate what you're doing, Dawn. I'm sorry we haven't had a chance to talk and be with each other more. Are you okay with everything? Anything you need?"

"No. I'm fine." she replied. "I really was frightened and worried when I heard about your close call in LA; that was scary."

"Yes, that was scary!"

While they were enjoying the day, the moment, the cider, and each other it began to snow. Then the sun decided to hide behind some clouds. A bright day became darker, much darker. At first, the light snow was delightful; the two were so engrossed with each other, it just added to their enjoyment. That changed fairly rapidly; the snow became heavier, visibility became poorer. Trace finally acknowledged to himself that he and Dawn needed to get back to LI's Lodge before the snow and visibility got worse.

They left the hotel's café, retrieved their snowmobile and began their trek back to LI's Lodge. Visibility wasn't good; the snowmobile lights did not project far enough ahead for safe driving. Trace was having difficulty seeing, but his sense of direction was good. After five or so miles they hit the narrow trail that led up over a small hill through a patch of trees. Trace remembered there was a hairpin turn just over the hill, so he reduced his speed and prepared to make the hairpin turn. As he made the turn, he, Dawn, and the snowmobile faced an obstacle in the center of the path. There was no way to miss it; trees were bunched up on either side of the trail. A collision was inevitable. He threw his weight sharply to his left so the snowmobile was not upright but was basically moving into the obstacle on its side. Dawn screamed. The snowmobile hit the obstacle a glancing blow and veered into the trees. Trace and Dawn were both ejected away from the collision and into the snow and the trees. A few minutes before there was the noise and the headlights of a moving snowmobile; now, there was silence ... silence and darkness.

Twenty-eight

Mutt and Jeff were arguing again. This seemed to be almost therapeutic to them. It's surprising they had been able to work together for over 15 years.

Jeff was saying, "Ain't this just great! 24 hours ago, we were in a hotel room in Las Vegas with all the pleasures of life just a few steps away. Then you get a telephone call from Henri, whoever that is, and then you take us to this isolated hotel where there ain't nothing but snow. You know how much I hate snow! What are you doing to us?"

Mutt replied, "Patience, Grumpy! Henri is one of Rico's guys. We won't be here long. You know we're not here for pleasure; this is strictly business. We've only been here two hours; I'm expecting a call any minute now."

Unfortunately, for Mutt, the call didn't come for another three hours. Both of the duo had stayed in their hotel room until noon watching some bad daytime TV shows. There wasn't much of a selection up here in the mountains.

When the telephone finally did ring, Mutt answered. Jeff watched again as the same routine unfolded as in Las Vegas. Mutt said nothing. The call was longer this time; it took over three minutes.

Jeff said, "Okay, big guy. What's the deal?"

"He's on a snowmobile a couple of miles from here. His girlfriend is riding on the same snowmobile. We need to arrange an accident."

"What are you talking about? Let's just shoot him and get gone."

"You know as well as I do that Rico stressed that we have to make everything look like an accident; we can't just shoot him."

"Rico, Rico, Rico! He takes something simple and makes it complicated. Okay, okay! What do you have in mind?"

"There's a narrow snowmobile trail about a mile or so from their lodge. We need to make something happen on that trail. Put your heavy coat and boots on, we ain't got much time. We gotta think of something and get there fast."

"I'm taking my gun just in case. To hell with Rico!"

It took only 20 minutes for Mutt to come up with a plan. Jeff didn't think much about plans; contracts like this one were simple ... just seek and destroy. He was impatient, but he'd let Mutt call the play for right now. Each of them rented something they'd never driven before ... a snowmobile. It took a little while, but they got the hang of driving it, even though their driving was a little clumsy. Mutt parked his snowmobile off the trail in a hidden part of some woods nearby. Jeff stayed put there while Mutt trudged back to the back entrance of their hotel. Mutt found what he wanted; somebody had left their snowmobile parked there, keys and all. He got in the saddle and drove the confiscated snowmobile back to where Jeff was waiting, and then the two snowmobiles were off to the LI Lodge.

.Matt's caller had assured him that there was only a single trail that Earl could use to drive his snowmobile back to the LI Lodge. The trail was easy to find, although it was beginning to snow and get dark. Once on the trail, Mutt found the perfect place for an accident. There was a hairpin turn just over a small hill providing hidden visibility, with trees closely bordering each side of the trail. He parked the stolen snowmobile in the middle of the trail, completely blocking the trail. There was no way Earl could avoid an accident, especially because he had been told how recklessly Earl drove cars...and probably snowmobiles.

Satisfied his obstacle was in place, the two men rode Jeff's snowmobile back to their hotel. They stopped just before reaching the hotel and picked up Mutt's rented snowmobile. It was pretty dark when they checked their rentals back in; it was also snowing heavily. Mutt couldn't have asked for better weather for his plan. The records showed he and Jeff checked out two snowmobiles for the day. The abandoned snowmobile on the trail belonged to someone else. Earl's accidental death was imminent. He thought he would ask Rico for a bonus.

Twenty-nine

The sound of one snowmobile hitting another was brief; the sound was drowned out by the continual gusts of winds and the swirling snow that followed. Trace was dazed. He was lying almost face down in a snowbank piled up against a tree. He was lucky. A few feet to his right was a tree without an accompanying snowbank. He was able to get to his feet, dazed but otherwise just a few sore limbs and bruises. *What about Dawn?* She was lying, face up, eyes closed, a short distance to his left. She was softly moaning. Evidently both of them had been thrown off, away from the collision, into some piles of snow. He quickly went to her side, with his knees in the snow, and gently removed her helmet and then brushed some snow from her face. That seemed to awaken whatever state she was in, and her eyes made contact with Trace's.

"What a lousy driver!" she exclaimed. "From now on, I'm the driver."

Trace's relief was so wonderful. He had to laugh and his laughter caused Dawn to laugh as well. He lightly cradled her face in his hands and kissed her very gently.

"Are you okay?" he asked.

"I believe so," she replied. "What did we hit?"

"It looks like some stupid person abandoned his snowmobile right in the middle of our trail. Ours is pretty much smashed. Fortunately, I have my phone. I'll call the lodge and get some help."

It didn't take long for a rescue team to come and take them back to the lodge. Both Dawn and he were fine, just a little sore. However, considering the circumstances they were very lucky. After they cleaned up, they joined Martin at the dinner table.

Martin said, "Earl, from what I saw, you did some good driving there. You two could have been killed or seriously injured."

Trace replied, "Yes, probably more luck than skill. How do you suppose someone could be so stupid to leave his snowmobile right in the middle of the trail?"

"Don't know. We cleared the trail for tonight. Me and a couple of guys will check things out tomorrow. Oh, yeah, Earl, before I forget it. I talked to Gordon about your accident. He was very sympathetic. He said it would be okay to come to our meeting tomorrow morning at 8:30 instead of 8:00."

Earl nodded his head, thinking sarcastically, *It looks like every time I'm hurting, I get a 30 minute reprieve. Great! What if I'm in the hospital? 60 minutes?*

The next morning Gordon and Martin started their 8 o'clock meeting at 6:45. After they covered some of LI's issues and problems, they turned their attention and discussion to Trace and Dawn.

"What do you think?" Gordon asked.

"You made some good choices, boss. Tr…er…Earl is really doing a good job. I told you about his conversation with Fontano … he didn't cow to him at all. Kept his temper and kept our position. It's all on tape; listen to it when you have a chance."

"What about Dawn?"

"Fine; not spoiled; good head on her shoulders. She's a sweetie. Got the staff here clicking their heels when she wants something. Nice personality. But, the elevator scare in LA really bothered her. And, now we have this snowmobile accident; it's not going to help."

"I understand. Did the elevator accident bother Earl?"

"Not to my knowledge."

"How are the two getting along together?"

"I haven't seen any issues or problems. Up until yesterday, they were just sorta friendly with each other. It may be a new ballgame now. At dinner last night, they were more than just friendly. Don't know where that's going from here."

"Hmm, okay. What about that accident last night?"

"Well, it doesn't look like an accident to me. There was nothing wrong with that snowmobile parked on the trail. It was completely tanked up and drivable in every way. Also, it was parked in the one place, the hairpin curve, that no one could see until the very last second. Let me tell you. Earl did a great job not having a head-on collision. After our meeting this morning, I'm going to take another look at everything and also find out who owns that snowmobile."

"Good! Let's not tell either Earl or Dawn that you have any suspicions about what happened. Right now it's just some stupid jerk that abandoned his snowmobile in the wrong place."

"Right!"

Thirty

At exactly 7:59, Trace strolled into the meeting with Gordon and Martin. He was not going to give those guys any satisfaction about a 30-minute time bonus.

Gordon said, “Well, well, how’s Evel Knievel this morning?”

Trace replied, “Sore, but lucky!”

Gordon said, “Yeah, I’m so glad you and Dawn weren’t hurt seriously yesterday. You have any injuries we need to take care of?”

“No! I’m really fine. No problems.”

“Great! This session won’t take long. I need to lay out what the next couple of weeks look like. The first week or so will be a combination of R&R and business. We will be on the company’s yacht, cruising and mooring along the French Riviera. After that we will be in Los Angeles for the premiere of a movie. There’s no prep for the premiere except to look at your picture book and learn who you are supposed to know. Our business discussions on the yacht will take more prep on your time. Stay loose this morning; I’ll meet with you for an hour or so later.

“I’ll let Martin give you an overview on our trip to the riviera in a few minutes. Before he does, I need to ask you a question about Dawn. What is your relationship with her? Are you guys getting along?”

“She’s a very nice, sweet girl. We have no problems unless I ask her to go riding again!”

All of them laughed; Gordon most of all.

Gordon continued, “I’ll tell you why I ask about Dawn. She needs to go with us to the riviera. I’m having our key management there to discuss our finances and the potential buyout of our company. And, as usual, our keys will have their spouses or friends with them … or at least they’re invited. Michael started having these annual business sessions in

Monaco this time of year many years ago before he died. We always have a good time, and we always accomplish a lot in our business sessions.

"Of course, Dawn needs to be there as your companion during our so-called free time following the end of each day's business session. That's important because just about everyone will bring their spouse or friend. We do a lot of social things as couples, and we want Earl to have a friend so he can join in those social things. The three times Earl attended he always had a female companion. A different one each time, I might add."

"I understand. That's great. I'd like to tell her after we have this morning's briefing."

"Sure. I was going to suggest that you do the inviting."

Martin had been just listening, but now it was his turn to do some talking.

He said, "Gordon wanted me to give you a few details regarding the trip. Gordon and I are charter members of this annual event, so we've tailored our experience to establish this year's plans.

"The business part of our agenda will take two and one-half days. But, we will be aboard a yacht along the riviera for a total of seven days ... so we're going to have a little R&R before the meetings start. We will fly to Marseilles and climb aboard the yacht, which will act as our floating hotel for all seven days. Our itinerary will include moorings at St. Tropez, Cannes, and Nice before our business session destination at Monaco. The business sessions in Monaco will be on the yacht and they will end every day promptly at two-thirty in the afternoon giving us a lot of time to enjoy the pleasures of the yacht, Monaco, and even Monte Carlo, if you have the urge to gamble."

Trace said, "That sounds wonderful. I'm ready for some sailing and sunshine."

Gordon said, "I'm ready, too, but I haven't had a chance to tell Martin that I won't be able to fly with you to Marseilles; I have an important bit of business to take care of before I can be there. I'll definitely be in Monaco for the business sessions, but I'm not sure if I can get there before then."

Martin said, "Something else, Earl. As a reminder, our two security guys will be traveling with us … Gordon said that those guys will be married to us for some time … at least until the BOD meeting."

Gordon nodded his head and said, "Right, and I don't want to hear 'until death do us part'."

Trace said, "Me neither!"

Gordon then said, "Oh, yes, Martin. I need to remind you of something."

"What about, Gordon?" Martin said, looking questioningly at Gordon.

Gordon replied, "Gambling losses are not legitimate business expenses; don't put 'em on your expense statement."

"Oh, yeah … I have a hard time remembering that."

"Do you need a written reminder?"

"Ah … no, I'll remember."

"Thanks Martin! See you guys later."

Thirty-one

Neither Trace nor Dawn had ever been to France much less the French Riviera; they were both excited to have some R&R and pleased it was to a place they had never been before. However, Earl had been here several times, so Trace had to act like he'd seen all this. In fact, when Gordon told Trace about this trip, he spent significant time on the internet educating himself on all the port cities where they might go ashore. Also, because LI had used this same yacht, named the *Synergie*, the last 10 years, Gordon gave Trace a folder describing the yacht deck layouts and pictures and names of all the crew members.

Upon arrival at the Marseilles airport, the three travelers, Trace, Dawn, and Martin, were met by a French security company that provided them with two bilingual bodyguards, Louis and Rene, who were to be with them during their stay on the yacht. A limo was waiting for them, and they took a driving tour of the city. Dawn's eyes sparkled as she did some window-shopping and people gazing without leaving the limo. Trace thought he would just throw in a comment. He pointed to an open café, and said, " Dawn, look to my right. See that café! That's one of my favorite places when I am here!"

Martin said nothing intelligible, but he rolled his eyes upward while his face was saying "forgive him".

Dawn didn't want the city tour to end so quickly, but Martin deemed otherwise. It was late in the day, and he wanted them to board their chartered yacht before dark.

The limo took them to the pier where their leasing agent was waiting. All the paperwork had already been taken care of so they got aboard an enclosed tender that took them to the *Synergie* that was to be their residence for the next seven days. Dawn found out later that the tender was one of two tenders that traveled with them on the *Synergie*.

A Frenchman, Paul Fontaine, was the *Synergie*'s captain and he greeted them warmly on their arrival aboard ship. Captain Fontaine knew Earl and Martin and was introduced to Dawn and the two bodyguards by Earl.

Captain Fontaine said he would personally escort them all on a tour of the yacht if they'd like to go. Martin declined as did Trace, although he really wanted to improve his knowledge of where everything was. Dawn happily accepted the offer; she was in seventh heaven.

Trace and Dawn were unprepared for the size and luxury of the yacht ... which was actually called a super yacht or mega yacht in the industry because of its size. It was over 270 feet in length and had four spacious decks for guests. There were four dining rooms: two indoor and two outdoor. There were two outdoor lounges, two indoor salons for social gatherings, a cinema room with a 65-inch screen, a library of music and movies, a fitness facility, a Jacuzzi and a piano bar. The décor and furnishings throughout the yacht were luxurious; the carpets and linens were all first class.

Captain Fontaine told Dawn he had a crew of 21 including a 1st Mate, a Chief Engineer, a Steward, a Bartender, two Chefs, a Housekeeper, a Security Officer, and a Medic. She met several of them on her tour and was quite impressed with their friendliness and command of the English language because most of them were French. Dawn had a fair speaking knowledge of the French language, so she knew she was going to enjoy speaking to them in their native language.

All the 16 guest staterooms were situated on the main or upper deck, each room having a large picture window allowing for perfect viewing. Earl had the master suite, the same one his parents used when they were alive. Gordon had the executive stateroom; Dawn and Martin each had a VIP suite; the two bodyguards each had a guest cabin.

If all this wasn't enough, the yacht had several jet skis, water sleds, water skis, snorkeling equipment, scuba gear, and fishing equipment.

That evening, after a gourmet meal, Dawn was telling Trace and Martin that she was living in a fairy tale or perhaps a wondrous dream where she hoped she would never wake up. She said, "This is fabulous! I know hardly anyone has the opportunity to live like royalty for a few days. I'm lucky; I love it!" Then she asked Trace this question:

"Earl, how is this affordable for Langston Industries? I realize you're having a business conference on this yacht later, but still ... how is it affordable?"

Trace's memory served him well; he remembered reading a copy of the yacht contract that was included in the Business Briefcase that he had studied while he was becoming Earl.

Trace replied, "Well, Dawn, at one time LI owned the company that owned this yacht and several luxury yachts like this one. Dad decided to sell the yacht company so that he could expand another part of LI's business. However, dad loved this yacht, and traveled on it many times. So, what he did was negotiate with the buyer of the yacht company such that LI could take one seven-to-ten-day cruise, each year for 12 years for 40% of the normal booking price. It's affordable at a 40% discount and I'll be sorry when the 12 years are up several years from now."

"Your dad was quite a good businessman, wasn't he?"

"Yes, he was, and he was a fine man besides."

Thirty-two

Meanwhile, Gordon was taking care of that important bit of business that delayed his flight to France. His business took him to the 1000 Islands where the real Earl was sheltered. He flew to Alexandria Bay, New York on his way to the Langston vacation home in the 1000 Islands. He was going to follow up on a telephone call he had received two days earlier when Trace and Dawn had their snowmobile accident. The Indian doctor, Dr. Khatri, who was tending to Earl was the caller.

Dr. Khatri was excited and pleased. He said, "Dr. Brewer, I have good news! In my judgement, Carl has almost completely recovered. I don't know anything more I can do for him. He does still have unplanned fainting spells that I am treating with medication. If he takes the medication, he doesn't faint. Attitude-wise, he's become very restless and even agitated at times. Mr. Link is working with him, but he needs to talk to you."

Gordon replied, "Good! It sounds pretty good. Tell me more about the fainting spells ... do they have a name?"

"Yes. It's called VS, *Vasovagel Syncope*. Under certain circumstances a person's blood vessels open too wide or the heartbeat slows, causing a temporary lack of blood flow to the brain. Sometimes when that happens, a person faints. Lying down usually restores consciousness quickly. VS itself is not dangerous, but a fall or a VS while driving could be. Before Carl faints, he has recognizable symptoms, so he is able to avoid injuring himself. VS is controlled by meds and over time preventable. In Carl's case, he just needs to stay on the meds for now."

"Anything we can do about it?"

"Not let him overdo things like sports, exercise, or even just standing. Minimize anything stressful. Keep him on his meds."

"Thank you, doctor. I'll be there in two days or so. Please tell Carl and Link I'm coming there to talk with them."

"Yes, I will."

"Thank you, doctor."

Gordon was pleased with Earl's recovery, but he was concerned Earl would unmask Trace or do something else detrimental that would mess up this whole complicated scheme.

Gordon's flight to Alexandria Bay was without incident. After landing at Maxson Airfield he rented a car for the short drive to Clayton where he rented a boat to complete his trip to the Langston vacation home in 1000 Islands.

Lincoln and the doctor were waiting in the massive den for Gordon when he arrived. After a short conversation with them, Gordon was ready to talk to Earl, but he wanted privacy. They understood; Link escorted Gordon to the back of the home where there was a glassed-in porch overlooking the South-end of the island and Lake Ontario.

"Nice view," Gordon volunteered.

"Yep," replied Earl, "but it gets old after a while."

"How are you feeling?"

"Fair. I don't have all my strength yet, although I'm on a pretty rigorous rehab program. I guess they told you about my fainting spells?"

"Yes, I know about the spells ... stay on the meds! You had a pretty bad accident. I'd say you're pretty lucky. The Porsche wasn't that lucky, there wasn't enough left to identify it as a Porsche."

"Yeah. Link told me a few things about the accident, but there's a lot he hasn't told me, also."

"What has Link told you?"

"'Bout the same things you said. That I was pretty lucky and there wasn't anything left of the Porsche. Oh, he also mentioned I was pretty stupid to be driving so fast on such a bad night. I guess I agree with all that. Then he talked about me being someone named Carl Bergstrom and told me that's who everyone here thinks I am except him. He also said I was to stay put here until you gave the go-ahead. He won't even let me use the telephone, the computer, or watch the news. I guess I don't agree with any of that. What's the deal, Gordon? Why am I a prisoner? Are you trying to take over the company?"

"No! You are not a prisoner, and, no, I am not trying to take over the company. But first, how's your medical staff and care? Any problems or complaints?"

"Nope!"

"What about Lincoln Smith?"

"We're on good terms. He's more than a good warden; we've become very good friends."

"Great! Now maybe I can answer some of your questions."

So saying, Gordon proceeded to tell Earl everything that had transpired since his accident, including the hiring of an actor to impersonate him. Gordon was surprised at Earl's reaction to everything that had taken place while he was unconscious. Earl had no reaction; he just listened and asked a few questions along the way. Most of the questions had to do with Trace and Dawn.

Then Gordon asked the big question: "Earl, I know you are unhappy here. But, now, knowing what has happened and why it happened, do you think you can be Carl Bergstrom and stay put here in 1000 Islands until the buyout issue goes away? It still means no phone calls and no internet communication whatsoever. I think your coming back on the scene now is an unnecessary risk and might blow the whole buyout problem. Please stay here and complete your rest and physical therapy so that you get the muscle strength back that you lost as a result of your accident and your long sleeping spell. I know you do not favor the buyout deal ... let me see it through the way it's going now. However, you're still the boss and I'll do what you want me to do."

"Gordon, once I became conscious, I was frustrated and angry because I didn't know what had happened and what was going on. I guess I've been that way until your visit today. You've resolved all the questions and concerns I've had. I don't disagree with the way you've handled things. I think if the word had gotten out about my accident and possible incapacitation our company would have had some major problems. I'll back you and stay here longer."

"That's just great, Earl! I appreciate your support. I'm sorry about the inconveniences."

"There are some things you could do to make my stay here a little better. I'd like to spend a lot of my time here understanding our company. I would like to understand company finances more. And, I'd like to read some books on leadership. Can you get that material to me?"

A surprised Gordon nodded his head in agreement. "Sure," he said, "I'll have our folks in Utah send that stuff to you asap."

Earl continued, "I've had a chance to do some heavy thinking about what I have done in the past and what kind of person I'd like to be in the future. I guess you can say I've had a real wake-up call. That's a long answer to why I'm supporting this deal. My Dad trusted you; I trust you now. I'll play it your way, just keep me informed."

Gordon had never had a conversation with Earl that had gone as well as this one. He had never dealt with this version of Earl before. Great! One big worry and fear evaporated. He was ready to join his R&R collaborators on the French Riviera after a couple of days in New York.

He talked to Link before he left.

"Link, I had a great conversation with our patient. Please get him any company material he wants from Utah asap. I'll send them an okay by email. Release the doc and his staff but keep the security personnel here until I get back from Europe. Thanks for your good work!"

Thirty-three

The *Synergie* cruised overnight and anchored in St. Tropez. Mid-morning a parasailing boat named *Insouciant* pulled up beside the *Synergie*. The captain of the *Insouciant* called out, “Ahoy, *Synergie*, is Monsieur Langston aboard? I'd like to speak to him, please?”

Hearing the request, Trace went over to the side of the yacht and saw a thin, wiry man looking up at him from the deck of his parasailing boat. He was balancing himself as the Mediterranean waves were causing his smaller boat to gently bob up and down. The captain smiled when he saw someone on the yacht, put his small megaphone down, and aimed a question at Trace.

“Are you Monsieur Langston, sir?”

“Yes, I am,” replied Trace. “And, who are you?”

“I am Captain Monfort, sir. I am captain of this parasailing boat. I have been hired by one of your friends, Monsieur Gordon Brewer, to take you parasailing this morning. He wanted to surprise you and he insists that you do this.”

Trace didn't have to wrestle with a decision. He replied. “Yes, that sounds like fun. Give me a few minutes and I'll be right with you.”

Trace had seen some videos on parasailing. It looked like an adventurous sport, so it was high on what he called his will-do list, a more upbeat term than a bucket list. He sought out Dawn and Martin to join him. But they both declined, saying they just wanted to read and relax on the yacht. However, Martin wanted Louis, one of the security guards, to go with Trace as a bodyguard and spectator.

Martin called out, “Ahoy! Captain Monfort!”

Monfort shouted back. “Yes, what is it?”

“Monsieur Langston is coming, but he will have a companion with him.”

"Oh, I'm so sorry. We can only have one passenger!"

"Just one?"

"Yes. Just one."

"That's too bad. Unfortunately, Monsieur Langston will not be able to come then."

"Oh, please let him come. My boat; she is just too small; we can only have one passenger! Just one!"

"Sorry, Captain. That really is too bad. Come back when you have a bigger boat!"

The conversation continued back-and-forth until finally Captain Monfort acquiesces. He reluctantly accepts both Trace and Louis as passengers. As soon as Trace and Louis boarded the *Insouciant*, Captain Monfort had his boat turn away from the *Synergie* and sail toward a nearby launching platform.

On their way to the launching platform the boat captain gave Trace some safety instructions and told him parasailing was just like flying a kite from the boat. The captain told him that boat speed, boat maneuvering, and length of the towrope would control almost all of Trace's flight. Trace was surprised and a little disappointed to learn he had almost no control of the parasail; it would be just a joy ride for him, very much unlike paragliding.

When they reached the launch platform, Monfort's helper, Matteo, put a life preserver on Trace and the flight harness that was attached to the parasail canopy by a towrope that led back to a reel on the boat, somewhat like a fishing reel. The boat captain said he would take Trace up high for 15 minutes or so, reel him down low to dip his feet in the water and then take him up high again. After another 15 minutes or so he would be cut loose for a gentle float down to the water where the boat would pick him up.

The parasail canopy fluttered behind the hitched-up Trace as he stood on the launching platform. When he said he was ready, the boat moved away from him. As the boat gradually accelerated it slowly took up the towrope slack. When the towrope became taut, Trace had liftoff; he was airborne.

From the boat deck of the yacht, the view of the beaches and the blue sea was merely beautiful. The view at 250 feet was stunning. And, the ride was fun and exhilarating. It would have been better if he could control the parasail, but that was no big deal. Sure enough, the captain slowed the boat gradually and the parasail was lowered so Trace could skip along the top of the water and dip his feet occasionally. Then the boat sped up and the parasail ascended this time to over 300 feet. This time the boat picked up speed and the parasail followed suit. In fact, the parasail speed made the ride a little uncomfortable and bumpy. Then, it happened. Trace felt like he was being shot from a slingshot; the boat had stopped, but he hadn't and worse still he was headed down toward the water at a pretty fast velocity. There was nothing he could do except brace himself. As he hit the water, he tried to release the harness, but the release was locked and wouldn't budge. The canopy flowed over him; he was trapped under it while the whole apparatus slowly began sinking. Then he lost consciousness.

Thirty-four

Mutt and Jeff had arrived in Marseilles the day before Trace and his companions. They were not interested in sightseeing or anything else Marseilles had to offer. Instead, they rented a car and immediately left the airport traveling east. They were in St. Tropez in a trifle over two hours. In another 30 minutes they located the place they were seeking. It was a small shack-like residence just on the outskirts of St. Tropez. A knock on the door fetched its resident, a small, balding man, probably in his mid-50s. The resident opened the door, looked at the two and said, with some irritation, "Que veux-tu?"

Mutt pushed the surprisingly smaller man aside and entered the shack. Jeff was right behind him. Mutt got in the small man's face. He spoke first. "Look, Frenchie, you speak English to us! None of that parlez-vous stuff. You know who we are and what we want!"

The Frenchman was not cowed. He simply said, "Maybe?"

Mutt said, "Are you Monfort?"

"Maybe?"

Jeff grabbed the Frenchman by the throat and pushed him against the wall with his feet dangling at least 18 inches off the floor. "Okay, Frenchie, zap the 'maybes'. Get real! I mean really real! We're here on business and I know you know Rico and I know you used to be cell mates with Rico's right-hand man Henri. We ain't got time or patience with your 'maybes'! Are you ready for business or ... maybe ... that would be our maybe ... somethin' else?"

The Frenchman couldn't talk but waved his arms frantically until Jeff rather reluctantly released his throat hold.

Jeff said, "Speak! Talk to my friend Mutt here!"

The Frenchman was now cowed. His posture was surrender. Catching what breath he had left, he said in a rasping voice, "Yes, I'm Monfort and I know Henri. He called me several days ago. I hadn't talked with him in several years. He described a job for me that would pay well. I said I might be interested. Are you gentlemen here to discuss that job?"

Mutt replied, "Man, you are dumber than you look. Of course we are! You got anyone else in this place?"

"Mais non!"

"Good! You got a parasailing boat business, don't you?"

"Oui!"

"Frenchie, knock off the French. Yes or no please."

"Yes. Yes, I have a parasailing boat business."

"Okay! So that there's no misunderstanding about the job, here's the deal. You are to arrange a parasailing accident for a certain person. That certain person must die because of this accident. He must die, do you understand? He must die! For that we will pay you 10,000 American Dollars tonight and another 15,000 dollars after the job is done."

"Yes, that is the job Henri described to me."

"Well?"

"It is dangerous for me and also, it might affect my business. If my parasailing license is suspended, I will need another $10,000. On that basis I will do it. Who is the person and when will he be here?"

"Wrong answer, Frenchie! That was a 'Yes' or 'No' question!"

"Yes."

"Good! We have an understanding! But, Frenchie, you are a poor host. We would like some wine and cheese while we go over the details with you. After the wine, after the cheese, and after the details, you will get our down payment of $10,000. Remember, Frenchie, failure is not an option!"

Jeff was the one who thought up the parasailing scheme. He remembered reading about a parasailer who died after the out-drive engine on the parasail boat failed, the boat abruptly slowed, and the parasailer crashed into the water. Of course, the problem was to induce Earl to try parasailing. If he had been disinterested, they would have to go to Plan B, which probably meant boarding Earl's yacht and assassinating him. However, Mutt thought up the perfect inducement for Plan A: Earl would not turn down parasailing if it were a gift from Gordon.

The two surly businessmen left after dining with their terrified client.

Thirty-five

Jean-Paul Marcelle trained his binoculars away from the busy beach and looked at some of the yachts that were moored in the harbor. It looked like another boring day for him and his fellow French coast guard crewmembers who patrolled the St. Tropez harbor. Of course, he did enjoy disciplining some of the rich vacationers, especially Americans, when they broke or bent some of the harbor's rules. He didn't mind the boring part too much; boring meant no paperwork ... no paperwork made Jean-Paul happy.

The boring day and the paperwork requirement changed in a matter of minutes. Jean-Paul saw the parasail and parasailer crash into the water. He alerted the crew, turned their boat, and they rushed toward the scene of the accident.

From the deck of the yacht Dawn had watched Trace's entire ride through her binoculars. It looked like fun; she was sorry she hadn't gone parasailing with Trace. Then she saw Trace's sail dive toward the water at a high rate of speed; she screamed, and her scream got Martin's attention. When Martin hurried to her side, she said nothing, she just pointed toward the parasail that was in the water. She didn't have to say anything; Martin knew that Trace must be under that sail. He quickly launched a jet ski and drove it toward the sail.

The "accident" was no surprise to Captain Monfort. The parasailing flight had gone as planned and the flight had moved further and further away from shore. Then it was the moment of a planned misfortune. Monfort, at the helm, caused the boat to make a very sharp turn. At the same time, he shut the boat engines off. The boat almost overturned. Monfort had braced himself but even he was thrown roughly to the cabin floor. A deluge of water drenched everyone in the open part of the boat.

Earl's bodyguard Louis lurched to the lower side of the boat and was thrown over the side into the harbor water. Monfort's helper, Matteo, managed to stay aboard, but he evidently had hurt his arm and was lying in a good bit of water that nearly had swamped the boat. Monfort was hoping, but not sure, that Earl had been killed or drowned. He started the boat's engines and turned the boat towards the half-floating, half-submerged parasail canopy. He was set to go there to confirm or ensure that Earl was dead, but then, he heard a shout for help. It was the bodyguard who had been thrown overboard. What was left of Monfort's conscience would not let him go off and leave a drowning Frenchman. He turned the boat back toward Louis and was able to fish him out of the water. Matteo was able to help despite what was obviously a broken arm. Louis was dazed and collapsed on the cabin floor. Before he passed out, he said, "Captain, we need to see about Mr. Langston! Let's go see about Mr. Langston!"

Monfort nodded his head, then turned the boat toward the fallen parasail. As he did, he saw another boat speeding toward the parasail. It was the Coast Guard! He knew it would be foolish now to go to the parasail; he would get there before the Coast Guard, but not in time to do anything except wait to be harassed with questions he couldn't safely answer. He made up his mind quickly; he told Matteo, "Look at that boat going toward the parasail. It's the Coast Guard! We'll just be in the way. I need to take care of you and see about the bodyguard." So saying, he had Matteo release the parasail from its towrope and headed the boat back to shore.

Thirty-six

As Jean-Paul's Coast Guard boat sped toward the fallen parasail, he noticed the parasail boat was headed toward shore; the towline had evidently been cut or pulled loose. He radioed his dispatcher, described the retreating boat, and asked that the boat and its occupants be detained.

It took about 10 long minutes to reach the fallen parasail. When they came along side, two of the crewmembers dove into the water to locate the parasailer. They found him under the canopy, still in the parasail harness, and on his back with his head and shoulders above water. He was breathing, but he was unconscious. The release on the parasail's harness was jammed, so it took the two crewmembers several extra minutes to get the unconscious man out of the harness and into the Coast Guard boat.

As Trace was being moved into the boat, Martin on his jet ski arrived. Jean-Paul, in a gesture of sheer annoyance, briefly put his hand to his head, saying. "That's all I need; civilian help, an onlooker, and more paperwork."

Jean-Paul used his native language to greet Martin, who used his native language to say he was an American and didn't speak French. Jean-Paul thought, *it's getting worse … now I have an American to contend with.* However, Martin squared his presence away in less than a minute. He told Jean-Paul that the parasailer was Earl Langston, a passenger on the nearby *Synergie*, moored near the entrance of the harbor. He suggested that Earl be taken to the yacht where they had a medic as a crewmember. Jean-Paul agreed; he knew that the injured party needed medical help beyond first aid right away. He turned the Coast Guard ship toward the *Synergie* with Martin still aboard as a passenger. One of the crewmembers rode the jet ski back.

The good news came quickly. Trace regained consciousness before they reached the yacht. He was still weak and shaky, but he was coherent. With the help of the crew, Trace was able to stand and climb aboard the yacht. The yacht's medic was ready and waiting; Trace was examined, and he was going to be all right. Jean-Paul and his crew were treated to a glass of wine and were thanked profusely by Martin and Dawn.

After sharing in the wine fest, Jean-Paul changed from rescuer to policeman. He questioned Trace for some 20 minutes, attempting to identify what happened. Trace was not much help. He had not noticed anything unusual and whatever happened, happened while he was high in the air. He was too high to see anything. He did mention that his bodyguard, Louis, was on the boat. Perhaps Louis could help.

Jean-Paul was annoyed, but then this seemed to confirm his impression of Americans ... friendly but not helpful. Jean-Paul and his crew left to retrieve the parasail as evidence and then went back to shore to interview the parasail's boat occupants. Then it would be paperwork. Always paperwork! How to explain all this in the paperwork? Damn the rich Americans anyway!

Thirty-seven

Carson Baker had finally decided what had to be done. His bad luck and Earl's good luck were almost impossible for him to fathom. How could Earl keep escaping what Carson had in store for him? Carson was frustrated but he wasn't worried; Earl would die, his good luck couldn't continue forever. In the meantime, he was going to punish Earl in another way: he would kill his grandmother. That simple, black thought energized him, made him smile.

It was about time he had some happy thoughts after his unplanned, hurried exit from Leo's cabin. That was a nice place to stay; that damn Jamie ruined it. This little place he was renting now was not bad, but it was a hunter's cabin and didn't have a lot of the conveniences that Leo's cabin had. However, it was in an isolated area in the Daniel Boone Forest, and he felt safe from prying eyes and the police. He was confident the police wouldn't be able to track him. He sold his car in Buffalo to make it appear he was going into Canada, but instead he took a bus from there to Cleveland and then one to Columbus where he bought a car to drive down to Lexington and onto this place in the woods. Thanks to Leo he had a fair amount of cash so there was no way to track him.

He didn't hurry down to Grandma Martha's; he liked driving so he just took his time; he wasn't going to give the police the opportunity to stop and question him. He had Grandma's address in Arkansas and a portable GPS; finding her place would be a snap.

It was late in the afternoon when he arrived in Little Rock. He drove around until he spotted a seemingly abandoned car. After a small wait time to make sure no one was paying any attention, he removed that car's license plates. Later that evening, he replaced his car's Ohio plates with the stolen Arkansas plates thinking that his car would attract less attention. He checked into a cheap motel to get a good night's sleep. Before he went to bed, he packed an attaché case with two of his favorite types of pistols and some small tools that burglars used for break-ins. Both pistols were favorites of Carson; both were loaded Glock 22 .40 caliber pistols, the ones he practiced with at Uncle Leo's. There was a silencer on one. He skipped the booze this evening ... celebration time would come later.

It was early in the morning when he left the cheap motel and made his way to the large resort community of Hot Springs Village. *My plan is simple. Break into Grandma's house, kill her and others who might be there, take any valuables, and head back to Kentucky. I will make sure that Earl is given all the details as to how his grandmother died after I make my escape.* Again, these thoughts energized him, made him smile.

The traffic up and down the hills of Hot Springs Village was busy but not really a problem and for Carson it was a plus ... his car blended right in. There was far less traffic up where Grandma lived. And, as he thought, Carson's GPS located Grandma's house easily. And, even another plus, it was isolated near the top of a hill with no nearby neighbors. *This will be so easy.* After two drive-bys, Carson noticed what looked to be a jeep trail about 100 yards down the hill from Grandma's house. *Perfect! I'll park my car there, off the main road where my car will not be seen, and then walk up to her house. Perfect! I must be living right!*

It was a pleasant day; Carson's walk up the hill was not difficult nor was he noticed by anyone. He was carrying the attaché case that he had carefully packed at the motel. Grandma's short, narrow driveway leading to her garage was vacant, which probably meant no visitors. He could see into her garage and saw there was only space for one car ... and there was one car in that space. *She's at home! Living right!*

He walked up and planted himself on the small front porch. He rang the doorbell, ignoring the handwritten instructions on the laminated placard posted above the doorbell which succinctly stated NO SOLICITORS OR STRANGERS! *C'mon, Grandma! ...Get real, Grandma!*

Carson waited a full 15 seconds before he angrily attacked the doorbell again ... he could hear it ringing, *why didn't she come to the door?* 10 more seconds! ... more anger ... Nothing! He pounded the doorbell another time ... more anger ... and this time he beat on the front door ... still no grandma!

Okay, grandma ... just like your grandson ... I may have to hurt you a little for this annoyance ... let's see what your backdoor looks like ... I'll be listening for your garage door going up, so don't try leaving ... I got so many things to tell you about your grandson!

Picking the lock and opening the latch on the back door was a breeze. He walked through the house carefully and quietly wielding the pistol with the silencer ... *no grandma, yet her car is in the garage? What's going on? Where's Grandma?*

He plopped down on one of the soft cushioned chairs in the den to think of a non-existent plan B. Nothing came to mind. *Well, I might as well get a bite to eat, maybe she'll show up to dine with me.* Her refrigerator beckoned. He answered but was surprised ... plenty of stuff in the freezer compartment but very little in the refrigerator compartment. Grandma must be on a trip. *Dammit! She's as lucky as her grandson.*

Thirty-eight

The next morning initiated a day that was a clone of the beautiful day before. *Perfect for any outdoor activity except parasailing,* Trace thought.

His body still ached from yesterday's crash; however, he was in excellent physical shape, and he was quite sure he would be able to do some snorkeling and play with the jet skis that were provided by the yacht.

Trace's accident changed the vacation plans for this 3rd day of the cruise. Gordon had been consulted and he advised them to cancel the short cruise to the mooring at Cannes and move on to Nice. They had nothing specific scheduled that day in St. Tropez except for a second interrogation of Trace and Louis in the morning. The two police detectives from Marseille were on board at 9am to conduct their interrogation. They were disappointed that Trace could not add any information to what had already been provided. Louis, the bodyguard who had an unexpected swim yesterday along with some cracked ribs and a badly sprained ankle, had been brought back on-board last night, was also unable to provide any useful information. Enzo, the lead detective, thought *My friend Jean-Paul is right ... Americans are friendly, but not helpful.* All was not lost: Enzo and his younger companion helped themselves to some excellent pastries and coffee before they left.

An hour after the detectives left the yacht, the *Synergie* was on its way to the port at Nice. It was a beautiful day for cruising and all the ship's occupants enjoyed it very much. Having skipped Cannes, the yacht's itinerary was back on its schedule.

Not everybody was enjoying the beautiful day. In a Cannes' hotel room, there was some spirited conversation between a tall, big man and a very short man. The tall man said, "Well, little feller, you came up short again!"

Mutt, the little feller, angrily responded, "Jeff, don't say that to me again! You know how I hate it!"

"Freedom of speech, little man, freedom of speech."

"Well, I don't like it; especially from a guy who looks like Sasquatch!"

"Okay, I'll cool it for a while. But, tell me, what are we going to do? It's about time we forget about the accident part; we just need to put Mr. Langston away without such complicated mickey-mouse. The runaway elevator, the snowmobile crash, and now the parasailing stuff have all failed. Let's just shoot him and get it over with."

"I'm about ready to agree. However, Rico told us very specifically: 'Make it look like an accident!'"

"Yeah, yeah, I know. But don't you think Langston's getting a little suspicious about the 'accidents'? And, we're running out of time. Our source said they're winding up this trip in a few days and most of those days will be in Monaco. I'd say we need to do something there."

"Okay, big guy! It's your dice! Tell me how we're gonna take care of Langston in Monaco. Tell me! Notice my heavy breathing? I can hardly wait!"

"Yeah! I'll think of somethin' and this one won't fail! By the way, how much did we get back last night?"

"About eight grand! I don't know where the rest of our dough went! He didn't have much time to spend it."

"Give me four! I'm telling Rico we got nothin' back. He owes us that for all the trouble we're goin' through!"

"Okay! That's fine with me."

Thirty-nine

The beautiful, sunshiny days continued. Yesterday's *Synergie's* cruise to Nice was very smooth, scenic, and enjoyable. Now the yacht was moored in Nice's port. There would be sightseeing, shopping, and nightclubs to visit and enjoy. This was the first time on the yacht Trace and Dawn had really had a chance to be together for any length of time and it became quite noticeable that they were becoming very fond of each other.

In mid-morning, Trace and Dawn took the yacht's tender into Nice. Trace insisted the two of them didn't need a bodyguard, so Rene shrugged his shoulders, and stayed on the yacht. The couple began their tour of Nice by going to the typical tourist sightseeing places: a walk through the old town, *Vielle Ville;* another walk-through Nice's famous flower market; a tour of the small *Marc Chagall* Museum to see his renditions of some well-known Biblical stories; and an elevator ride to the top of *Castle Hill* for some great views of the city and the harbor. Trace was disinterested in photos, but Dawn had a voracious appetite for pictures, so time and time again they stopped or paused so she could take photos. Tiring of walking, they stopped at a small outdoor café for a glass of wine and some appetizers; eating more would spoil the wonderful dinners they were enjoying on the *Synergie.*

While they were seated at the outdoor café, Martin spotted them and joined them for a glass of wine and some conversation. Martin told them that he had received word from Jean-Paul late last night that the parasailing incident was considered to be an accident. Captain Monfort and Matteo were absolved of any blame and were released after questioning. Martin asked Trace, "What do you think, Earl?"

"I have no idea. All I know is that my landing wasn't any fun."

"Well, how are you feeling? Any problems?"

Trace replied, "No, none at all!"

Martin said, "Great! Thanks for the wine. I'm off to the airport to meet Gordon who will be flying in later this afternoon. I suppose you guys don't want to join me?"

He paused and then continued, "You don't have to answer that...I'd rather have fun, too. Ciao!"

Trace and Dawn chorused a goodbye.

After some more leisurely time at the café talking and people watching, they left their table to continue their tour of Nice. Trace quickly found out that Dawn had exchanged her sightseeing shoes for shopping shoes. Several of the crew members had suggested two touristy shopping places: the *Galleries Lafayette* and a flea/street market. To Dawn it wasn't an either one or the other choice. She had Trace take her to both places. Dawn was having the time of her life; Trace was not a shopper, but the atmosphere of the French markets made it enjoyable. Dawn had been warned not to buy any lace curtains at the flea market ... *once in the washing machine they will disappear!*

In late afternoon, just before leaving the flea market for the tender, Dawn began negotiating with a shopkeeper for a small ceramic flower arrangement. After a few minutes, the price was agreed upon; so, she reached in her shopping bag for her purse ... it wasn't there! That's when she discovered Trace wasn't by her side as well. Then, she saw him. He was about 25 yards away: he had just delivered a blow to the head of an athletic, muscular young man, who ungracefully fell face down on the ground. Trace planted his right foot on the middle of the stretched-out man's neck and then leaned over him and stridently said "The purse, please! The purse!"

The young man struggled to get up, but Trace had immobilized him. The young man answered Trace's requests with an anguished, "Non, non, mais non!"

Trace repeated his request, "The purse, please! The purse!"

The answer was the same. "Non, non, mais non!"

Meanwhile, the shopkeeper motioned to a burly man stationed at the end of an aisle and he quickly came to Trace's side. He said to Trace, "I am a guard here. Please let the man up.! What's the problem?"

Trace said nothing. He removed his offending foot and then he and the burly guard helped the young man to his feet. Then Trace pointed to the inside of the young man's jacket and there was the cause of all the commotion: it was Dawn's small purse! The burly man nodded his head in approval and appreciation of Trace's keen observation and quick reaction as he led the young man away. Dawn thanked Trace profusely; it was the first time she had ever been a pickpocket victim.

Shortly after the pickpocket incident, Trace and Dawn were on the tender on their way back to the *Synergie.* Of course, before they boarded the tender, Dawn managed to obtain a small ceramic flower arrangement.

At dinner that evening Trace and Dawn were joined at dinner by two Langston Industries' executives and their spouses who had arrived from Asia for the business sessions scheduled to start two days hence. Gordon and Martin missed the dinner because Gordon's plane had been and still was delayed.

The conversation with executives and their wives went well. None of the four new arrivals suspected that their younger dinner mate was an imposter. After dinner, each of the three couples went their separate ways. Trace and Dawn were tired after their day in Nice. They elected to see an on-board movie together; then they went to their separate cabins for a good nights' rest.

Later that night, and after Trace and Dawn had retired for the evening, a tired, but still sociable Gordon arrived at the airport greeted by Martin and two Langston bodyguards, Bryan and Winston. After they loaded up their rented limo with the luggage and were on their way to the yacht, Gordon asked, "How's it going, Martin?"

Martin gave a half-smile and responded haltingly, "Pretty good, Gordon. Everything has gone well except for the parasailing incident I told you about yesterday. The police called it an accident. I'm not believing it. First the elevator, then the snowmobile ... now, this."

Gordon replied, "Yeah, I understand ... and, I'm going to add to your concern."

"What's that?"

"After you called last night and told me what happened, I became concerned also. So, this morning I thought I would discuss the incident with the Marseilles police who did the investigation. Nothing different about the incident itself. However, guess what? The parasailing boat captain ... I think his name was Monfort ... was shot and killed last night in his home. His home was ransacked, wrecked. The police are considering it a burglary gone wrong. Seems way too coincidental to me."

"Wow! I guess so! That does look bad!"

"Give it some thought. Let's see if we can do something about all these so-called accidents."

"Right, Gordon. Glad to have you with us. Maybe we can talk more in the afternoon? We'll be in the Monaco Port the next three days, and I have to deal with local security people in the morning. Also, I'll be getting a French bodyguard to replace Louis, who got hurt in our parasailing accident. Louis is not in bad shape, but he is physically unable to be a bodyguard now."

"Good! I'm ready for the yacht and a bed right now."

Forty

Like most days it had been a dull, uneventful day in the offices of Hot Springs Security Services. Shift supervisor Clayton Kershaw got up from his absent boss's executive ergonomic desk chair to grab a quick cup of leftover, overcooked coffee. He microwaved the half-filled cup of coffee for 44 seconds and then returned to his boss's chair to enjoy it along with a *Payday* nut roll, his favorite candy bar. *Oh! Oh! Red alert! Looks like it's Mrs. Langston's place; her motion detector sensor has been activated. Probably one of the many false alarms we get, but best check it out!*

Clayton opened the HSSS call book and noted that Mrs. Langston had left a week ago for Connecticut; if a problem came up there were two of her friends to call. So, following the prescribed protocol he made the two calls, but no answer. *Okay, the mobile unit will have to check it out; I've done all I can do. ... Drat! My coffee is already cold!*

Buford "Butch" Smith, the semi-retired policeman in Mobile Unit 1422, took Clayton's call and said he would check out the Langston place and call him back later. He knew which house it was, he'd been there four or five months ago when she'd forgotten to turn off the motion detector after coming home from an afternoon bridge game. But, this time was different; Clayton told him Mrs. Langston was in Connecticut. Butch drove up the hill to her place and parked in her driveway. *Everything looks fine from the outside. Car is in the garage.* He peered in one of the front windows but didn't see anything. Then he tried the front door, but it was locked. *Should I call for backup? Nah, I don't think so. We haven't had any break-ins for several months now ... and when we did it was usually some unarmed druggies looking for some pawn material. Since there's no car around, if it was a break-in, they're probably long gone by now. Those guys get in and out in 10 minutes. I'll just walk around to the back door and check it out.*

After raiding the freezer for some meaningful food, Carson searched for some beer to wash it down, but had to settle on a couple of Dr. Peppers instead. *Grandma sure don't know how to treat her guests!* Then, he toured the house to see what valuables might be there. He was disappointed. *Yep! Like the bare refrigerator told him, she must be on a trip ... no cash, no jewelry of any value ... everything small must be locked up somewhere else or she has it with her.* However, there were two items left in her locked rifle cabinet that Carson broke into. There was a small caliber pistol worth a few bucks and a 12-gauge shotgun he would keep. *Well, Grandma, thanks for your hospitality! Being the nice guy I am, I'll leave without doing any damage to your house. I'm sure you and your beloved grandson will worry a lot about your home being violated. I'll thank Earl in person for everything when I see him later.* Carson loaded the shotgun and got ready to leave. It was then when he heard someone rattle the front doorknob. He could see a car parked in the front and a man dressed in a khaki uniform with a sidearm on the front porch attempting to enter the house. *Well, it ain't Grandma and it looks like a very unlucky hillbilly. I hope he likes surprises!*

Bad guys never warn the good guys they're going to shoot them. And, that's what happened this time. As soon as Butch entered the unlocked back door sporting his pistol in his right-hand, Carson shot the semi-retired policeman one time with his newly acquired 12-gauge and watched his face disappear and his body reel back from the blast, his pistol clattering some 40 feet away. Butch never saw Carson nor knew what hit him; he was seriously wounded lying near the backdoor on the cement patio. Carson was still feeling generous, he left through the front door without looking back to see if his victim was alive or dead.

Forty-one

The passengers on the *Synergie* went to bed in the port of Nice and woke up the next morning in the port of Monaco, the final port of their cruise. Early in the morning Gordon and Trace met for an hour over breakfast where Gordon briefed Trace regarding the upcoming work sessions that would begin tomorrow. The 2-day business sessions were to start at 8:30 in the morning and finish each day promptly at 2:30pm. Gordon would conduct the meetings; the agenda would cover financial planning, goals, and obstacles for the coming year. Each of the eight execs would have 60 minutes to discuss his or her responsibility, highlighting the obstacles they faced and how he or she would handle it. Four execs would discuss their work on the first day, the other four were scheduled for the second day. In addition, the corporate attorney and as well as Gordon would discuss the tender offer from Kesterson Industries. Two of the eight execs were women; they brought their spouses so they could enjoy the trip's perks together. The spouses and friends brought by the execs stayed with them on the yacht at night but were tendered to Monaco during the work sessions for shopping or touring as they pleased. After 2:30pm the rest of the day was free for what anyone wanted to do either ashore or using the amenities provided by the yacht and its crew.

After Gordon gave Trace an overview of the business sessions, he asked, "Earl, do you have any questions about the work sessions?"

Trace replied, "What will be my participation? How did Earl handle himself in these work sessions?"

"Excellent questions. In the past Earl would interrupt, ask a few good questions or some really bad questions. More bad than good, I'm afraid. I asked him repeatedly not to interrupt so much, but he did anyway."

"How do you want me to play it?"

"Definitely not like Earl! With your study and IQ, I suspect you know more about Langston Industries than Earl himself does. Don't worry, I trust you and your judgement. Continue on as you're doing. Treat everything as if it were your money but ask only a few questions. All the execs will notice and be surprised … and maybe even curious, but they will be **so** pleased!"

"Got it!"

Now Gordon switched topics; he asked, "Earl, do you have any questions about people: the ones on the yacht you've already met or the ones who will arrive at different times during the day?"

"No, I can't think of any, Gordon. Thanks to the Business Bible you gave me, I've seen all their pictures, memorized their names, spouses, and friends … I've had little trouble so far and really don't expect any today or the rest of the trip. So far it's been good. Do you know if anyone is suspicious?"

"Haven't heard … if they are, they're keeping it from me."

"Great! Anything else?"

"Yes. How are you and Dawn getting along? Any complaints?"

"Great! She's terrific! Probably the second-best hiring decision you've made on this project."

"Thanks! You not only look like Earl, you're starting to talk like him. Enjoy your day, anyway. I'll see you this evening at the reception."

"Okay, see you later!"

Gordon was pleased that Trace and Dawn were happy together; it would have been a problem otherwise. *I am worried, though. I had hoped the Hudson Building elevator "accident" had not been aimed at Trace, but the snowmobile and parasailing incidents made it likely that someone wants Trace aka Earl dead. So far Trace has not seemed overly concerned but I certainly hadn't enlisted him to be a target of some conspiracy. I did talk to Martin about it. We decided that all of us need to be more careful now … maybe we'll be lucky and the police will apprehend the perps. In the meantime, we'll have the French police help with the security of the yacht. I hope Trace and Dawn listen to us. We told them to not leave the yacht without a bodyguard.*

Forty-two

As all vacation and recreation days do, the hours of the day passed quickly. The remaining business executives and spouses arrived during the day, and all were present for the reception that evening. There had not been any new faces in this group of Langston execs for three years, so it was like a reunion of sorts, and they enjoyed each other's company. Morale was good. The friendship was honest, not contrived. As far as the business sessions tomorrow, Gordon was completely relaxed. He knew his managers; they were all competent and made good business decisions. He had three worries: the buyout bid, the unmasking of Trace, and the safety of Trace and Dawn. However, Gordon was smart enough to not let worries drive his judgements or decisions. He was confident that even if unexpected bad things happened, he would be able to respond quickly and appropriately.

Trace's first full day in Monaco had already been planned. Dawn took care of that two days ago. She wanted to spend all day sightseeing in Monaco, and she wanted that day to be with "Earl". Trace readily agreed, although he didn't realize that in Dawn's mind, actually in every woman's mind, sightseeing includes shopping. (This is part of the learning curve for young bachelors.) Dawn had relied heavily on the internet to plan the places she wanted to visit. Her first choice was to travel out of the city onto the very scenic mountain highway, *Moyenne Corniche*, to the medieval hilltop village of *Eze*. Gordon, however, asked her to stay within the city; he felt it would be safer there. Not discouraged, she went to plan B.

Plan B was great. She, Trace, and the ever-present Rene left early in the morning exploring *Le Rocher*, Monaco's old town with its winding, cobblestone roads and alleys, and quaint shops and cafes. They visited the interior of *St Nicholas Cathedral* with its white marble throne, and the burial places of

Princess Grace and Prince Rainier III. They walked through several flower-laden gardens and to the *Palais du Prince* just before noon to watch the changing of the guard in front of the Prince's Palace. The ceremony had all the formal trappings of Buckingham Palace, just on a much smaller scale. Instead of their white uniforms, this day the guards were snazzily dressed: bright blue helmets, black jacket with red cuffs, and blue, red-striped trousers. Rene was very careful with his charges at this point because this venue was always crowded during the guard ceremony.

Then they had a leisurely, people-watching luncheon at an outdoor café followed by a visit to the glamorous Monte Carlo Casino and Opera House. Of course, there was shopping in between the tourist venues, but Dawn was mostly looking and evaluating; she would do her serious shopping the next day. They decided they didn't have enough time to tour the famous *Musee Oceanographique* that had the huge aquariums housing rare and exotic fish; they could visit it on their last afternoon in Monaco. However, they managed to squeeze in a walk through the hillside *Jardin Japonais,* a true replica of a Japanese garden with its rushing waterfall, a pond with koi fish and water lilies, and teahouse. They returned to the yacht, tired but happy. Plan B had worked well.

During the daylight hours almost all of the remaining invited parties arrived. There were a few who would come later that evening. The "later" ones would miss the reception. The reception went well for Trace. He was congenial, knew all the players and spouses thanks to the Business Bible. There were no surprises. None of the executive group he talked with hinted in any way that Earl was not Earl. So, shortly before the end of the festivities that evening, Trace was celebrating, by himself, seated alone at the bar in the yacht's lounge, enjoying a martini. He was unashamedly congratulating himself on what a good job he was doing playing the part of Earl with all of Earl's business associates and their spouses. He had almost finished sipping his martini when thoughts of his success suddenly turned into an anxiety attack. His musings were interrupted when a nice-looking, middle-age, slender woman approached his table, smiled, and playfully said, "Earl, I am hurt. Why are you ignoring me? I thought you and I were best buddies? Oh, even more than just buddies! Has someone else taken my place? No hugs? No caresses? I'm really hurt!"

Ah, *Success is fleeting!* Trace's face went flush, his mind went absolutely numb; he closed his eyes for a brief instance, and tried to think of a generic, if not witty, response to someone he did not know or recognize. *Where was Gordon's calm, cordial, and careful response?* Precious seconds sped by in slow motion! *Nothing! Nothing! I'm dead! It's over!*

Forty-three

"Earl! Earl? Are you okay?" The determined woman continued, demanding a response from the comatose-acting person seated before her. "Perhaps you should stop drinking so early in the day?" she said. "May I order you an American coffee?" she asked, again in a playful manner.

"Oh, I'm sorry," Earl managed to reply with words flowing from a mouth seemingly encased with cotton. "It's been such a beautiful day. I was just daydreaming I suppose."

The woman pouted. "Is that the best greeting you're going to give me after you've been away from me a whole year? Now I know for sure someone else has taken my place. Again, no hug! No caress! You'd think we'd just met!"

Earl rose to his feet, leaned over by the neighboring bar stool, placed his hands on either side of her waist and gave her a short European kiss on each cheek.

"It really is so nice to see you," he said. "I apologize, I'm not myself today. Won't you join me?" he asked, hoping for a refusal. Even as they talked, Trace's mind was beginning to go full throttle as he tried to place who this nice-looking gregarious woman was. She looked like she was a trifle older than he and she spoke her English well but with a slight European accent; an accent that Trace was unable to place with a language.

The woman's cheery manner turned into a rather puzzled look. She bowed her head ever so slightly and grasped her chin between her thumb and index finger of her right hand as she stared at Trace for a few seconds. "No, No," she said. "I think not right now. Perhaps we can get together later."

Her smile returned. "Ciao!" she said cheerily as she turned and left a very worried Trace standing by his bar stool.

Trace watched her as she left the lounge to goodness knows where. "*Dammit!*" Trace's voice box yelled silently to his brain. "*I've blown this one! I need to see Gordon right away! I don't know who she is and it's quite evident she doesn't know who I am either … and, the worse problem she knows who I'm not! We need to instigate damage control asap."*

The martini didn't taste as good now as it had minutes earlier. He gulped it down anyway. He thought about getting something stronger but knew that wouldn't help solve any problems and probably just give him thoughts of inadequacy. He walked to the port side exit, through the same door the woman had left, and peered aft down the side of the yacht. He spotted her talking with Gordon. *Not my day,* he thought. *I wanted to see him first and give him an early warning signal as to what was coming his way. Oh, well, this has been good while it lasted.*

Gordon and the nice-looking lady were just finishing their conversation. She was smiling and laughing with Gordon just as she had been with him earlier in the lounge. Gordon saw Trace and waved to him to stay put, so whatever was going to transpire would happen soon. Trace was relieved; the masochist part of him wanted whatever problem he had to be over quickly. Trace never did like long dying scenes in movies either.

Gordon arrived and steered Trace back into the lounge where he chose a table farthest away from the bartender and two couples who had just wandered in for a nightcap. They jointly decided on a tap beer; Gordon waited until they were served and were alone before he began their discussion.

"How's the day going?"

"Well, Gordon. You probably know how my day is going better than I do."

"You're right. I do. I'd say your day was going pretty well until about an hour ago. All the execs and their spouses have accepted you without question or concern. And, even now you seem to have your A-game back. What happened to your A-game here in the lounge?"

"I just got blindsided … A woman came to my table, and she evidently knew Earl very well ... I didn't know her at all; I was at a loss for words. I know she knows I am not Earl. What can I do to fix it? Who is she anyway?"

"Who are you talking about? What's her name?"

"I don't know! You were talking with her just before you came to the lounge."

"Oh, her. Yeah, I know her. That's Johanna. Don't you remember her picture?"

"No, Gordon, I do not. I have never seen her picture! She's an attractive lady and I can assure you I would have remembered her."

Gordon looked at Trace intently as if he was trying to remember or recall something. "Rats!" he said. "This is my fault. I know what happened now and I apologize. I failed to put Johanna's picture in your Utah books and, worse, we haven't discussed her at all. One of my problems is that I'm extremely business oriented. You've probably noticed. I really don't talk about family very much. You see, Johanna is my wife of some 14 years. We are still happily married although we are separated by my work and her desire to raise our son in her small hometown village of Alpbach in Austria. We always get together during this annual planning session and at a few other times when it is possible for me to get away. I am looking forward when I can retire from this job and move to Austria. We hope I can do that soon. In the meantime, Johanna maintains a gift shop in Alpbach and raises Josef our only son."

"What a relief! I did such a sorry job; I was really worried."

"Yes, I understand. I need to tell you one other thing. Johanna knew you were not Earl when she saw you today."

"What? You mean ..."

"That's right! From what she told me it sounds like she out-acted the actor. She's one-up on you! I'll admit she has an interesting sense of humor ... more like a practical joke kind of thing."

"Well, Gordon, how did she know? How did I give myself away?"

"You didn't give yourself away; I told her. Johanna arrived today; we were able to have lunch together. She has been like a big sister to Earl; she helped him a lot, especially after his father and mother passed away. She knows him so well I was sure she would immediately know you were not Earl. So, I told her who you are and why we were going through this charade. I wanted to let her know what was going on so she wouldn't express her doubts to someone else."

"Wow, what a deal! She got to me really good. You have a beautiful wife, but I'm not going to trust her sense of humor. What an evening!"

"Our charade is totally safe with Johanna, just as it is with Martin and me. And, there is someone else who knows. In the morning I will have Johanna introduce you to Katrin. Katrin is Martin's Austrian friend. They have been coming here together the last few years at this annual meeting. It's one reason I look forward to coming here. Johanna and Katrin will be party to your and Dawn's masquerade. They are aware that Dawn knows nothing about the charade. I assure you that our secret is safe with them. They will not talk about it with you, Dawn, or anyone else. I'll have them meet Dawn in the morning to invite her to go shopping with them tomorrow."

"That sounds really good. No more surprises I hope?"

"Nope! Good night, Earl. See you in the morning."

Forty-four

The second day in Monaco was the beginning of the first business session. The night had passed without any problems for the yacht or for its occupants. As expected, breakfast was sumptuous, splendid and other words describing extravagant, but, then again, that seemed to be the standard of everything about and aboard the *Synergie*.

The business sessions began promptly at 8:30 with Gordon as host. He had assumed being the host and that of session facilitator and moderator following the untimely death of LI's founder, Earl's father. Earl was there as the interim CEO; he had no presentation responsibilities.

The Langston managers on stage during the first day made effective presentations. In addition, Gordon provided the LI managers with current and factual information about the proposed buyout. He dispelled some of the rumors as to LI's stance opposing the buyout: He explained it was LI's intention to move forward as before, protect its employees, and not allow the company to be broken into pieces.

The first day session finished promptly at 2:30 pm; no major issue or obstacle loomed ahead with the exception of the tender offer. Trace had little difficulty playing the part of Earl. Despite Earl's executive title, all the Langston executives knew Earl had little to do with actually making any executive decisions, so the Langston people were accustomed to Earl being in their meetings but not really being a part of their meetings. In fact, in this first day of meetings, they were pleased that the Earl they knew so well and who had such poor knowledge of LI's businesses hadn't interrupted presentations or discussions with some inane questions.

After the session, Trace joined several of the group to go to the casino until it was time for the scheduled evening meal. Earlier in the day, just as Gordon promised Trace last night,

Johanna and Katrin met Dawn in the morning and insisted that she go shopping with them. After all, the two Austrian ladies were experienced Monaco shoppers. *Now what young woman could possibly refuse that invitation, especially since Gordon had given her a generous shopping budget?*

The shoppers didn't arrive in the city until late in the morning. There were other wives with the same intent and schedule, but Gordon's trio of ladies left together and stayed together during the day. Unfortunately, Johanna told Rene, the bodyguard, that he was not needed, so he stayed aboard ship and later accompanied the casino players; the ladies were on their own.

Shortly after noon, the three shoppers decided to have a wine and cheese lunch at a very nice outdoor café. The weather was beautiful, the shopping had gone well, so, they agreed to rest a bit before they continued. About halfway through their meal, a waiter approached the table asking to no one in particular, "Mademoiselle Young?"

Dawn replied, "Yes, I am Mademoiselle Young. What do you want?"

The waiter turned his full attention to Dawn. "Mademoiselle, I have a very urgent call for you. I don't know who it is. The phone is inside, go left, and the phone is near the backdoor exit."

A concerned Johanna immediately said, "Oh, Dawn! Do you want us to go with you?"

"I don't think so. I can't imagine who it is. I'll be right back!"

Dawn got up and made her way to the rear of the café while a puzzled and concerned Johanna and Katrin watched.

About 40 yards down the street, a short man lounging in the shadows of an alley between stores, was looking through binoculars watching the "Mademoiselle" event being played out. "Perfect!" he said, "Perfect!" Mutt continued gloating, *Thataway, Baby, you're doing great! You might not like what's comin', though. Just follow the instructions Jeff will give you so we can introduce ourselves.*

Mutt and Jeff had almost come to blows after their third failure to fulfill their contract. Out of frustration and on short notice, they decided to kidnap Dawn, then either kill or neutralize rescuer Earl through the extension of a yet-to-be-fully-defined convoluted scheme.

Dawn had no trouble locating the phone. She picked up the receiver and said, "This is Mademoiselle Young. Who are you and what do you want?"

The caller hurriedly replied, "Mademoiselle Young, I am police detective Beaumont, Antoine Beaumont. Your friend Earl Langston is in danger and needs help. You must come immediately to help him. Do you understand me? You need to come to help Mr. Langston right away. I do not have time to tell you anything more. You have no time to waste or to return to your table and tell your two friends. Leave out the back door immediately, a black Mercedes is waiting about two blocks down the street. Hurry! Hurry! Goodbye!"

A very frightened Dawn dropped the phone and opened the back door. Sure enough, there was a black Mercedes a block down the alleyway. The Mercedes was moving slowly toward her. She began running toward it, but she only took a few steps before she stopped. She panicked and froze for a few seconds. The Mercedes picked up speed as it rolled toward her. Terrified, she turned to go back inside the café. As she turned, she saw the Mercedes bearing down on her, but she was able to safely get back into the café. The Mercedes rammed into the back of the café, but quickly backed off and fled the scene. The driver did not attempt any further action.

Dawn was quite shaken about the event and her two new Austrian friends were horrified. Shopping was over. They left the café immediately and returned to the yacht via the tender.

Boarding the yacht, Dawn was immediately surrounded by the yacht's medical staff and then its security people. She was shaken but not hurt. Subsequently the Monaco police interviewed her, but she could only say "It was a black Mercedes"; she could provide nothing else helpful.

Before the evening meal, Trace spent some time consoling Dawn and told her he wanted to always be ashore with her from now on. She readily agreed. Gordon and Martin caught up with the couple before the meal to hear what Dawn had to say about the encounter. After hearing her description of the event, Gordon asked Dawn, "It sounds like you almost took the bait. What made you change your mind?"

Dawn did not answer immediately. Finally, she said, "Oh, Gordon, I'm not sure. Things didn't add up. I didn't like the way the emergency was presented to me. How did someone know I was at the café? Why would Earl be in danger? Wasn't Earl in the business meeting? Why was I the one called if Earl was in danger? How did they know my two friends were at the table and why couldn't I tell them what was happening? Why the backdoor, instead being told in person at the front?"

Gordon laughed and said, "Thank you for not saying it was a woman's intuition. I get that a lot. You processed a lot of information, and you made the right decision. We're all so pleased that you are safe and sound. Please let me know if you need anything or if we need to discuss this further."

The attempted abduction was the talk of the yacht in the evening, but it didn't stop the evening entertainment. There were some humorous skits performed by a local group, movies, and music for dancing.

Dawn was tired; she retired early, as many of the other LI group did.

Much to the dismay of two understanding Austrian ladies, Gordon and Martin spent much of the evening discussing security and safety issues. Neither Gordon nor Martin linked Dawn's abduction attempt to all of the recent LI-related "accidents". The local police had convinced them that attempts to kidnap wealthy Americans for ransom is not an infrequent event in Europe, severely damaging their "accident" conspiracy theory. You can't win 'em all.

Forty-five

The third day in Monaco was the beginning of the second and last business session. Another night passed without any problems for the yacht or for its occupants. And, the business session went well; so well, in fact, it finished early, shortly after 1 o'clock.

Trace and Dawn went ashore to spend a little more time sightseeing, accompanied by Rene, of course. Martin had forcefully reminded them not to go ashore without a bodyguard. After yesterday it was a no-brainer. Most of the afternoon they spent just walking and looking; but they did take in the *Musee Oceanographique* with its huge aquariums and its large number of rare and unique ocean creatures. Dining on the museum's *La Terrasse* rooftop restaurant was out because of their early dining plans that evening, but they did have a glass of wine there and enjoyed the remarkable and wonderful panoramic views of the coastline. All in all, a nice sightseeing afternoon visit to the city. Uneventful again; Rene happy again.

They returned to the yacht fairly early because they had to prepare for the LI get together at the *Terrace Exclusive Equivoque* that evening. Dr. Langston had always had a dinner at various top-rated Monaco restaurants for everyone as the final LI event of the planning sessions; Gordon was continuing that tradition. So, it would be dinner and entertainment for everyone beginning at 7pm.

The food, music, entertainment, and atmosphere were first class, a good way to wind up this year's planning session. Some of the participants went back to the yacht immediately after it was over; others sought other entertainment for their last night in Monaco. Trace had already made arrangements for Dawn and him to have a moonlight drive through the cliff areas overlooking Monaco and the Mediterranean. Gordon nixed the drive at first, but finally caved to Trace with the unnegotiable proviso that Laurent and Andre, Louis' replacement, ride shotgun as chauffeur and bodyguard.

The view and the scenery were spectacular. The almost full moon played its part. It was beautiful. It was romantic. Laurent, the chauffeur, was familiar with the mountain road and knew where to stop to allow Trace and Dawn to step out of the limo in order to have a full view of the rocky cliffs that dropped below their feet all the way to the bright lights of the city and beyond the city to the ships in the harbor.

After three prior viewing stops, Laurent pulled the limo over to a small viewing area and parked. He announced, "This is it, Mademoiselle and Monsieur. This is the last viewing place I am to take you. The hour is late. I am advised it is almost time to take you back to your ship. I suggest we stay here only 15 minutes. Enjoy the view!"

The view was great, but a person with vertigo might have felt differently. Right below where Trace and Dawn had been standing there was a sharp drop-off, and it was that way not only in this area but also along the road they had been travelling. A bench beckoned nearby. They took advantage of the bench as they enjoyed the view.

Dawn said, "It's a beautiful view, isn't it, Earl? This whole trip has been great even with yesterday's scare. I feel like Cinderella and midnight is coming and I'll have to go home. The party's over, but I don't want it to be over."

Trace responded, "I don't mind the party being over, but I don't want our relationship to end. And, our relationship doesn't have to end here; I want it to continue until you say it's over. I hope you feel the same way, Dawn."

"Oh, Earl, I do. I do. I do feel that way!"

Suddenly the view was set aside as the two collapsed in each other's arms and tenderly kissed, more than once. In a few moments, Trace noticed that Dawn had become sort of teary-eyed.

"What's the matter?" Trace asked.

"I'm sorry, Earl. So sorry." she said. "I really have fallen in love with you, but I feel there are some problems in our relationship. You have done nothing wrong; I don't think I have done anything wrong; and I feel like I have done the job I was hired to do. Yet, I sense Gordon and you are hiding something from me that I need to know. For instance, all these accidents that keep happening. Then, you're the CEO, but Gordon seems to be calling all the shots, like hiring me and like you seemingly getting permission to do things. Then, your skill in doing impressions and your subduing the pickpocket like you did ... I haven't heard anything about your background that would suggest any of that. I'm sorry, Earl. I'm so in love with you, but all this has just boiled up in me."

An anguished Trace thought how he could best answer Dawn's legitimate concerns. But he knew he could not reveal the truth at this time. No, the party wasn't really over until after the BOD meeting. Hopefully when she heard the truth she would love Trace, not the Earl who was the billionaire he was imitating.

Trace finally responded, "Dawn, I found out yesterday when you thwarted that abduction attempt what a perceptive person you are. Yes, there are some things right now that I can't tell you. I do love you. I do hope you trust me. I hope you will continue to trust me until I can answer your questions. I hope that very much."

Dawn responded with a nod of her head, and they cuddled a few minutes on the bench until Laurent said, "Mademoiselle and Monsieur, it's time we leave."

Trace and Dawn returned to their place in the back of the limo. Nothing more seemed worth saying. Trace felt things would be sorted out in the days ahead. Laurent and Andre took their places in the front seats. The limo pulled forward into the right lane to begin its journey back to the yacht. The limo got up to speed and travelled about 200 yards when a car suddenly came up behind them and hit the left rear of the limo a glancing blow in such a way it caused the limo to spin counterclockwise out of the chauffeur's control. The limo rolled over once and then began a journey off the road, off a cliff into the wilderness below. The last thing Trace remembered was hearing the other passengers' screams.

Forty-six

Fortunately, the limo landed in some small shrubbery on a narrow ledge, a drop of less than 25 feet; otherwise, there would have been no survivors. The limo landed on its side, driver-side down, punishing more severely the chauffeur and Dawn. All airbags had discharged. There was no fire nor did there seem to be a likelihood of fire. Andre never lost consciousness. He disentangled himself from his airbag and, despite his bleeding face and other hurts, began attending to the other passengers. There was nothing he could do for the chauffeur Laurent; he was dead. Andre climbed up and through the passenger door to see to the passengers in the back seats. He was able to open the back door and with difficulty carefully pulled an unconscious Trace and an unconscious Dawn out of the wreckage and lay them side-by-side on the ground. Andre was hurting. He lay down beside them. He needed help. He called 112.

Five hours later, in the ER Section of the Monaco *Princess Grace Hospital Centre*, Martin had just heard the medical reports from the young, white-robed Frenchman in front of him. Martin asked, "Anything else, Doc?"

"No," the ER Doctor answered, "that's all. She will be moved to a hospital room shortly for further testing and observation. Her vitals are good, so I don't expect to find anything major. She still goes in and out of consciousness, but I expect her to snap out of that shortly. She's young and healthy. I think a couple more days in the hospital and she'll be good as new."

"Thank you, Doctor." Martin replied.

The doctor nodded and left.

Martin turned to the figure occupying the lone bed in the ER curtained area marked "Urgences #4". He said, "Okay, Earl. I guess you heard the report about Dawn. It sounds like she's banged up and will be in the hospital a while longer, but she'll be back to normal in a few days. And you? You'll be out of here as soon as they work your discharge papers. You were mighty lucky: mild concussion, chest and arm bruises, negative chest and head X-Rays, sprained left ankle. Are you still feeling okay?"

"Yes, I guess I just conked out for a while. I'm glad Dawn is okay. I would like to see her and stay in Monaco until she recovers."

"Okay, I'll pass your request on to Gordon. I expect him any minute. I talked him out of spending the night here like I did. I promised I'd have a full report for him around 6 o'clock. Knowing him, he'll be here promptly at six.

It was 6 o'clock twenty minutes later. That's when Gordon joined Martin and Trace in Urgences #4. Gordon talked to Trace for a few minutes, but it was Martin he wanted to talk to, so they left the curtained area and went to a corner table in the hospital cafeteria where they could talk in private.

Gordon was curt and grim, not in the mood for chit-chat.

"Okay, Martin," he asked, "what do we have?"

"We've got a lucky guy and his girlfriend who survived a bad crash without serious damage; the guy is being released shortly but the girlfriend will be staying in the hospital a few more days. We've got a chauffeur who was dead at the scene and a bodyguard who has been patched up and detained in ER for further observation. Andre, the bodyguard, did some heroic work at the scene, pulling the others out although he had a broken nose, broken fingers, face lacerations, and three broken ribs.

"We've got only one witness, the bodyguard, who told the police their limo was hit from behind by a second vehicle causing their limo to spin out of control and go over a cliff, luckily landing on a ledge below. He saw no one or nothing else, although he said he thought the vehicle that hit them was a black Mercedes. The cops think it's a hit-and-run case probably by a drunk driver. I've asked the cops to release no information until they've talked to you."

"Okay, tell me more about Earl and Dawn ... what are their injuries?"

"Yeah, I'll be glad to tell you."

And, that's what Martin did. He concluded by saying, "They were very lucky, and we are very lucky. I see nothing in our current plans except Dawn being delayed a few days before she can return to the States."

Gordon nodded his head and then said, "Thanks, Martin, I got the picture. Give me 30 minutes to get some breakfast. Then, come back and let's talk about what needs to be done. See if anyone can give you more precise info about Dawn's stay in the hospital and have Earl stick around for a session with us after we talk again."

"Right, boss."

Forty-seven

Martin seated himself at Gordon's table exactly 29 minutes later. Gordon was more relaxed; Martin could sense Gordon had matters well in hand. This would be primarily a one-way discussion.

"Martin, I thank you for staying up all night and handling this situation. I'm sorry I let those two go on a drive last night. All my doubts about these so-called accidents and coincidences are out the window. And, would you believe it, we have another one of these LI-related circumstances. Your call was not my only wakeup call in the middle of the night. About an hour after your call, I was told that Grandma's place in Arkansas had been broken into and a security guard was killed on the premises. It's fortunate she was visiting her sister in Connecticut before the BOD meeting in New York. The killer's picture is on her home video security system. It's the same guy who killed our caretakers in California."

"What the hell is going on, Gordon?"

" I don't know. The Arkansas guy and these accidents may not be related. At least, we know who the Arkansas guy is and maybe the police can apprehend him before he kills someone else. Now, as for these accidents, I have no doubt that someone or someones are trying to kill our founder's son. That would be Earl, although because of me, it's really Trace who is in danger. After we talk, I'll talk to him to see if he wishes to continue. Dawn deserves the same consideration, but we'll wait until she is well before I have that conversation with her. In the meantime, here's what we should do:

"Make sure Dawn has a private room; set up security 24/7.

"Cancel her trip to LA for the movie premiere; Trace will go-it alone.

"Trace will not stay here; he is to return to the States today as planned.

"You, Katrin, Johanna, and I will cancel our 3-day getaway in Austria; we will vacation in this area instead. I want friendly faces around Dawn.

"We will use the police position on what happened; it was an accident.

"We need to encourage the police and the hospital to leave LI company and LI names out of their release to the media.

"Because our planning sessions are over, all our LI folks should be informed of this accident; but they should continue with their current plans.

"Have our financial and insurance people investigate the needs of the chauffeur's family and of the bodyguard. Provide me with recommendations accordingly.

"Have a couple of LI reps at the chauffeur's funeral.

"And, keep the bodyguard available, I'd like to visit with him in about an hour or so.

"I think that's it. Any questions? Have I left anything out?"

"Everything sounds right to me. I continue to be very concerned about Trace and Dawn. I suggest we limit their public exposure and conceal their travel plans to all but a few people. I think we both know who's behind these accidents. I'd like to challenge those guys, but I think it would only put them on guard and probably move their actions from accidental to deliberate."

"I agree. We're not in position to challenge them now."

"Also, Gordon ... I don't think they will, but what if Trace and Dawn bail out?"

"Dawn's leaving is not an issue. Earl has had a lot of girlfriends ... this one has lasted longer and more celebrated by the paparazzi, but her absence will be easily handled. Our backup for Trace will be Earl himself. I might make that change anyway, but at this moment I'd like to stay with Trace."

"Okay. Are we ready for Trace?"

"Yes, but have the waitress come at the same time. I'm ready for some refreshments."

After Trace was seated at the table, Gordon expressed his concern about the accident and his injuries, hoping that he was okay. Then he and Martin proceeded to give him a complete rundown of all the accidents and LI-related incidents, including Grandma's break-in. They wanted to be sure he knew all the facts in order for him to realize his life had been and was in danger.

Then, Gordon asked Trace the question, "Knowing all this do you want to continue? I didn't recruit you to be a target or a fall guy. I never expected any attempts on anyone's life. Earl had no part in this masquerade plan; he knew nothing about it. It was strictly my plan and I solicited you on my own and I stand ready to meet my financial commitment to you. If you want out now, I will develop a plan B and make other arrangements. I will say you have handled this chore extremely well and I couldn't be more pleased ... but, I don't want to endanger you nor do I want you to continue under false pretenses."

"Gordon, do you want me to do anything different?"

"No. We will make the changes we have to make. Do nothing different except be more careful. We need to decide about limiting your activities and your public exposure. And it's on that basis I want you to return to the States today and not stay in Monaco."

"Ouch! Negotiable?"

"Non-negotiable."

"Gordon, I trust you and Martin. This has been a great experience. I'm glad we have been able to pull this off. I learned a lot about danger during my eight years in the Marines. I'm prepared to take the risk. I don't want this to end until we have completed this assignment. If you're happy, I'm happy. Let's have at it!"

Forty-eight

Langston's sleek Gulfstream G650 skidded to a stop, the ending to a perfect landing at the LAX airport. It was early in the afternoon, but the rain made Los Angeles' early afternoon look like it was dusk. After a complete stop, Mary, the perfect hostess, unfastened her seat belt, stood up from her middle cabin seat to announce, "Okay, Gentlemen we have arrived, we will be disembarking in a few minutes." The gentlemen were Gordon, Martin, and Trace.

Gordon and Martin had to be exhausted; they had flown from Nice with one bump in-between to Salt Lake City, rested a short while, then flew from there to LA. Trace came from LI's Utah's Mountain Lodge and joined them at Salt Lake for the flight to LA. All three were in LA to attend a movie premiere and other scheduled activities by one of Langston's subsidiaries.

Dawn wasn't with them. And Gordon didn't tell Trace where Dawn was. She never arrived in Utah from Monaco. Something was wrong. When Trace asked Gordon, all Gordon would say, "Everything is okay. No more questions about Dawn, please." Hardly comforting. Martin and the Utah people seemingly knew nothing either. He was worried; he didn't like worry.

Gordon was going to be the visible Langston executive attending the premiere. He would stand before the cameras and the reporters as they ask those difficult, penetrating, and sometimes inane questions about the accident, the tender offer, Earl's whereabouts, Dawn's identity, and the upcoming BOD meeting. Martin's job was to take Trace stealthily into the theater, hoping no one would see him. Gordon was limiting Trace's exposure to the public as a security measure.

Outside the *ArcLight Hollywood Theater* there was the usual crowd pushing against each other and the golden rope holding them back from the dignitaries and stars lingering on the red carpet for their fans, pics, and sycophantic TV interviews. The crowd was also jostled by a small group of vocal, disruptive protesters who had something against the controversial director, Dimitri Rossi, who had been at odds with the public over his environmental views. Inside the theater, a sense of quiet excitement reigned. The patrons were enjoying conversation with their friends while they downed the free non-alcoholic beverages and popcorn.

For the Langston executives, everything went as planned. Just minutes from the viewing, the three men met again in an enclosed, private viewing area in the balcony of the theater. The name of the movie was, "*The Cabin by the Lake* ". Trace had given little thought to the movie or title they were about to see, but when the movie began, under the movie title there was this introductory phrase by Benjamin Franklin, *"It is easier to suppress the first desire than to satisfy all that follows it."* The phrase caught Trace's attention*: I've seen that before*, he thought. And, as the movie continued, and the plot began to take shape, he realized the movie must have been adopted from a short story he read several years ago. *I remember the story fairly well. It's about an unfaithful wife and her lover taking steps to murder her husband. A familiar plot, but the story did have a twist or two in it. Not a classic. Not a feel-good story either.*

The plot continued as Trace remembered. Then, something unanticipated happened. Trace's actor genes took over. Trace forgot about the story and began to focus on the key actor and actress: their actions, their facial expressions, how they were playing their parts. *They're doing a decent job, but I think Dawn and I would do just as well if not better. What they are doing is a piece of cake compared to the acting that Dawn and I are doing now. And, ironically, there's only a few people know it. When I think about that, I realize I have reached the pinnacle of my career. There will be no acting role in the future that will ever satisfy me again. This is it. This will be my last acting job. I don't know what will come next, but I want Dawn and me to live an unscripted life in the future, no more just reading someone else's lines or being moved around like puppets, I like people, but I don't want to be cast in the role of just entertaining people; surely there is more that Dawn and I can do besides acting and entertaining.*

There was a loud explosion, courtesy of one of the last scenes in the movie. Trace's thoughts were disrupted; he returned to reality as to who he was now, not who he wanted to be.

The end of the movie generated decent applause. The movie wouldn't win an Oscar, but it was okay. After the applause died down, the stage floodlights came on and the movie acknowledgements and principals were introduced. The producers, director, and the stars all had their time on the stage and made a few remarks. In closing, it was announced there was a shuttle bus to take those who had been invited to a planned garden party at the Blackstone Estate. The announcer reminded the audience that one must have a registered ticket in order to attend the party. The moderately successful premiere was over.

Most of those going to the party had their own transportation; a few took the shuttle. One of the riders was a large man, who somehow had forgotten how to smile. The grim man was Carson. The grim man was convinced he would see Earl at the party, and he would have his revenge at last. He was wickedly persistent, and frustration personified.

Forty-nine

Carson knew his bad luck had to change sometime. *I know, I just know it will. Earl is here. He just has to be at the premiere, but where? I never saw him, and it looks like the media or crowd didn't sense he was here. Well, I'm going to go to that party, now. I'm sure ole Earl ain't goin' to miss a party. And, I'm not goin' to miss it either. But, that man who wouldn't sell me his ticket is sure enough gonna miss it; maybe he'll miss more than that party. He'll probably regret he turned down my money offer when he wakes up … if he does wake up , that is.*

The post-premiere party was at the Blackstone Estate, the movie producer's large estate. There were a little over 300 tickets registered and required for entry. A medium size party by Hollywood standards. However, entry to the estate did not mean a person could enter the 12-bedroom, 36,000 square foot home itself. Entries to the house were guarded by technical devices and security personnel. If they didn't know you, you could enjoy the garden party; but you didn't have access to the interior of the house.

Carson didn't see Earl at the garden party outside. He was turned away at the house politely the first time he tried to enter, rudely the second and third times. The security was too much for him. He waited outside for a couple of hours, but he finally gave up and left the estate premises.

Dignitaries, stars, critics, and trusted media personnel were thus isolated and protected from most of the "lesser" public at the party. The elite in the house were able to freely go in and out of the house, but the "lesser" could not. Limited access into the house was strictly enforced at all times.

The Langston people took advantage of that. Gordon went in and out; Trace and Martin stayed inside the whole time. As he had decided earlier, Gordon was media accessible, and he took care of all the media questions. Trace was made media inaccessible. Trace did have some social, small talk with others in the house. He talked briefly with Charles Blackstone and his wife Jodie, who Earl had met before. He had lengthier conversations with the other movie principals who Earl had not met before. Dimitri Rossi was an interesting man to talk with, inquisitive and knowledgeable. Conversation with the movie stars was fairly confined to themselves, as if they were doing an audition. The movie's PR man, Faire 'Deal" Lewis, gave a flattering review of the movie and even the protesters. "You just can't buy publicity like that!"

Arlo Tuffin was there. He hurried over to talk with Trace, who was sitting in a chair in what was called the third game room.

"Earl," he said, "I'm so glad to see you. We've been trying to get in touch with you. Harold and I want you on our show again."

"Sorry, Arlo. Nothing deliberate, but our staff decided to keep me out of the limelight until we have our Board of Directors' meeting. We didn't mean to be rude. We've been very busy. But, yes, I'd like to do your show again. I'm available sometime after our BOD meeting; I'll have my folks set up a schedule with you. I look forward to it; I enjoyed our last get together, but I really feel very bad about the elevator accident, especially losing your hostess ... Jane... er,ah ... Jane Munroe?"

"No, Jane Munson. Yes, that was a big loss to us, she was not only an exceptional hostess, but she was also a good friend of mine and my family as well. Her dad and my dad are USC alumni. Her dad is inconsolable; he's giving the LA police detectives fits because they say it wasn't accidental, yet they don't even have a person of interest much less a suspect. We replaced Jane with her assistant, Irene Goodson. She lacks Jane's experience but so far is doing a credible job."

"Yes, credible job ... credible job ... I'll try to do better with names, Arlo. It is Arlo, isn't it?"

Arlo laughed. "It is. Still handy with the quips I see. I have a question. What's with all the accidents happening around Langston?"

"I honestly don't know. We're hoping somebody will figure it out soon. Meanwhile my staff advises me to stop wearing my Langston t-shirts in public. That's off the record, Arlo."

"Gotcha! Yeah, and one of those was a parasailing accident?"

"Yes, it was. Scary, but I was fortunate. I wasn't hurt too bad."

"That is fortunate! Well, I really want to have you on the show again as soon as you're available. Incidentally, bring Dawn with you."

"Nice try, Arlo. You're meddlin' now!"

"Yep! Not too subtle, I guess."

"I do appreciate your nice invitation, Arlo. I'll make sure my staff honors it. Nice to see you again."

"Yes! Looking forward to our next get together."

Trace did have a conversation with a young woman Gordon told him to be wary of. The young woman was Frieda, Earl's ex-wife of one year. Trace didn't know her current last name. *Maybe she doesn't know it either! She's been married at least twice since Earl, and she may be in between marriages now. Gordon told me to be careful; she's smart and ruthless. She likes money any way she can get it. She may decide I'm not Earl.*

Frieda sought Trace out and engaged him in some chit-chat about 15 minutes after he talked with Arlo. She came up to Trace, assumed the Mae West sensual, alluring posture, and softly and fetchingly said, "Hello, big guy. In case you don't know, I'm Frieda. We used to be married, that is Earl and I used to be married, but you ain't Earl. You look like him, honey, but you ain't him."

"But, I do know you Freida. Always playing the seductress to get what you want. Always plastered. What's your last name these days?"

"That's none of your business, honey. I don't tell my business to anyone I don't know. I sure don't know you, but I'd like to get acquainted. Let's be friends. Close friends. Introduce yourself. Then maybe I'll tell you my business. All my business."

"Sure. I'm Earl Langston. I think we could be close friends if we lived maybe a thousand miles apart. That would be plenty close enough for me. It sounds like you skipped your last AA meeting or was it your shrink's appointment this time. Did you cancel or just forget?"

"Ease up, big guy. Admit it! Earl don't have your sense of humor. Who are you?"

"I'm Earl. How soon you forget. I guess you weren't listening. Take your amnesia and go elsewhere. There's plenty of prey in here."

"I'm in no hurry. I just might leave after you show me that ski scar on your left leg."

"Nice try, Frieda. I don't have a scar on my left leg."

"Okay. Your right leg, then."

"I might do that. After all these years you're not making a pass at me, are you?"

"Do you want me to?"

"No, Frieda, What I want is for you to leave me alone. You're not part of my life anymore. Shove off!"

"Not until I see the scar, baby doll. Not until I see the scar!"

"That's an offer I just can't refuse! You got it, hon!" He rolled up his pants on his right leg. The scar Dr. Janssen had carefully sculptured on Trace's leg was there.

Trace said, "Okay Frieda, keep your promise; time to go. Now if I wanted to make sure you're Frieda I'd ask to see that tattoo on your left hip, but I imagine there's lots of guys who know about that tattoo, don't they? Now, leave me alone; let's see if we can live without each other, okay?"

Frieda left, there was nothing more to say.

Around one o'clock, Martin told him he had called for the limo. The limo would probably be there in 10 or 15 minutes. Trace was more than ready to leave. While he was waiting for the limo, the head butler, Jefferson, came into the third game room and said, "Mr. Langston? Sir, I hate to bother you, but a telephone caller insists it's an emergency and he has to talk with you."

"At this time in the morning?"

"Yes, sir. He won't take no for an answer."

"Well, okay. I'll take the call. Who is it?"

"He wouldn't give his name, sir. He said he would only talk with you."

"Fine. Do you have a place where I can take a private call?"

"If this place is adequate, I can bring a phone to you."

"Yeah! That'll work. Thanks, Jefferson."

Less than a minute later, Jefferson returned with a portable phone, plugged it into the wall port, and gave the instrument to Trace.

Trace nodded his thanks and then spoke into the phone.

"Hello! This is Earl Langston."

"Hi, Trace! How ya been doin'? I've been wantin' to talk to you for weeks now, but you've been dodging me! You haven't answered my telephone calls or my e-mails. I just wanted to tell you what a great job you're doing playing Earl Langston. Now, you don't have a problem with me congratulating you, do you, ole buddy? "

The caller's first words put Trace's mind into an emergency response mode. *"What had Gordon told him the first day he started this job? He said, 'Be calm, cordial, and careful!' Should I hang up or continue talking to this guy?"*

Fifty

There was only a slight delay in Trace's response to this caller and his threatening accusation. *Be calm, cordial, and careful! Well, cordial is out, but let's find out what this guy wants!*

Trace answered. "Well, for starters I'd say there's more than one problem. I don't know you; I don't want to know you. I'm not dodging you, and you're certainly not my ole buddy. Also, I don't go by the name of Trace ... other than that, there's probably no problem. Maybe you should seek medical help ... I suggest calling 911!"

"Hey, that's a pretty good comeback, but you're a skillful person, so it's not unexpected. However, it doesn't change the facts: you are the actor Trace Reinhardt, and you are masquerading quite successfully as Earl Langston, the CEO of Langston Industries."

"Is that so? And who are you? And who are you masquerading as?"

"My name is Sam Lector. You haven't forgotten ole Sam, have you?"

"Well, I haven't forgotten anyone who I didn't know. Let me tell you something, Mr. Lector. You're doing a very good job of being foolish. Is this a hobby of yours where you bust into a private party, seek out one of the hosts, and then tell him he's not who he says he is? Must be fun. You probably do over ten or twenty of these a year, don't you?"

"No, it's no hobby; it's more like a profitable enterprise that will help my standard of living."

"I see. ... Well, take your enterprise and target someone else! Don't call me again! It's harassment and I don't have the time or patience to deal with cranks like you."

"Okay, Trace. I won't waste anymore of your time and don't you waste mine with your pretenses and denials. I'm an actor like you and unknowingly you were mentoring me while you were performing. I've seen just about all your stuff. I've seen you perform impressions many, many times. I never saw you do Arlo Tuffin before, but when you did him on his show, I knew I was watching ole Trace Reinhardt, not Earl Langston. The two of you do look astonishingly alike and for some reason you are imitating Earl. Is it because of the tender offer and the buyout being discussed right now? Oh, heaven forbid! ... You didn't kill him, did you?"

"You better watch your tongue, Mr. Lector ... it's about to get you into big trouble. You said a lot of words, but I didn't hear any of them offer proof of your theory. You better take this 'feeling' you have and bury it; it has absolutely no value."

"We disagree again, but I really didn't expect a man of your talent to be easily swayed. No, I think I'll just tell everybody about my feeling. But, as you suggested, I'm willing to bury this feeling. It's negotiable. All it takes is $100,000 in cash. That's probably cheap since otherwise you're gonna mess up a billion dollar buyout. Just bring the money in $100 bills to me tomorrow night at 6 o'clock. I'll be waiting on the 3rd floor of the LA Central Library on 5th Street. Incidentally, the library shelves all their fiction books on the 3rd floor. A nice touch, don't you think?"

"You are absolutely deranged, Mr. Lector. Don't expect me to be there, I wouldn't be able to identify you anyway."

"Oh, that's a clever comment ... I'll make it easy for you. First, I'm bringing an actress friend who costarred in a play with you ... I think you were even a couple for several months. Second, just for grins, we'll be carrying canvass tote bags and wearing LA Dodger baseball caps. And, Trace, I just can't stress this enough. Tomorrow night at 6 o'clock at the LA Central Library. No show ... no silence. No money ... no peace. $100,000. Can you spell **fraud**, Trace?"

"Yes, I certainly can. Can you spell **extortion**, Mr. Lector? Or, better yet, can you spell **prison**? Goodbye!"

Fifty-one

In the next evening at 5:45pm, there were eight people in an oblong room on the 3rd floor of the Los Angeles Central Library. One of them was seated alone at the end of a rectangular 8-person table. Unlike the others, he was dressed nattily wearing a conservative sports coat excepting a tie. Unlike the others there were no books or magazines in his possession or even near him although he seemed to be reading a copy of *The Wall Street Journal*. Occasionally he would look up from his paper and briefly survey the entrance to the hall leading to the elevators.

Four of the seven others were most likely college students working together, gathered around two laptops and several open books, bounded by animated, but quiet, conversation. There was a lone middle-aged man, dressed flamboyantly, seated in a comfortable chair in the corner, looking through some magazines. And, there was a young man and woman seated at a small table, obviously more interested in each other than books, magazines, and other people.

The man at the rectangular 8-person table had been there since 5 o'clock, as had the others. At first, the young couple had his attention, but their appearance and demeanor caused him to disregard them like he did the others.

At 6:18pm a man and woman haltingly entered the room peering at all the occupants. They, too, did not have any books, but each of them was carrying a canvass tote bag. Unlike everyone else, they were wearing LA Dodger baseball caps. His peering completed, the man of the pair scowled, made fists of his hands and put them on his hips in a threatening manner. The rather attractive woman with him quietly stood by his side saying and doing nothing.

The man at the table facing the couple did not rise from his chair but he put his paper down, raised his right arm and motioned to the couple to come to his table. When they neared his table, the seated man spoke, "Please sit down. I am Dr. Gordon T. Brewer, Chief Operating Officer of Langston Industries. I have been expecting you. You are 18 minutes late. Being late is intolerable in my business."

The couple seated themselves on either side of Gordon. The man spoke, "Brewer, huh? We got no business with you! What we ..."

Gordon interrupted, "Sit down and shut up, **boy**! You are Lector, aren't you? You **do** have business with me!"

Turning his attention to the woman, Gordon asked, "Who are you and **why** are you here?"

Gordon's brusque manner made the woman nervous. She replied in a soft tone, "I'm Linda Lane. Sam asked me to come with him to visit with a friend of mine, Trace Reinhardt."

"Nice to meet you, Miss Lane. I'm sorry to see you are mixed up in this extortion plot. And, unfortunately, you'll not be visiting with your friend this evening, whoever he is."

Again, Lector tried to bull his way into the conversation, "Now wait a minute, Brewer ... I want ..."

And, again, Lector failed. Gordon exploded with his interruption: "Mr. Lector, for a man who arrived late to an important meeting, why suddenly have you become so impatient? You will meet the party you're so anxious to meet in just a few minutes. Before he joins us, I am telling you how angry I am that you two have succeeded in wasting the valuable time of two of Langston Industries' executives. I warn you that it will cease after tonight's meeting or there will be unpleasant consequences for you. Both of you! Trust me ... that's not a threat; it's a promise. And, I keep my promises!"

"Well, Brew ..."

"**Don't** interrupt me, boy! You have made a mistake in attempting to blackmail Mr. Langston. I have your telephone conversation on tape. If you persist, I will see both of you prosecuted to the fullest extent of the law. That's a warning shot over your bow, boy. The next shot will be a direct hit!"

Gordon paused to let his words sink in. Then he motioned with his left hand. From the entrance hall came Earl. He came to the table where they were sitting and then remained standing at the opposite end of the table from Gordon. He looked back and forth at the couple while saying, "I am Earl Langston, the CEO of Langston Industries. I've forgotten your name, sir, but I guess you're the guy that called me last night ... and I don't believe I have met your lady friend."

The looks and demeanor of the would-be extortionists were priceless. The woman spoke first, "Oh, Sam, what have you gotten me into? He's not Trace. He looks like Trace ... but he's not Trace!"

Earl smiled at the woman. "Well, at this moment I wish I were this guy named Trace. I'm sure sorry that you're not a friend of mine. Maybe we could fix that ... the night is young and there are better places to get acquainted than the library."

For the first time, maybe in months, Sam was paralyzed in speech and body. He looked down at the table, saying nothing.

Gordon got up from his chair. "Folks," he said, this little session is over. Mr. Langston and I are leaving. I don't expect to hear from either of you again. Remember that we have your call on tape as well as this little get-together. And, Miss Lane, if that is your name ... I would think long and hard about keeping this guy as a friend, much less as an extortionist."

So saying, Gordon and Earl left the two would-be blackmailers sitting there: an attractive but indignant young woman and a perplexed and subdued young man, never to bother Langston Industries' employees again.

As they made their way to the elevator, they were joined by the flamboyantly dressed man and the three of them took the elevator to the ground floor.

Gordon asked Earl, "I bet you're tired. Your first trip out in a while, and it was a long one."

"Yeah, I'm not quite up to par. But it was worth it! I enjoyed it!"

"Thanks for making this quick trip to LA. I'm sorry you have to return and stay cooped up a little longer but it's best for right now. Rest up, it's almost over."

The elevator reached the ground floor. As Gordon and Earl made their way to an awaiting limo, Gordon said to Earl, "Have a good flight back."

Earl replied, "Thanks. This trip was fun and educational. I did learn something about you."

"What was that?"

"I learned that if you make Gordon Brewer angry, further discussion is over and you become a listener."

"Maybe. Perhaps there is some truth in that. I do know I enjoyed the evening. It's the most fun I've had in several months! If we're lucky, maybe Trace will get another call like this one!"

Fifty-two

Trace exited the New York City Essex Hotel elevator and found his way to the first-floor coffee shop. Gordon and Martin were already there, seated at a small, round dining table. They exchanged pleasantries and then Trace seated himself and readied himself for this scheduled 8:30 morning meeting. The Continental Breakfast for the three of them had just arrived, so they had coffee and Danish with their social conversation before they began talking business.

Gordon began the business conversation. He said, "Well, guys, I haven't seen or talked with you since our LA trip. All went well. The movie survived the amateur critics and most of the professional ones. No forecasts on gross receipts but it looks like it will be moderately profitable. Nothing in the film will cause any controversy. With Rossi directing I sweated that one a little bit. Mr. Blackstone's pleased about the movie. Mrs. Blackstone's pleased her house and estate survived the party. My conversation with the media passed muster. Always a good thing. So, no major issues. These public appearances are worrisome; I'm glad it's over!"

Then, Gordon turned and looked directly at Trace. He didn't grin as he said, "And, how is the blackmail victim this morning? I'm sorry, but the company just can't afford that $100,000 your actor friend wanted. I guess we may have to take some of that $100,000 out of the money coming to you."

Trace grimaced, then replied, "Oh, that's not good. Not good at all. Blackmail sure pays a lot better than I thought it did."

Gordon paused, then laughed as he told them all the details of the library confrontation. He told them, "We used a guy that looks just like you to completely intimidate and embarrass the would-be extortionists. We won't have to worry about that pair anymore. It was really fun, a nice ending to my LA trip."

Trace said, "You saved me! I'm grateful. Thanks for handling that, but you sure have a way of worrying people sometimes."

It was Martin's turn. He reported on security issues at the theater and estate. He said, "There was really nothing much at the theater, just a few protesters doing what protesters do. At Blackstone's, there were a few party goers who partied too much, and some gate crashers joined in for the free booze and maybe some upfront visits with the celebrities. No damage there. The police reported several crowd injuries, and one man was beaten around the head evidently for his Blackstone ticket. Police are investigating that one with help from the Blackstone people. Almost a no-nothing night."

Trace told Gordon he talked to Arlo and consented to be on his show after the BOD meeting. Gordon nodded in agreement. Then, he told him about his *tete-tete* with Frieda. Gordon laughed when he told him how that went. Trace said, "She's something else. Thanks for the warning, Gordon."

Gordon switched topics away from LA. "Now, the bad news. Nick Fontano ... you know who Nick is, don't you?" Trace and Martin nodded. They knew all right ... he was the leader of the three Florida BOD members who wanted the Kesterson buyout and who were violently opposed to its rejection.

Gordon continued, "Well, it seems like Nick's been in town on business but returning to Florida early this evening. He has a tight schedule but wants a face-to-face with me and Earl to talk about the tender offer for about 30 minutes this afternoon. As usual he won't take no for an answer. The problem is that I will be in a meeting with our lawyers in Boston at that time; a meeting I can't put off or reschedule. That leaves you, Earl. I hate to feed you to the lion. What do you think?'

"Well, I did have that one phone call with him. I'm game ... maybe a bad word to use ... let's just say I'm okay with it, but I'm not going to be passive and let him run over me. I can handle it."

"Good! Teatime is 4 o'clock this afternoon in the hotel lounge."

They spent more time and Danish going over some details regarding the BOD meeting scheduled for the morning a week later. No surprises in the details; everything seemed to be well in hand. Then, Trace got some information he wanted to hear, but had been reluctant to ask a second time.

"Okay, guys, looks like things are in good shape. I'm going to wrap this session up by telling you about Dawn. I know I've kept you guys out of the loop. But I wanted to have firm ground before I told you anything. Dawn has done her job well. I couldn't ask for anything better. I've had several conversations with her since Monaco. Best I can tell she's recovered. I gave her every chance to quit if she wanted to. She's a strong young lady. After the car wreck, she had some fears and doubts. Who wouldn't? But, bottom line, she wants to stay until this is over. Ah, ... I think she sorta likes Earl."

Trace interrupted, "I think Earl sorta likes her, too!"

Gordon, ignoring Trace, continued, "Dawn will be arriving later in the week. Grandma will be with her. You know, Grandma is a jewel. When she heard about Dawn's plight and I was going to keep her in Utah to recover, she insisted, ... no, she demanded that Dawn visit and recover with her and her sister in Connecticut until the BOD. Dawn never went to Utah, we took her directly to Cheshire Village, Connecticut from Monaco. Currently Dawn and Grandma are scheduled to arrive at the Essex the day after tomorrow. It will be in the afternoon; I'm not sure of the exact time. They will have a suite together here at the Essex."

Trace said, "Nice to hear, Gordon. What's her telephone number?"

"Sorry, Earl, I don't seem to have that handy. One of us needs to be more patient. I'll let you know when they plan to arrive. That's it, gentlemen. Oh, Earl … nowhere in the city without the bodyguard, huh? Winston's on duty. He's waiting for you in the lobby. Okay?"

Of course, Trace understood. *I have a date with a bodyguard, not a girlfriend.* Sure enough, Winston was sitting in one of the comfy chairs near the hotel entrance reading one of the hotel-provided newspapers.

"Okay, Winston" Trace said, "Let's take a walk down to the Theater District. I want to see what's playing this week."

"Won't this newspaper help?"

"Nope."

"How about a cab, then?"

"Nope, it's only about 12 to 14 blocks. Let's walk."

And, off they went.

Hotel Essex was a great hotel, probably not one of the really showcase, newer elite hotels that New York City offered, but it was still a nice 5-star hotel. Michael Langston did not always have his BOD meetings in the same NYC hotels, but he always chose a hotel where he or his friends could walk in Central Park or walk down to Times Square and the Theater District and not have to yellow-cab it everywhere. Gordon felt the same way and was continuing Michael's tradition. Trace was pleased he could take advantage of their location acumen.

Later, that afternoon, at precisely three minutes before 4 o'clock, Trace entered the sparsely occupied hotel lounge that adjoined the lobby. He had no trouble locating Nick. He was seated in the last booth in the corner. He recognized Nick from the material Gordon had supplied. It wasn't difficult. Nick was a big guy, somewhat resembling Earnest Borgnine in size and shape. He was neatly dressed.

Trace strode over quickly to the booth, extended his hand in welcome and said, "Good afternoon, Mr. Fontano!"

Nick did not stir nor provide his handshake in welcome. He merely nodded his head, saying, "Where's Brewer?"

Trace sat down in the booth, directly across from Nick. "Sorry, sir. Gordon had to be in Boston for a meeting with our lawyers this afternoon and evening. He told me you had some business you wanted to discuss?"

"This is typical ... you guys don't respect all I've done for this company. I can't get you guys to sit down together with me and the Brunos to talk business. I might as well be selling Bermuda shorts to Eskimos."

"His absence was not preventable. Again, I'm sorry, sir."

"Look, since Brewer's not here, I don't need to talk long. I'm not sure how much you'd remember, anyway. Here's ..."

"Mr. Fontano, please. Please say what you need to say, even if Gordon is not here. I will remember."

Nick was taken aback. Earl had never interrupted him or ever talked to him in that way. In fact, no one had ever talked to him in that way.

"You're a real wise-ass aren't you son. Your dad woulda never talked to me like that. You really don't know who you're dealing with. You better watch what you're saying."

"And, what business did you wish to discuss, Mr. Fontano?"

"Okay, buddy boy! I'll bring this down to your level. You and Brewer and all your tiddlywink friends need to understand something. This buyout needs to happen. This company ain't gonna survive with Brewer and Michael's idiot son running the business. It's time and it's necessary that we turn this company over to businesspeople who know what they're doing."

"Mr. Fontano, I have **not** changed my mind since we talked on the phone a couple of weeks ago. Kesterson is a raider company; they will gorge on our assets, destroy our business, and get rid of most of our employees. The buyout is morally and economically bad for our company."

"This ain't about women and fast cars, son. What makes you such an expert on buyouts and business?"

"Sir, regarding our company, I **am** an expert! I certainly **am** an expert on ***my*** opinion!"

"Well, let me just tell you about ***your*** opinion, **boy**. I think your opinion won't be around much longer. You just think about that, son."

"No! I'll be thinking that our company will be doing quite well on its own, without Kesterson. That's what I'll be thinking about."

Teatime was over.

Fifty-three

After dinner, following his first full day in New York, Trace returned to his hotel room to rest and then retire for the night. A busy day. *I hope Gordon will accept my aggressive position with Fontano. I wonder how Earl's dad kept him and his Florida buddies under control.* Trace was about to find out what Gordon thought of his conversation with Nick. The phone rang; it was Gordon.

Sure enough, Gordon asked, "How did your session with Nick go?"

Trace answered his question by telling him the dialogue he had with Nick. He then asked Gordon, "Well what do you think? Was I too forceful or rude?"

"Let's just say you've teased the bear. From a company perspective, it's okay. From your personal standpoint, it's not okay. I worry about his threat to you regarding your opinion not being around much longer. You need to be extra careful this week ... he may try to hijack you or your vote before the BOD meeting. He's a dangerous man; I know Michael thought so."

"What's done is done. I'm glad you feel I wasn't off base as far as the company was concerned."

"Nope! All okay. I appreciate you handling that for me. My sessions here went fine. I'll be back tomorrow. Take the day off. Take it off with your bodyguard, though."

"Yep. Thanks, Gordon."

Gordon's call made Trace feel better ... he turned on the TV, watched the news for a little bit and then went to sleep.

After an early breakfast, Trace called his steady. His steady bodyguard, that is. A quick phone pick up and answer.

"Hello. This is Winston. Is that you, boss?"

"Yes, it is. I'm taking yesterday's suggestion."

"What suggestion?"

"We're going out today. And I want to ride where we're going. We're not walking this time. How about meeting me in the lobby at 10?"

"Sure."

"Great! Put on some recreation clothes. Then meet me at 10."

Winston got to the lobby five minutes early. Being late to meet your boss was not an option. However, Winston was surprised that his boss had a companion with him. *It was Martin. What's going on?*

Trace answered the unasked question.

"Winston, today will be a good day ... but, only if my Houston Astros can whip Martin's Damn Yankees. We got a day of baseball ahead of us. Yesterday Martin and I talked at breakfast about going to the game. He got us some great seats down the first base line in one of the field-level suites by the Yankee dugout. We'll leave shortly. You and I will cab with Martin and put up with a business errand he has to run at the NYSE, but then we'll be on our way to Yankee Stadium in time to watch some pregame stuff before the game begins. Martin wouldn't let me tell you earlier ... there seems to be some secret stuff going on about my whereabouts."

A smiling Winston replied, "Oh, absolutely no problem. I love this secret. I love this surprise."

Martin said, "Okay gents. Time to go. Let's adjourn to the curb outside. I have a limo and driver waiting."

Across the street from the Essex, there were two men walking toward the hotel about half a block away. The short man stopped, held the tall man from walking further and said, "Well, there he goes again. Where to now? I don't believe we could catch him in a closet."

"Yeah, I see him. That's okay, Mutt, not to worry. Rico told us he'd be at the Essex, and he's at the Essex. He'll come back and we'll be waiting."

"Who are those two birds with him?"

"The big guy is probably a bodyguard. I think the other guy is Martin, a big shot in Langston."

"So, what's the plan?"

"It's a simple one. We wait till they come back, then kill him and kill any unlucky guys he happens to be with."

Fifty-four

The three men enjoyed the afternoon baseball game as well as the amenities provided by the lounge tickets. They had perfect field-level viewing seats, along the first base line, near the Yankee dugout. The amenities included a private entrance, a private restroom, and all-inclusive food and unlimited non-alcoholic beverages.

The ballgame itself was entertaining; but much to Trace's chagrin, the Yanks pulled it out in extra innings: 6 to 5.

Martin had the rest of the day planned following the ballgame. He had Logan, the chauffeur, drive them to his favorite NYC restaurant, *Emery's Fine Dining,* in Upper Manhattan. As the limo rolled to a stop in front of the restaurant, Martin said, "Okay, gents, Logan's going to see our limo is parked, then he will join us for dinner. Now, this is an upscale eating place. We'll have to wear sports coats, but no ties. I had Logan bring each of us a sports coat; so, suit up, gentlemen. Let's enjoy a good meal."

All of them added the required clothing. Logan gave up the limo to a valet; then the four of them entered the elegant eating place together. The tuxedoed maître d' knew Martin and greeted him by name. Martin returned his greeting and gave him a monied handshake.

The maître d' said, "Good evening, Mr. Wheeler. I see there are four of you. Are you ready to be seated now?"

"Yes, we are," replied Martin.

"Upfront on the right side, as usual, sir?"

"Yes, that will be fine."

"Follow me, please."

The four dutifully followed the maître d' and were seated at a table that had a panoramic view of the other diners and overlooked a musical quintet seated on a small stage in front of the diners. When he was seated, Logan made an embarrassing mistake that in this setting would have to be called *a faux pas*. Addressing the maître d', he said, "Say, I'm really thirsty. Would you bring me a glass of ice water, please?"

The maître d' was 6 foot 3 inches tall. He made himself look even taller as he stiffened up into what military people call a brace. He had lost his pleasant face. He glared down at poor Logan as he stridently and emphatically said, "Sir, **I … am … the … maître … d'**. Your **waiter** will be here shortly!"

Logan's companions had a difficult time stifling their laughter. Logan not only had to endure the scolding of the maître d'; he also had to suffer through most of the meal with the grins of his fellow diners.

After really a great, sumptuous meal accompanied by soft instrumental music, Logan retrieved their limo and then he gave his fellow diners a little tour along the Hudson River through Greenwich Village, Lower Manhattan and to a great view of the Statue of Liberty at night. So, it was almost 11 o'clock when their fun day ended, and they returned to the Essex. As they exited the limo, a man standing at the hotel door called out, "Martin, Jasper needs to see you. He needs to see you asap. He's in the lounge."

Martin replied, "Okay!" He gathered Trace lightly by the arm and began walking him to the lounge. He said rather casually, "Let's go guys; this will only take a few minutes."

Trace thought, *what's going on? We were just saying how tired we were and how ready we were to go to bed … and, now this? And who in the world is Jasper? Never heard the name or saw it in Gordon's stuff.*

To compound Trace's bewilderment, Martin didn't look right or left when he entered the lounge. He went straight to an empty, round booth in the rear, a booth where its seating faced the lounge entrance. Martin nodded at Winston and got a nod back in return. When Trace started to say something, Martin put a vertical finger in front of his lips and shook his head back-and-forth.

Just a few minutes later, Trace and his companions heard some loud shouting in the hotel lobby punctuated by gunshots, lots of gunshots.

Fifty-five

Two hours after Jeff and his short buddy had spotted Earl leaving the Essex, he had fleshed out his simple plan. He and Mutt were seated in a small bar down the street from the Essex.

"Okay, Mutt ... here's what we're goin' do. I found out through the desk clerk at the Essex, that Earl and his buddies went to a baseball game. Now, that's what big shots do instead of working. And I expect big shots like them are doing somethin' else before they return, but to be safe, I'll say they could come back early, as early as, say, nine o'clock. Now, I don't expect the lobby will be crowded then, so we'll hide somewhere, and when they come in the lobby toward the elevators, we'll just put 'em to sleep right there. Anybody walking with Earl will be armed; we take them out first, because I don't think Earl will be carrying. I also found out there's no armed guard in the lobby at that time. After this they'll probably hire one. Now that's the easy part. The hard part is not gettin' caught. Of course, since the lobby is an open, public place, we'll disguise ourselves in some way. We'll wear some easily identified clothing over some other regular clothes. And we'll make a beeline to a place in the alley I'll show you later. I called Rico. He knows what's goin' on and he says forget the accidental stuff; take Earl out. He said he'd provide the getaway car and a driver named Henri. Henri will be parked in the alley in a black Ford sedan; he'll take us to a nearby place out of the city up the Hudson."

Mutt yawned. "What a great plan. Did you usta work for the CIA?"

So, the two would-be assassins wasted the remainder of the daylight hours before they returned to the Essex. Mutt wore a Texas straw hat and a colorful Hawaiian shirt. Jeff wore a baseball cap, a bright orange Syracuse University pullover sweater with dark running pants and tennis shoes. Their fake beards looked like fake beards. Horn-rimmed glasses completed the effect Jeff wanted. It was about 9 o'clock. They walked individually through the lobby, about five minutes apart. They walked through the lobby, then up the stairs by the elevator to the 2nd floor. Even though they "disguised" themselves, Jeff thought it best not to wait downstairs in the lobby where they might attract attention; it was smarter to be more secluded on the 2nd floor. They were in luck. The 2nd floor was quite busy; people were informally dressed, and they were milling around in small conversation groups. Their garish costumes seemed to fit right in.

Jeff's plan was to rush down the stairs and take care of the Langston trio as they left their limo and walked to the elevators. Mutt sat down in a plush chair by the right-hand staircase; Jeff sat in a similar chair near the left-hand staircase. They could see each other and also easily see the hotel front entrance. Then they waited, and waited, and waited.

At last. At last. Fortune, or more likely fate, came their way. Mutt saw the limo arrive and nodded to Jeff, who had already risen from his chair in anticipation. They were ready to attack as soon as the trio got closer to the elevators. *But they were going toward the lounge instead?* Jeff looked at Mutt quizzically, and not getting a quick response, rushed down his assigned stairs toward the lobby and adjoining lounge, pistol in hand. Mutt followed down his assigned stairs. They reached the lobby floor and made a move toward the lounge when all hell broke loose. First, there were several cries of "Halt or we'll shoot!" and "Stop! Stop!" but the only replies the callers got were a hail of bullets aimed at their voices. Lots of shooting and yelling continued for a long 15 seconds. Then it was quiet. Very quiet. The short man in the Hawaiian shirt lay in a slowly increasing pool of blood about 20 yards from the lounge entrance. The tall guy in the orange pullover sweater was 10 yards closer to the lounge entrance, and like the short man he wasn't moving. There were a few others in the lobby but only one was injured. Evidently one of the shooter's stray shots hit him in the right hip and he was experiencing pain.

Martin broke the silence in the lounge. He said, "You guys stay here. Winston, watch Earl."

Martin left the table, gun in hand, and he walked toward the lounge entrance.

Trace asked no one in particular, "Would somebody tell me what's goin' on?"

Winston answered, "I'll tell you what I think. I think that our guys just stopped somebody trying to kill you, Mr. Langston."

"What?"

"Yep! When we got here one of our guys warned us there was imminent danger … he used our code word for that: 'Jasper'. Jasper didn't know who or where the danger was, but Jasper told us to go to the lounge, an area that was safe. So, that's all I know now … we'll get the rest of the story as soon as Martin returns. I know everything is safe now. Meanwhile, would you like somethin' to drink?"

"Ah … no, thank you … I'm not particularly thirsty right now."

Trace was tired. It was a couple hours after the shootings, but there were still NYC detectives and policemen roaming outside the yellow '*CRIME SCENE*' tape that encircled the crime area. The EMTs and ambulances left about 15 minutes ago. Trace was tired but pleased. *Those guys were gunning for me because they thought I was Earl. The guy who hired them thought I was Earl, also. Good acting has risks.*

Martin returned to the table where Trace had taken residence during this whole incident. He said, "We're wrapping everything up for now. Here's what I know. The Feds were looking for these guys as suspects in the death of Captain Montfort, the attempt to kidnap Dawn, and the so-called drunk driver incident. And, incidentally I think I saw one of those guys when the elevator crash happened. Anyway, one of these smart guys threatened the hotel's front desk clerk so much he reported it to the police. Yeah, the clerk told the police that the tall guy confronted him in the men's room and threatened him not only with his life but also his family's life if he wouldn't tell him where we went today and when we were coming back. The clerk told him, but he was not intimidated. He wasn't going to let that guy get away with those kinds of threats. He told the police about the threats and described the person who threatened him. Thanks to his info, the police got the Feds involved and they put an APB on these fellows, focused on this area. Our guys asked them to be here when we returned. The only slip, and it could have been a big one, was not matching these two disguised goons to the police pics they had. It seems there is a big duplicate bridge tournament in town this week and the bridge folks had their registration and information desks on the second floor. The floor was busy; lots of people, almost all of them very casually dressed. So, these two goons sat up there looking like badly dressed tourists and got overlooked. Could have been bad. Anyway, it's over. They're both dead and we only had one policeman injured, not seriously. The incident is over, but questions remain ... who hired 'em and why?"

"I certainly appreciate what and who did everything. I'm going to bed. I'll see everyone later in the day. Thanks a bunch, Martin. You too, Winston."

"Sure. I imagine you'll have a call from Gordon waiting for you when you get up. Good night or is it good morning?"

"I don't know. It's been a good one, except for the Yankees. Yeah, and remind me not to play bridge anymore."

Fifty-six

It was almost 10 o'clock before Gordon and Trace made contact with each other. Gordon was still in Boston but expected to return to the Essex by late afternoon. Gordon had already been briefed on the shootings by Martin.

Gordon said, "I need to tell you about another worrisome thing. The police told Martin the man who killed the guard in Arkansas is the same guy that killed my friends in California ... and, he's still out there, motive undetermined. The guys killed last night had no part of those other murders."

"What's going on?"

"I wish I knew. I have no idea. But this does bring up the main topic I want to discuss with you. We've had these talks before, but we need to talk about this again."

Gordon paused, then broke Earl's identity cover asking, "Trace, how do you feel? How do you *really* feel? Are you okay?"

"Well, both good and bad. You have some good guys protecting me and I expect the accident perpetrators are history. That has to be good. But I'm afraid there is more to come. I think the folks behind these two thugs will probably try something else. And now it sounds like there's another player. That has to be bad."

"I agree. I worry about that. I really can't ask you to continue on under the circumstances. This is not your fight. When we first talked, I had no idea that you would be faced with the danger you have travelled under, and which does not seem to be over. I think we should moth-ball you and get Earl back in the picture."

"I appreciate that, Gordon. However, my dad taught me to never quit any job that I willingly took. And the Marines sorta reinforced that ... oh, brother, did they! So, I'll make it your call. I'd like to make it through the BOD meeting. Your call!"

"It's an easy decision for me. Sure! Absolutely! Let's proceed! I very much appreciate your attitude and willingness to go on.

"Now, here's the agenda for today. You'll be glad to hear Dawn is arriving this afternoon with Grandma Langston. Jessica is playing chauffeur today; she's driving them down from Cheshire Village, Connecticut. As I told you before, they will have a suite together here at Essex. I've arranged for us to have dinner with them this evening. My staff got four tickets to the Broadway play, *Mystic Magic,* for you, Dawn, Grandma, and a bodyguard. My staff also arranged for you and Dawn to have a carriage ride through the park after the show. Tomorrow night, more of the same except Grandma won't be with you. Tomorrow's show is a drama called *The Dragonfly Chronicles*. Our dating service is now closed; henceforth, you make your own arrangements. Most of today is yours. Any questions? "

"None! Thank you, Gordon!"

Trace couldn't wait for dinner.

Meanwhile, the Florida Signore Council was also having a mid-morning meeting. Cigar smoke was heavy. So was the conversation. There was no merriment.

Dario was saying, " You just can't find good help no more."

Marcellus replied, "Tell me about it! I told Rico those two jackasses he had couldn't find their way out of a privy. They've spent a month doing nothing except attracting a lot of attention. We don't need no attention and we certainly don't need no failure."

Nickolas agreed, "You guys are right. In the old days, this job woulda been done and over within a few days. Now, we gotta big problem and there's just a few days left to fix it."

Dario said, "Let's get the Bangor brothers! I don't like either one of 'em, but they get the job done although sometimes they're messy."

Marcellus agreed, "That's okay with me. Let's call 'em."

Nickolas said, "Wait. Let's not get hasty. I'm angry just like you guys are, but we need to be angry and smart. Let's call Rico and see what he's got."

Marcellus said, "He's got nothing but lip. I wouldn't trust him to lick a stamp. I say we include him in the contract we give to the Bangors!"

Dario said, "Hey, that's a good idea. Beats paying him, too."

Nickolas replied, "Gentlemen, let me remind you. We didn't get where we are by running to a bad decision without looking to see if there's something better. I care less what happens to Rico. He's not the priority ... Earl still is ... the buyout still is. Let's just be patient a little bit and see if Rico has anything. If he has nothing, the Bangors sound okay to me."

Dario said, "Okay, that don't cost nothin'. I'll call him. He's got several numbers; let's see which one works."

The second number rang only twice before Rico answered. As soon as he did, Dario put him on the speaker phone.

Dario said, "Rico, this is Dario. You're on the speaker here with me, Nick, and Marcellus. We're sittin' here waitin' to hear what a good job you're doin'!"

Marcellus added, "Yeah, Rico, we're excited!"

Rico replied, "News travels fast, don't it?"

Dario said, "Bad news always travels fast! Newspapers tell us somethin' bad happened to your two worthless buddies yesterday. That's strange. We thought they were the hunters, not the victims. Something's crazy goin' on up there in the Big City. You want to help us understand?"

Rico said, "I'll just say this. The police beat me to it. I put up with their failures across two continents and all they ever gave me were poor excuses. I'm not going to play that game. I'm not going to give you a poor excuse now. I'm going to give you a piece of news that you won't believe. And it guarantees from here on out we **will** be successful."

Nickolas spoke for the first time, "Rico, I hope what you're going to tell us is true and will solve the problem we have to fix. In fact, I'm going to try to believe you. I'm betting your life I will."

Rico responded, “I’ve never failed you guys. I will not fail you now. Here’s what I have to tell you. Earl ain’t Earl. The Earl we’ve been trying to snuff ain’t the real Earl Langston. I don’t know who the guy is, but he ain’t Earl! I don’t know who all knows that, but it looks like most of the bunch he runs around with are fooled.”

Nickolas said, “Rico, if this is some crazy story you just cooked up, you are a dead man! I don’t take to lies or liars.”

Rico replied, “I know better than to lie to you. And let me tell you the rest of the story. The real Earl is hiding in that little vacation house you got in 1000 Islands. How does that grab you?”

Nickolas said, “You may have just saved your life!”

Fifty-seven

Rico responded to Nickolas' comment, "Who do you think you're dealin' with? I ain't no Mutt or Jeff. I always deliver."

Dario asked, "Well, how you know so much, big shot? How come you know something nobody else seems to know?"

Marcellus chimed in, "Yeah, who you in bed with?"

Rico replied, "Okay, okay. Here's how I found out. I had a source inside the Blackstone Estate when they were having the big party a week or so ago after the movie that Langston was backing. My guy overheard a telephone conversation that seemed like Earl was being blackmailed. The payoff, or whatever was going down, was going to be in the LA library two days later. He told me about it, so I sent my right-hand guy, Henri, to check it out. He sat in the same library room with some guy and gal who evidently were trying to shakedown Earl. Earl didn't come in the room until later. Guess who the negotiator was. It was Brewer ... Earl brought the heavy guns. Whatever Brewer said made the guy and gal back off; in fact the gal started crying. Well, Henri wasn't close enough to hear anything, but he could tell whatever the guy and gal were going to do was shut down. Henri is smart. He followed Brewer and Earl out of the library to the parking lot. Imagine this ... Henri even rode the elevator down with them. They had a limo waiting, but Henri was agile and quick enough to get a cab and follow them to the airport. Earl gets out, Brewer stays in and the limo leaves to who knows where. Long story short, Henri was able to follow this Earl all the way up to the 1000 Island area, where I believe your company has a vacation house. That's evidently where this dude has been staying. And, he's not there as Earl Langston, he's there as Carl Bergstrom ... that's the name of the guy in the hospital that you told me about. He's the patient who was spirited away before Mutt and Jeff got there to bag him. So, what does this tell you? Carl Bergstrom is the real

Earl. The Earl in New York is someone else. Case closed, gentlemen."

Nickolas said, "Rico, I like you a little bit more than when we first started this conversation. I think you're right. Brewer has pulled off a switch right in front of everybody's eyes. You stay on the phone while we talk this over. I'm turning off the speaker, but don't hang up."

Marcellus spoke first. "One choice would be to continue as is, and then expose the deception in the BOD or maybe even earlier. However, it might expose our role, even criminally dangerously expose our role, and would delay any buyout, perhaps for a long time."

Nickolas agreed. "Hurting the company is just hurting ourselves. Exposing them would sure be entertaining, though."

Marcellus asked, "Is there any option where we can do the buyout regardless of Earl?"

An irritated and frustrated Dario answered, "We've talked about this forever! **No**, there ain't no other options. Earl has to be out of that BOD meeting. He holds the deciding votes. I say he's cooked. Now, you guys can keep talking, but all roads lead to Earl. I say **kill him**!"

Marcellus asked, "Which Earl?"

Dario said, "Both of them, dear brother. Both of them."

Nickolas said, "Okay let's vote. It's a vote to kill both Earls. Put your vote in the bean jar."

Marcellus asked, "We voting to kill anyone else?"

Nickolas answered, "Not yet. Not for this vote."

As before, each of the three men voted surreptitiously, placing their hidden bean in the dark blue jar on the coffee table. The men voted quickly. There was no waiting to see the results. As soon as the last man voted, the jar was flipped over to expose three black beans.

Nickolas picked up the phone and turned the speaker on.

"Rico, you have two targets now. Both are named Earl. Both Earls before the Board of Director's meeting. No mistakes! No excuses! Got it?"

Fifty-eight

Later that same day, much later, almost midnight, a horse-drawn carriage arrived at the road entrance to the Essex. It was a large, white ornate open carriage with red trim and red interior. The magnificent white horse pulling the carriage was held in check by the tuxedoed driver who sported a high hat like the ones pictured in the game of *Monopoly*. Soon after the first carriage arrived a second carriage arrived and stopped directly behind the first carriage. The second carriage only deviated from the first by being black in color with yellow trim. It was pulled by a black horse. The drivers sat up high in front of their seated passengers like the stagecoach drivers you see in cowboy movies.

The single passenger in the second carriage hardly waited for his carriage to stop before he jumped to the pavement and made his way to the first carriage. He helped the joyful young couple out of their carriage. It had been a wonderful evening for Trace and Dawn. The dinner, the Broadway *Mystic Magic* musical, and ride through the park made for a perfect date; it had been wonderful. Bryan Oliver, their bodyguard for their carriage ride, enjoyed the evening as well. There were no incidents.

A man seated in a luxurious armchair by the lobby entrance looked up from the paper he was holding, but not reading. He saw the carriages arrive and their three passengers come into the hotel and make their way to the elevators. Carson was pleased and somewhat excited. *So, I finally see Earl, after I've missed him all these weeks. I didn't know where he was until the media said he was at the hotel where all the shooting was. I could take him out now, but he needs to be talked to first. He needs to suffer first. I lost my sister; he needs to lose his girlfriend first. I think I'll find out something about those carriages they rode in.*

Carson left the lobby and walked out to the hotel entrance where the Essex doorman reigned. He casually lit up a cigar, fitting in with the three other smokers on the sidewalk.

"Sir?" he said, drawing the attention of the doorman. "What's with the carriages that were just here? I liked them. I'd like to rent one tomorrow night."

"Well, they're like yellow cabs. There are plenty of 'em. They nest around the park. Wait 'til they're open in the morning. Won't be any problem."

"Yeah, I gotcha ya. But, I don't want just any ole carriage. I want the white one I just saw here."

"You're outa luck, my friend. Langston Industries has exclusive use of those carriages while they're in the city. Edward and Ramon have been under contract with Langston a long time ... probably 12 to 15 years."

"I see. Well, Edward and Ramon, you say?"

"Yeah!"

"Well, I'd still like to talk to them. Where can I find 'em?"

" I can tell where their normal pickup station is but calling them might be better."

"I'll try their station first. Could you tell me where it is? I'd appreciate your help."

"Okay, I'll be right back."

The doorman went inside into the lobby. He came back in a few minutes with a business card and gave it to Carson.

"Here you go, sir," he said. "Straight from the concierge's desk."

"Thank you," Carson said, "you don't know what this means to me."

Fifty-nine

"Yesterday couldn't have been better!" Trace was responding to Martin's question. Martin and he were having breakfast coffee together and Martin wanted to know about Trace's dinner, show, and carriage ride.

"Yeah, it was great. It was nice to see Dawn again. I think she has recovered nicely. Last evening we had a great meal at *Trattoria Dell'Arte* near Carnegie Hall. Great Italian food in a wonderful setting, sort of like an artist's studio with pictures on the wall and some oversized sculptures. Then Grandma joined us for a very entertaining new musical, *Mystic Magic*. Then Dawn and I closed the evening with a carriage ride through the park. As I said before, yesterday couldn't have been better! Today I am planning and hoping for a repeat: an afternoon of sightseeing, then dinner, showtime, followed by another carriage trip around the park."

"What show are you going to see this time?"

"Well, Gordon's staff got us tickets to *The Dragonfly Chronicles*. It's supposed to be a really good dramatic play; we're looking forward to it."

"You mean you have the audacity to date a beautiful girl and have great entertainment planned, while poor old Martin is working his tail off?"

"Duh ... yeah, something like that!"

"Okay, okay. Let's talk about this get-together with Arlo. I expect him to be here shortly. When he comes, we'll order breakfast and then schedule your next guest appearance on his show."

"Right. Is this what Gordon wants us to do?"

"Yes. Regardless of our situation, if you know what I mean; we would just cancel if necessary."

"Got it!"

It was only five minutes later when Arlo arrived. He had someone with him. After Arlo greeted them, he said, "Let me introduce a friend of mine. I've known him even before I had the late-night show. His name is Mark, Mark Munson. I know we set up this session to see if Earl would come on the show again, but Mark asked to sit in. He has a question or so about Earl's last appearance on the show."

Trace replied, "No problem, Arlo! Glad to meet you, Mr. Munson. Please sit down. Let's order some food. All we've had is coffee so far."

After the meal and some social conversation, they discussed Arlo's request for Earl's next guest appearance. There were no issues, so it was just a matter of scheduling ... and they agreed it would be six weeks after Langston's BOD meeting, but not publicized until 10 days before his appearance.

Then, Trace turned to the quiet Mr. Munson.

"Sir," Trace said, "what can we help you with?"

"Thank you for having me, Mr. Langston. This has been a delightful breakfast and I hate to bring unpleasantries into it. But, here's the situation. My only daughter, Jane, was the young woman killed in the elevator crash after your appearance on Arlo's show."

"Oh, my!" Trace interrupted. "I'm so sorry!"

Munson nodded in appreciation, "Thank you, sir."

He continued, "The LA police have not ruled out a deliberate act, but they have no clues regarding intent or people of interest as they call them. In no way am I blaming you, your company or Arlo. But, I am a vengeful person, Mr. Langston. If that was a deliberate act, I want to do everything in my power to find the killers and anyone behind them and see that they get the punishment they deserve."

Trace replied, "We certainly agree with you, sir."

Munson then asked, "Here's really why I came to see you at this time. I saw on TV that there were two men killed in the Essex lobby. What I saw and heard was that the two men were not yet identified, and the object of their attack had not been determined. Do you know if those two men have been linked to the elevator crash?"

Martin answered before Trace could. "Mr. Munson," he said, "the answer to your question is no. We know little. If the shooters have been identified, we are not privy to that information. The lead NYC police detective working this shooting told me last night they had nothing new to report. They have reached out to the LA police, but nothing has been resolved. There is some concern it was a terrorist attack, but that's only one of the theories being explored. The detective said it's a top priority case, so I expect we will know more in a couple of days."

Martin continued, "Mr. Munson, as Earl said, we are very sorry about your daughter and what happened that night. I wish we could help, but we're not able to. It was a very tragic thing that happened in LA. We hope the LA police will give it their full attention. Like you, we want it to be resolved. If we hear anything, we'll let you know. How can we get in touch with you?"

"Well, you can't call me directly. I'll be on the road for the next three weeks. Here's my business card; call the number there and they will contact me. I have some business here and then some business in South Carolina and Florida before I return back to Texas." He paused. "I really do appreciate the time you gave me today. If we meet again, I hope everything has been resolved."

Breakfast was over. The men stood up and shook hands. They were going their separate ways when Martin hollered, "Oh, Mr. Munson, wait a minute, please. I have a question about your business card, sir."

Trace and Arlo left immediately; Martin caught up with Munson and they had a short conversation before the two of them left.

As Trace was leaving the dining area, he passed the FSC members in a booth, eating breakfast. Trace stopped and greeted them. "Good morning, gentleman. I didn't realize you were here yet."

"Yeah," Dario replied. "We came up late last night. We missed all the excitement, though. Sounds like somebody else don't like you."

"I can see why, Dario," Marcellus volunteered. "He just don't *loo*k or even *act* like the Earl we know. Must have been that accident he had; he's definitely changed. What do you think, Nickolas?"

"Oh, yeah, Marcellus," Nickolas replied. I see what you mean. He just looks different. Doesn't look like he normally does. And people tell me he *acts* different. Maybe he stayed in LA too long. Are you okay, Earl?"

"I'm fine, thank you," Trace replied. "I'd like to join you for coffee, but I have a meeting to go to. Enjoy the day." *I got caught by surprise. Those guys know I'm not Earl. I wonder how? I thought of a good comeback related to the three stooges; wish I could have used it ... but no, be calm, cordial, and careful ...*

Marcellus hurled a parting shot as Trace was leaving. "Oh, too bad you have to rush off, Earl. We'd like to see some of those impressions you did on TV; we didn't know you could do that. Maybe you'll have more time the next time we see you."

Meanwhile, Rico and Henri were having their breakfast in a cabin, in Sleepy Hollow New York, about an hour away from the Essex.

Rico was complaining about his telephone conversation with the FSC members. He said, "Those guys think they're so smart. Yeah, so smart. They wouldn't have ever known there were two Earls if I hadn't told them. And what did I get? Nothing! Nothing but their disrespect! Henri, I may want to take care of them after this job. Wadda you say?"

"Whatever. Just as long as it pays well. Up to you."

"Great. Okay, here's the deal we got with Nickolas. We know there's two Earls. I'm going to take care of the New York City Earl. I'm going to grab him and bring him up to this cabin. I'm thinking there might be more money in this job than just a simple hit.

"I want you to go to 1000 Islands and kill the other Earl. We don't need to keep two of them around. Take him out anyway you want to. You followed him up there. You know where he lives; take him out. Don't let anyone get in your way. Do it right away. It has to be done right away. Come back here when you're done. Any questions?"

"Nah! How about passing the coffee pot, will ya?"

Sixty

It was a different Carson that was in the lobby of the Essex the next afternoon. For one thing, he made himself look much older; the unneeded walking cane helped. And he did not seem to be in a hurry. For an impatient man on a mission, today's Carson was an anomaly. He was seated in a different plush chair in the Essex lobby. He got there about 2 o'clock the next afternoon. He sat quietly, people-watching. He disregarded all except the three clients of Edward and Ramon last night. He was calm; he felt like he was in a deer blind back up in the Adirondacks waiting for his prey. He saw Earl and his girlfriend take a cab around five. *Easy targets, but not what I want. I think I got this figured out. They're going to dinner and maybe somewhere else. The carriages be picking them up at some point for their park ride and return to the hotel. Now if I'm lucky this time, their bodyguard for last night will be going to the nearby carriage pickup point and ride with the carriages to meet Earl. I want the bodyguard.*

After Carson saw Earl and his girlfriend leave, he made a move based on his theory. He left the hotel and walked to a park bench near the targeted carriage pickup point. *Now my bet is that the same bodyguard will be riding with them tonight. I don't know his name; I don't care to. I just want to see him coming this way toward me.*

After a few more hours Carson began to revert to his normal, impatient avenger mode. He didn't like being out in the open where he might be recognized. He didn't like waiting. He worried that he had figured out tonight's scenario incorrectly. He hadn't. He saw the bodyguard come toward him where he was sitting.

Carson rose awkwardly from the park bench. He had a cane. He almost fell and said, "Say, mister. Can you help me? I need to go to the restroom, and I need some help getting there."

Bryan Oliver was the helper-type. He said, "Sure!"

That would be Bryan's last act of kindness. As soon as they reached the restroom, Carson brandished a gun, forced Bryan into a stall, and shot him twice. The second bullet was not necessary. Fortunately for Carson no one else was in the park restroom. That and the gun's silencer meant Carson's attack was neither seen nor heard by anyone else. Carson stripped Bryan of his wallet, all of his identification, his pistol, and his telephone. He propped Bryan on the commode, shut the stall door and left to go meet Edward and Ramon. He was excited, the frustrations of California and Arkansas were behind him; tonight he would avenge his sister.

Carson had already verified that the carriage business card address and the carriage pickup point were one and the same. He wasn't acting the old man now; he was a bodyguard. He saw Edward first.

"Are you Edward or Ramon?" he asked, although he knew he was talking to Edward.

"I'm Edward. How can I help you?"

"I'm Brad Joiner. I'm Earl Langston's bodyguard tonight. Bryan Oliver got sick suddenly and couldn't make it. Martin sent me over in his place. He told me I'd be riding with Ramon tonight and to stay with Earl and his girlfriend until they got back to the Essex."

"Well, Brad, I guess it's okay. They usually call me. Do you have any ID?"

"Sure! What do you need? Here's my Langston security badge and their security phone. We might be able to call Martin, although he was in a hurry to get to a bigwig dinner meeting in some other hotel. Here's the phone if you want to call him?"

"No, I guess not! Make yourself comfortable right now. When Ramon gets here, we'll go pick up our young couple and have a nice, leisurely ride through the park. If it's like last night, they won't even know we're around."

Carson nodded. He sat down in one of the four uncomfortable chairs nearby to wait. *Perfect so far! Phase I is complete.*

The seating in Ramon's carriage proved to be far more comfortable. However, the ride to the theater where *The Dragonfly Chronicles* was playing was slow for Carson's taste, but that was his impatient gene gaining control again. After they had reached the theater, it was another labored 60 minutes before the show was over. Trace and Dawn came out of the main exit. Carson was waiting for them there. He managed to get in front of them and say, "Good evening, Mr. Langston. My name is Brad Joiner, I'm riding shotgun tonight; Bryan got sick suddenly and couldn't make it. Our carriages are parked around the corner, sir. I'll take you to them."

Trace said, "Wait! Wait! I don't know you. You look familiar, but I don't know you. I don't remember seeing you around the hotel. What's your name again?"

"Brad Joiner, sir. I'm one of four new security officers that Martin brought in after the shooting at the hotel. I've had 3rd shift duty in the hotel until Bryan suddenly got sick tonight."

"You have any ID?"

"Sure. Here's my Langston security badge and their security phone. If you need to call somebody, I suggest Martin. It was a last-minute thing with Bryan, and Martin was on a tight schedule; I'm not sure who else knows besides them. Would you like to use my phone, sir?"

"Yes, I would. He picked Martin's name out of the contact list and made the call to Martin. After several rings, an automated voice told the caller to leave him a message and he would call back as soon as possible.

"Okay. Brad. Let's find the carriages. Oh, you probably haven't met Dawn." Trace made the introductions and then they headed for the carriages.

As Brad (Carson) led Trace and Dawn around the corner to their carriages, he was thinking … *Perfect so far! Phase 2 is complete. Good thing I replaced Martin's phone number with my ole prison mate's phone number; I knew he was back in prison again. Good thing Langston didn't call anyone else!*

Sixty-one

Once the carriages had their cargo, the horses began their slow-paced journey east on 46th Street and then turned left on 7th Avenue toward Central Park. It was a beautiful night. Carson was the only one who ignored the beautiful night. After the busy traffic died down, Carson was ready to begin Phase 3. While his carriage was still moving, Carson leapt to the pavement onto the sidewalk and began yelling, "Stop! Stop!" He ran forward alongside Edward's carriage continuing to yell, "Stop! Stop! Get out of the carriage now! Hurry! Now!"

The suddenness and the strident message paralyzed everyone at first, but then Trace left his carriage before Edward was able to halt his horse. After the drivers were able to halt their horses, actually stopping in the middle of the street, Trace helped Dawn to the sidewalk. Panic ruled. Carson moved into the street in front of the lead carriage and was furiously trying to wave down a cab. There didn't seem time for an explanation. Carson was successful almost immediately as a cab pulled over by the sidewalk.

Carson then told Trace, "Mr. Langston get in the back seat. Miss Young, please sit up front with the driver. I'll sit in back behind you."

Then Carson told Edward, "It would be best if you and Ramon leave 7th and take another route to the park. Be careful, I was warned of a possible ambush."

With those instructions, Carson joined the others already in the cab. The cab driver seemed to be unfazed by all the shouting and the quickness in which his passengers had joined his cab.

He said, "Look, the lady needs to be sitting in the back. What's with you guys? What's with all the drama? You ain't from around here, are you?"

Carson replied, “No, we’re not! What’s your name, wise guy?”

“It’s Dwayne spelled with a y.”

”Now you listen, Dwayne spelled with a y. We are goin’ ride just like we’re sitting and you ... you are gonna take us wherever we want to go without any further conversation from you! Got it?”

“Okay, mac, okay. Don’t get in a dither. Just tell me where to go.”

“Go to Columbia University. I’ll give you the address nearby Columbia when we get near there.”

Trace spoke up. “Okay, Brad what’s goin’ on?”

Carson answered, “Sorry, Mr. Langston. I got an alert that there was a possibility there were shooters somewhere on 7th Avenue. I was told we should abandon the carriages, catch a cab, and go to a safe house located near Columbia University. We are to stay there until we get an all clear.”

“Thanks, Brad.”

After a few blocks, Trace and Dawn settled down and just made some idle chatter. Carson and the cabbie were quiet. But when they got to 67th street west of the park, it was Trace that ordered the cabbie to pull over and stop.

Carson asked, “What’s happening, sir? Is there a problem?”

Trace said, “Maybe. What we’re doing is not clear to me. Who called you and told you about the shooters?

“It was Martin, sir.”

“And, to leave the carriages, catch a cab, and go to Columbia?”

“Martin, sir.”

“And, tell me again, what’s at Columbia?”

“We have a safe house near there that no one in Langston knows anything about except Gordon, Martin, and us bodyguards.”

“I see. Well, we’re not going any further until I talk to either Gordon or Martin. Dawn, give me your phone, please.”

Dwayne had pulled over into a pedestrian walking area and stopped. He then disgustedly put his left hand on his face resting his elbow on the door arm rest. He looked upward and began silently moving his mouth.

Carson said, " I can't let you do that, Earl. That's not part of the plan. We need to get you up there at Columbia and let you tell me why I shouldn't kill you for killing my little sister."

While Carson was talking, he pulled a gun from his coat pocket and had the nose of the gun resting on the back of Dawn's head.

"None of you move now. Any attempt to do anything but sit will cause my gun to shoot this pretty little girl's head off. I'm sorry, Miss. You've heard of the wrong place, the wrong time. This is it!"

Dawn began to cry out; she stopped when Carson tapped her harshly on the back of her head. Trace almost leapt forward, but his seat belt restrained him to the point he realized he would be unable to disarm him before Dawn would be shot.

"Carson threw a pair of handcuffs to Trace. He said, "Put 'em on, Earl. or your girlfriend gets it!"

Trace felt he had to comply. Carson locked the cuffs while continuing to hold the pistol pointed at Dawn.

Trace said, "Okay, whoever you are. I don't know you. I don't know your sister. You have made a bad mistake. Put the gun up. Let's go back to the hotel and talk."

Dwayne said nothing, but his eyes widened, and he nodded his head up and down.

"Well, Earl, it's clear you're a hit-and-run date. You've probably been in trouble since the Cub Scouts. I want to talk first about your background. I'm sure your lady friend doesn't know it or she'd be far, far away."

"Well, who are you? Who's your sister? I don't know you!"

"Okay! You're right; you don't know me. But you did kill my little sister. She was at one of your drug parties. You gave her drugs. She ODed on cocaine and died. I was in prison at the time, or you'd already be dead by now."

"Now wait just ..."

"Don't interrupt me again, Earl. It makes me unhappy. I don't like to be unhappy. Say nothing unless I ask you somethin' ... that goes for you two onlookers, too."

Carson adjusted himself in a more upright position before continuing.

"Of course, I'm not Brad and I'm not one of your bodyguards, although you now have an opening for one. My name is Carson Baker, my sister's name was Isabel. She started going to your drug parties when she was 20; she got hooked; she died. There were three of you rich party boys that were blamed for the party and her death. The other two were convicted and are in prison now. I plan to meet them in the near future. But, Earl baby, you got off ... you got off ... you had the big bucks that gave you a leg up on justice.

"I know your bio. Had the big buck privileges all your life. Your daddy worked hard to give you those privileges and the opportunity to build on those privileges, but you chose to chase women and drugs Probably got your habit early, continued in your first year of college. Got married, didn't make it through second year college; didn't make it through one year of marriage. Parties and fast cars were your way of life; you are a womanizer and addict. You and your drug parties killed my sister and have probably done tons of damage to many others. Now we are going to a place up by Columbia University where I will hear your defense and then we'll decide what to do."

Early on Dwayne wanted no part of these people. As Carson talked, he was able to free himself from his seat belt and stealthily unlatch his car door. As Carson concluded his monologue, Dwayne flung the door open and ran directly across the street into the car traffic. Carson's reaction was quick; he pointed the gun at the fleeing cabbie and got off two shots. Dawn fell to her right against the passenger door; Trace, however, slammed down his handcuffed hands as hard as he could on Carson's left wrist and hand that held the pistol. The force of Trace's blow caused Carson to drop the pistol. Trace began yelling, "Run, Dawn, run. Run! Run!"

Dawn was scared but when she heard Trace yell, she was able to quickly get out of her seat belt, open the passenger door and run. She ran into the nearby park amidst some onlookers nearby. She was really scared, but she was safe.

Carson suffered a few more blows from Trace's handcuffed hands, but he moved away from Trace before he could do more damage. Trace was still restricted by his seat belt as well as his handcuffs. He was no match for Carson who got out of his seatbelt, slugged Trace twice with his fist, then knocked him unconscious with the butt of his pistol he retrieved from the front seat. *I have my quarry, forget the others, although I would have enjoyed hurting the girlfriend while Earl watched. It's time to get out of here!* The keys were still in the ignition; Carson became the driver. The cab with its two occupants sped off toward Columbia University.

Sixty-two

Carson knew he was in trouble. *The survivors and onlookers are going to give the cops plenty of information about this cab. The girlfriend will tell them I was in a yellow cab, going to Columbia University. Well, we're not going to Columbia now. I need another car, or I need to shelter this one. Getting Earl into another car will not be easy; I think the best bet is to find a 24-hour self-parking garage. That will give me a little recreation time with Earl. I can't play with him like I wanted, but I can give him a little pain before I shut him down and leave this sorry city.*

With those thoughts in mind, he crossed over a few streets and turned back toward Lower Manhattan, the direct opposite direction of Columbia. He drove to Greenwich Village before he found the unattended, underground garage he wanted. He took the meaningless parking ticket as he entered, then drove down to the 6th level before he found the parking space he wanted. It was not near the elevators and partially concealed by an interior building wall. After he parked, he turned his attention to the dazed and barely conscious Trace in the back seat, who was still confined by a seatbelt and handcuffs. He ripped off Trace's shirt and undershirt, losing a few shirt buttons in the process. He then gagged Trace, who was too dazed to resist. He slapped Trace a few times to get him out of his dazed condition; Carson wanted Earl fully awake before he delivered *la finalite de la mort*.

Carson made himself comfortable. He got in a sitting position in the passenger seat, back against the passenger door with his legs extended on the seats toward the driver's side. He retrieved his gun from his waist belt, then toyed with it and the silencer as he was deciding how to proceed. His thoughts were interrupted as a couple exited from the elevator and got into a nearby car. Trace was fully awake now and made some extra efforts to free himself. Carson shot an area in the back seat by Trace saying, "No, no, Earl. You be quiet now. Don't be so selfish … you're gonna get some other people killed if you're not quiet."

Carson was ready, but two cars entered the 6th floor, and he was forced to wait a bit longer until they drove down to the 7th floor. Now, it was time. He began berating Earl again. Finally, he said, "Earl, I wish I was in that place near Columbia. I woulda had more time and more things I wanted to do. You've never cooperated in this whole mess. Not only did you kill my sister, but I also had to kill that couple in California and that guy in Arkansas because you weren't around. And that stupid guard got in the way tonight. You are the cause of a lot of problems; you don't deserve to be around any longer. So, here's what's going down: Listen carefully. I'm shooting you in your right leg first; then I'm shooting you in your left leg. We'll wait a short time and while we're waiting, I'll talk to you about pain … the pain you caused me and my sister. Then, it's your turn again. I'll shoot you in your right arm, then in your left arm. We'll rest awhile, and we'll go from there."

Carson had been leaning over the passenger seat talking to Trace. He lifted his gun to follow through on his threat. Two shots were fired and heard; both bullets coming from a gun without a silencer; both bullets from the gun of a policeman crouching by the partially open driver's door. The passenger door was flung open, Carson's body fell backwards onto the garage floor. Other policemen joined the scene. Trace's fright night was over; New York City's calvary had arrived.

Sixty-three

Resting, back in his hotel room at the Essex, Trace found out why he was probably the luckiest person in New York City. Martin was with Trace while Gordon was offering his explanation; Dawn was not present.

Gordon said, “Well, you are asking how we found you. Of course, we knew you were last seen in a yellow cab. But, where? I have to ‘fess up to something we didn’t tell you. When Dr. Janssen molded the fake scar on your leg, Martin and I decided to embed a small transmitter that would enable us to determine where you were. It was a last-minute thing, and, honestly, I had no intention of ever monitoring you and didn’t until tonight. Sometimes you just get lucky; the transmitter saved your life. The transmitter signal led the police to the parking garage and the noticeable parked yellow cab did the rest. The police drove two unmarked cars up and down the parking levels until they spotted the cab. Fortunately, they were in time. They were able to stop this guy Carson, who you and Dawn told us was avenging his sister. I’d like to hear all the allegations he made against Earl; Dawn is very upset by what she heard. I understand you never broke character. We’ll talk about all that later. It’s after midnight, it's time for everybody to rest. See you later today.”

Earl, the real Earl, was in a good mood. He had an unexpected guest that afternoon. It was Lincoln Smith, his former watchdog and caretaker who had overseen his safety and health while he was at 1000 Islands. He had become good friends with Link during his recovery and rehabilitation time. Earl had just finished telling Link about his quick trip to Los Angeles and the thwarted blackmailer story. Lincoln really laughed at Earl’s description of the angry Gordon Brewer and the subdued and scared blackmailers.

Link said, "So, don't mess with Gordon, huh?"

Earl replied, "That's what I learned."

Link then said, "Earl, let me tell you the main reason I came by. I didn't really have a chance to talk to you before me and my security team left. This is more than just a social visit. I hope I'm a good enough friend I can be serious with you for a few minutes; I may step on your toes a bit, but I need to just say a couple of things to you. I had heard some stuff about you before we spent some time together the past several weeks. Frankly, I was surprised. I thought I was going to be baby-sitting a self-indulgent, wild, immature kid. I'm sorry, Earl, but that was your rep when I came in. Maybe the accident knocked that out of you; I don't know. You almost died, but you didn't. Anyway, I found a young man who has a lot of capabilities but hadn't found his role in life yet.

"I was a great friend of your dad's. I saw up close and personal what he could do and did. He had a great mind for business and for people. I've had a lot of bosses. He was the best. I was one of many who mourned his unexpected passing at the prime of his life. I am saying all that to tell you I honestly believe you have the same qualities as your dad's, but you're wasting them chasing a life that will end up being meaningless. I see no reason that you can't eventually take full control of Langston Industries."

Earl was almost in tears. It took him a few seconds to control his emotions. He replied, "Link, I think you've hit it spot on. I can't really account for or defend my past behavior; I know I have a bad rep. I'm probably regarded as the spoiled son of Langston's founder. I got off on the wrong foot in college and didn't learn from it; just continued it. I loved my dad, but I lived in awe of him. I was afraid I couldn't live up to his expectations. And instead of trying I just gave up. I knew I was wrong.

"I do appreciate what you've said and the confidence you have in me. The accident did knock some sense into me. I have changed. Gordon sent me a lot of material about the company; I've become well-versed in the operation and finances of

Langston. I have read several books on leadership and management. I want to be the man my dad wanted me to be. I'm almost fully recovered. I would have already come back but Gordon and I thought we should wait until after the BOD meeting. After I return, I will rid myself of my sordid reputation."

Link smiled and said, "There's no doubt in my mind that you will. It's nice seeing you Earl ... and even nicer knowing where you're headed."

Earl replied, "Thanks for the visit, Link. One of our boats is at our dock; do you need it to get back to the marina?"

"No, I rented one, I'm in good shape."

" Great! Stay in touch."

Link said, "I will, Earl. I'll let myself out. Do you want the front door locked?"

"Yeah, please; the caretaker won't be here for a couple of hours."

"Okay!"

Earl read for a while longer but grew sleepy and went to his bedroom and changed into his pajamas. He had no trouble going to sleep. After several hours of sleeping, he was rudely awakened. There was a man standing near the end of his bed. Even though the room was almost dark, Earl could see the pistol the man was holding.

"Wake up!" the man exclaimed loudly. "Wake up!"

"Who are you? What are you doing here?"

"First things first. Wake up but don't get up!"

"Now wait just ...."

The intruder shot his gun once, the bullet shattering a dresser mirror. He said stridently, "Now shut up! I own this conversation! Shut up! I'm doing the talking now."

He continued, "I got excited when I first saw you in Los Angeles. That guy looks like Earl Langston. The resemblance is awesome! I need to find out who he is. It took a lot of effort on my part, but I found out: it was you, Carl. Imagine. Carl

Bergstrom. A look-alike to that billionaire, Earl Langston. So, what were you doing in LA, Carl?"

" I go there occasionally; what's it to you?"

" I'm talking about recently."

"I don't remember."

"Oh, I suppose you don't remember seeing me there recently."

"No."

"Not even me sitting in the library ... and even riding downstairs in the elevator with you. How rude. How snobbishly, unthoughtfully rude."

Earl remembered. The extravagantly dressed man. "Okay, what do you want besides time to insult and lecture?"

"Nothing really. We got it figured out. You're the real Earl. The guy in the City having all the fun is a fake. You made your way here from the hospital after a bad accident. You got knocked out as Earl and woke up as Carl. Magic! Imagine that! I want you to sleep sound now and realize this charade is over."

Saying that, the intruder hit Earl hard enough to daze him, then quickly chloroformed him into unconsciousness.

Henri had enjoyed his little monologue with Earl. *Now after I set this fire, what's left of Earl will be in his bed, a victim of a terrible fire. Yeah, and he'll have company. I chloroformed that old guy downstairs also; I was afraid he might interrupt my conversation with Earl. I don't know who he is, but it doesn't really matter. He's a goner just like Earl.*

Now I'm going to search the house and see if there are any valuables. I have at least two hours. There's no rush. I don't like driving at night, so I'll wait until it's almost dawn before I set the fire. Then, it's back to Sleepy Hollow. I'm going to ask for a bonus for taking care of two guys instead of just one and making it look like an accident. I do such good work.

Later Henri lost his glow; he became angry and very disappointed. After searching the house thoroughly, he found little of portable value. He took his anger out on a few beers from the fridge. Then, as dawn approached, he started a fire in the kitchen. The fire spread quickly. He went outside in front of the house away from the flames to watch the house burn. He watched until the outer walls caved in; he saw no survivors. He left the island using the boat that had brought him to the island, *Mission fait accompli*.

Sixty-four

Trace slept to almost noon without interruption. *I'm glad to be alive. That guy was crazy; it's just unbelievable what he did to get Earl. And what's so pathetic, he didn't know what he was talking about. He was nuts. Gordon told me all about Earl when I was learning to be him. Yeah, he was introduced to drugs, but not until his first year of college ... and, probably the drugs influenced him to marry that ball-of-fire Frieda; man, she's something else. They lasted over a year. He did leave college for a drug rehab program. He did go to friends' parties where drugs were prevalent, but after rehab, he didn't use drugs again. And in all that time, he never provided drugs to anyone else. Guilty of using drugs, he was innocent of being a supplier. He never knew that guy's sister, except to see her at some of those parties. Guilty of being stupid; but innocent of any part of the death of that guy's sister. He was never charged with any complicity in her death. Not a good resume, but not as bad as our abductor described him. All of that stuff has given Earl a bad reputation. Recent problems with his immature behavior are probably related to the death of his father. I need to talk to Dawn to explain all that. I'm obligated to defend Earl. She may have believed all that garbage that maniac said to us last night. I'll call her.*

Trace dialed the phone number of her suite.

"Hello." a feminine voice said. "This is Demi. May I help you?"

"I think so. Demi, this is Earl. Earl Langston. I'd like to speak to Dawn."

"I'm sorry Mr. Langston, but she's not to be disturbed right now."

"Hmm! Well, Demi, when can she be disturbed?"

"I'm not sure , sir."

"Demi, I don't believe I've met you. How do you know Dawn?"

"Sir, I'm one of Langston's security personnel. Dr. Brewer wanted someone to stay in her suite today; to stay with both Dawn and Mrs. Langston. I know who you are, sir; but right now I'm to see that she is not to take calls or visitors."

"I understand. When it's appropriate, please tell her that I called, and I would very much like to talk to her."

"Yes, sir."

"Also, Demi, can you tell me how she's feeling; how she's doing?"

"I think all right, sir. She hasn't talked much, but she seems okay."

"Thank you, Demi. Bye-bye."

"Goodbye, sir."

Trace did something he hadn't done during the whole course of this job. He decided he'd stay in the suite, eat lunch, read the papers, and watch TV. So he ordered lunch, and he spent the rest of the afternoon in the suite.

It was after 5 o'clock when Trace began to be despondent. *Well, I had an uninterrupted afternoon. But now I worry. Dawn hasn't called. It sounds like she's angry about those lies she heard last night. I can't say I blame her. I need to talk to her, but I think it would be wrong to bulldoze my way in to see her or even call her right now. I just can't let her go on thinking of me the way it was portrayed last night. So, I'll tell her who I am … and then she learns I'm just an actor? Spare me! I probably just need to talk to Gordon before I get caught off base here.*

Calling Gordon and even calling Martin didn't help. They weren't in. No one seemed to know where they were. He was still tired from last night, so he took an unplanned and unexpected short nap. He didn't sleep too long because a loud knocking at the door woke him up. He opened the door. It was a young man, dressed in a hotel uniform.

"Mr. Langston?"

"Yes, what do you want?"

"Sir, I have a message for you. They told me they tried to call you, but you didn't answer. Here's the message, sir."

He handed the hotel envelope to Trace; Trace waited until the young man left before he opened the letter addressed to Earl. The handwritten note inside simply said, *Earl I need to see you. I'll be in the park by the Imagine mosaic until dark. D*

Rats! How long have they been sitting on this note? It's almost dark now!

It took Trace only a few minutes to get his act together. He was out the hotel and the doorman got him a cab immediately. The drive was a short one. The mosaic was a short walk into the park. He was there. She wasn't. *Where is she? Maybe I missed her? There's a couple sitting on that bench. Maybe they've seen her?*

He described her. No, they hadn't seen her.

How about the old lady on a different bench?

No, she hadn't seen her.

Maybe the young woman standing by a baby carriage had seen her?

No, she had been walking through the park and had just gotten there. She hadn't seen her.

Maybe the middle-aged man with a cane on another bench?

"Well, maybe son. Why don't you sit down and tell me again slowly what she looks like. Is she in trouble?"

Trace was agitated, but he did sit down on the bench to describe her again.

."That's the best I can describe her, sir."

"Oh, yeah. That's plenty good enough, Impostor!"

The man plunged the needle into Trace's arm as a bewildered Trace was thinking *How does this guy know I'm an impostor …* and suddenly everything was dark, and Trace slumped forward on the park bench.

The middle-aged man motioned to a slender man standing on part of the mosaic. Hey, mister! Can you help me with my friend, sir? I think he drank too much!"

"Yeah," the skinny guy replied. "I can help!"

The two men gathered Trace between them and walked him out of the park. The couple on the first bench, the old lady on the second bench, the young woman alongside her baby carriage, and all the other tourists and New Yorkers visiting the *Imagine* mosaic didn't seem to notice.

Sixty-five

Gordon was concerned. Trace was supposed to meet him for breakfast, but he's a no-show. *This is a first for Trace. He's 30 minutes late. He's always been prompt. Maybe yesterday's bout with that maniac has something to do with this. The newspapers are all over that story, especially since the police have linked that nut to the California and Arkansas murders.*

His thoughts were interrupted when a waiter brought a telephone to his table, plugged it in, and said "You have a call, sir. A Mr. Evans from Alexandria Bay, New York said it was an emergency. Sorry to interrupt you, sir."

That's up by the marina at 1000 Lakes. What's going on?

"Yes, hello? This is Dr. Brewer."

"Morning, sir. My name is Blake Evans. I am the Alexandria Bay head of 1000 Islands Security. I have some bad news. Your Langston operators forwarded my call to you to tell you that news. The Langston house in 1000 Islands caught on fire. The fire is still smoldering, although the fire has already leveled the house. Basically, the house is gone."

"Wow! That is bad news!" (pause) "Mr. Evans, we have a caretaker and one of our employees staying there. Do you know if they're safe?"

"No, sir, I do not know. There are a lot of onlookers, but none of them seem to know anything about who was in the house. We'll be able to search through the rubble in about an hour or so. Hopefully, we won't find any bodies."

"You probably don't know what started it, do you?"

"No, sir."

"Thank you for calling. I appreciate you letting us know right away. If you don't mind, I'll turn you back to my office staff to get your number and location up there. They'll give you a contact person for today; tomorrow we'll have two people up there. Thank you again."

Wow. I hope Earl and Orlando are okay. What a way to begin the day! I need to get Martin down here and let him "enjoy" some of this day with me.

Martin joined Gordon in ten minutes. Two hours later the bad news had gotten worse, regardless of their efforts. The search through the rubble at 1000 Islands had yielded a badly burned unidentified body. Earl was either dead or missing. The transmitter in Trace's leg had not transmitted since shortly after midnight. The last transmission came from somewhere north of Central Park. Trace was either dead or missing.

Two fine young men either dead or missing. The BOD is tomorrow morning. It's on occasions like these that I miss the steady hand of Michael. He was more than just my boss; he was my mentor, my friend. He never panicked nor seemed to worry. He told me several times 'God is Greater than any Problems I have.' I'm going to draw on his Christian faith as well as my own right now."

He decided to call Grandma. *I hate to worry her, but she's entitled to know what's going on.*

"Hi, Grandma."

"Good morning, Gordon."

"Not really, Grandma."

Gordon then proceeded to tell her the alarming and worrisome news. Grandma listened patiently, asked a few questions, but said little. Finally, Gordon asked, "How is Dawn doing? How did she take all those lies that maniac said about Earl?"

"Not too well really. She has gone through stages of anger, confusion, and depression. The danger and stress have not treated her well."

"Grandma, have you talked to her about Earl?"

"Some. She probably thinks an old lady like me doesn't want to think her grandson can do anything wrong."

"Grandma, what about telling her about everything? What about telling her all the bad things about Earl. No sugarcoating: Frieda, college, rehab and the works. Then tell her the Earl she loves is not Earl; he is an actor named Trace."

"Gordon, I've wanted to tell her everything very much. Thank you. She and I will have that little talk this morning. Now don't you worry about our two young men. They'll be all right. And I'll take care of this young 'un."

"Thank you, Grandma."

Grandma did take care of that young 'un. Dawn came out of her depression signaled by some tears of relief.

"Oh, Grandma, I've been such a dork. Earl ... I mean Trace, called yesterday and wanted to talk, but I was angry, and I didn't want to talk to him. I didn't call him back as he asked. So now, he's missing, and I can't talk to him and tell him how I really feel. I'm so sorry. I'm so worried too."

"Yes, all of us are worried. Let's pray and hope."

In mid-afternoon, Gordon turned his attention to the BOD meeting scheduled for tomorrow morning. He called Roland Turlington, Langston's Chief Corporate Lawyer and Secretary of the BOD. *I'm not really friends with Roland and I know he's on the other side of this buyout question. However, I've found Roland to be an excellent attorney, fair and straight-forward in all his dealings.*

"Roland, this is Gordon. Have you heard the news?"

"Yes, Gordon, I have. Any updates? Has Earl been found?"

"No, he hasn't. That's why I'm calling. I want to understand the ramifications of Earl not being at the BOD tomorrow."

"You would be the moderator, in charge of the agenda and the meeting instead of him. Basically, business as usual."

"Doesn't the bylaws speak to the absence of the CEO and Chairman of the Board in any other fashion."

"No, it does not." *Strike 1!*

"What about a quorum? Will we have a quorum?"

"Yes, as far as I know. The bylaws require at least four of its eight members to be present. We could miss three more and still proceed and have legal, binding votes on all business matters. I've not been informed any of the others will not attend." *Strike 2!*

"Well, Roland, how about rescheduling tomorrow's BOD to another day."

"No, Gordon we're very restricted as a corporation in this regard. We have published a date and we are unable to change that date, barring a major disaster, unless it's at least seven days before the scheduled event. The meeting must go on as scheduled." *Strike 3!*

Sixty-six

It was mid-morning before Trace was able to become fully awake. Being awake didn't help much. He was tied down, probably to a bed. He wasn't sure because he was blindfolded. He had a headache, but the pain that bothered him the most was his right leg. It felt bad, it felt like he had been cut. *What have I got myself into this time. The last thing I remember I was in City Park trying to find Dawn. Oh, no. There was something else. A man called me an impostor?"*

Trace sensed someone was near his bed. "Hey!" he cried out. "Help me! Help me!"

"You gotta be kidding," a voice said. "I've helped you all I'm going to. I don't see you need nothin'."

"Where am I? Who are you?"

"Son, you ever heard of *The Legend of Sleepy Hollow*? It's a favorite of mine. Pretend you're *Ichabod Crane,* pretend you're reliving his story, his sleep; pretend you're going to sleep and wake up ... well, you ain't."

"I don't know what the heck you're talking about! Let me talk to your boss!"

"I **am** the boss, stupid! You are my prisoner. Not much else to say. I've already told you that you are in Sleepy Hollow. You probably won't be leaving Sleepy Hollow. We'll see how that works out; it'll probably take us a day or two. Now, I'm leaving. If I feel like talking, I'll come back and visit later. If you feel like talking when I'm not here, I will gag you. If you talk loud, I might even hurt you like this ... ." The "this" was a sharp hit on the place on Trace's leg that was hurting him so much. Trace yelled in pain.

"You get the picture, son? I can hit harder, you know. See ya later, son. Don't go away! Try to think pleasant thoughts."

Trace heard footsteps that moved away from his bed. A door opened and closed; he didn't know if his "boss" had left the room or not. It was frustrating not to know, not to see.

What Trace did not know or see was the rural area he was in. It was Sleepy Hollow alright. The Sleepy Hollow village of 11,000 or more was about an hour's drive from the Essex in New York City. Trace was in one of the two bedrooms of a rustic cabin located in a wooded area, far removed from the village and a half mile from any other cabin or house. Isolated.

Man, that guy hurt me. I think I know why. He knows I'm not Earl. He must also have known about the transmitter implanted in my leg. He must have cut it out and taken a lot of my leg with it. I hope I'm wrong, but that makes sense. I can't think of a way out of this right now ... I hope something will come to me.

After a while, the voice came back. The voice had been drinking; he was loud and slurred some of his words.

"Well, Mr. Impostor, how's it going? Enjoying your visit here? Maybe we'll have a chance to visit Washington Irving's grave. It ain't too far away. I guess not; I probably couldn't trust you to behave. Guys playing games like you just can't be trusted and your kind sure don't like to take orders."

"What do you mean 'my kind'?"

"You tell me! You're the one playing games!"

"Okay, you got the best hand. I'm listening. What do you want with me?"

"Well, Imp, you don't mind me calling you Imp, do you? Let's just say you're a bargaining chip. I'm fixing to see how much you're worth."

"You should be calling me Earl, not Imp."

"Oh, c'mon, Imp. Game's over, don't insult me."

"Who are you bargaining with? Maybe I can help."

"I don't need no help, Imp. I'll see you later! Bye!"

"Wait! Wait! Maybe I'm worth more than you think?"

"Nice try, Imp, but you ain't part of the bidding process."

"How about some help with the pain in my leg?"

"Looks good to me! But surgeons always like the looks of their surgery. I can help it like I helped it this morning if you want me to. Maybe not, huh? Bye, Imp!"

Rico left the back bedroom, entering the den that led to the kitchen and the front bedroom. The bedrooms were separated by a single bathroom. The den was large; it had a large fireplace at one end, near the front entrance. At the other end of the cabin was the kitchen area which had an outside entrance. Rico's helper, Patch, was half-drunk, rummaging around in the kitchen. As usual, Patch was complaining about doing work and not getting paid for it. Rico was tired of dealing with Patch. He didn't like his bitching and he didn't trust him to keep his mouth shut.

"Patch," he said. "Did you finish that job I gave you?"

"No, Rico. I got tired. That's a big grave you asked me to dig and the ground's really hard."

"Patch, get your butt outside and finish that job. I don't want to see you inside until that job is done. I'm not paying you to sit in the kitchen and drink beer all day long."

"Oh, Rico, let me ..."

"Get going, Patch. Don't make me angry. You don't wanna see me angry!"

Around 1 o'clock in the afternoon, Rico was ready to make a telephone call to his clients. He was in a good mood. *I'm gonna put it to that Florida bunch*. He went in the front bedroom on the other side of the cabin where Trace couldn't hear the conversation. He called the new number he'd been given. It was Nickolas' number.

"Hello, who is this?"

"It's me, Nick. It's Rico."

"Have you got good news?"

"Yes and no. I haven't heard from Henri yet. I don't know what's going on at 1000 Island."

"We haven't heard yet either, but our company learned our house up there burned down. Maybe there's good news waitin' to be told."

"Yeah, sounds promising."

"What about the fake Earl?"

"The impostor? I got him. He's tied up. He ain't going nowhere."

"What's the deal? You know what to do!"

"Not so fast, Nick. You owe me big time. I got a lot of expenses. I lost two men. I told you about the two Earls; you never thanked me or rewarded me. That wasn't nice. That was disrespectful. The problem you got has gotten much bigger over the last month or so. And the guys who shot up the Essex have made it a lot more dangerous to me."

"What are you leading up to? Are you welshing on me?"

"No. I'm just explaining that you're shorting me on this job."

"If you're trying to make me angry, you've succeeded. I'm not haggling with you or anyone else."

"I understand, but I'm not going to haggle either. The old contract is dead. I want 500 grand to make sure both parties won't be at your BOD meeting tomorrow. If they don't show up, I want 500k. Put 200k in my account to show we have a deal. No 200k in my account and I'll turn this guy loose, maybe the other one too if he ain't dead. That's it. It's a little after 1 o'clock now; I'll call back at 7. If the 200k is in my account, we have a deal. No dollars. No deal. 7 o'clock"

"Where are you? I wanna talk face-to-face!"

"No! I told you the deal. Where I am makes no difference. Listen! It's simple! If you put up the money, we have a deal. If you don't, no deal. If it's no deal, I can assure you my impostor is near enough to be at your meeting tomorrow. Nice talking with you, Nick. My regards to your two partners. I'll call back at 7 o'clock."

Sixty-seven

About an hour after Rico's call to Nickolas, Rico heard someone come into the front of the cabin. He pulled out his pistol and stealthy left the kitchen to confront his visitor. It was Henri. They exchanged greetings; then Henri asked, "Where's your Earl, Rico? I saw the makings of a grave outside, but there ain't nobody in it. You ain't done nothin' yet?"

"Not to worry, Henri. My Earl is trussed up in the bedroom. He's goin' to take up residence in that hole outside sometime tonight. When we get through talking, we'll pay my Earl a visit. What about your Earl?"

"Well, if this was the Olympics, I'd get a gold medal. I burned his place down with him in it. It'll drive the cops nuts. Didn't leave no clues or nothin'. My part of the deal is done. Let's take care of your Earl and go somewhere else. Contract's done; let's get our money."

"I'm not ready to go yet. I've told our client we need more money, or we'll turn my Earl loose. They have a lot of money at stake. They'll pay. I ain't worried; they'll pay."

"They better, Rico! I'll be very, very unhappy if they don't. I want some dollars; I don't work for free. And if I'm unhappy, I'll see that you're unhappy too."

"My, my. Here I'm trying to get us some free money, and my partner don't like it. Have a little faith, bro."

"I do, but my faith is an impatient faith. When are we goin' know something?"

"I'm goin' call 'em back at 7. I'm expecting 200k in my account then as a down payment of 500k. At 11 we take care of my Earl and then we leave."

"The money sounds good. I can wait 'til then."

"I knew you could. Let's visit my Earl."

They took the short walk to the bedroom. Trace had been napping but the opening and closing of the bedroom door woke him up.

"Who's there?" he asked.

"There are two of us, now, Imp. My partner wanted to see you. He just got back from 1000 Islands. He brought some bad news for you. There was a terrible fire there; it seems it was Langston's place out there on one of the islands. It seems like a guy living in that place didn't make it. That's too bad. Hope it wasn't anyone you knew."

Trace's heart fell. *These guys are killers; Earl deserved better. I'm going to be quiet. No use giving them any satisfaction.*

Henri said, "Glad to meet you, Imp. I thought your name was Earl, but I was never any good with names. Are you enjoying your rest? Need anything? Why so quiet all of a sudden?"

Trace remained silent.

Rico said, "He's not being nice right now."

He viciously hit Trace's leg where the wound was. Trace yelled. It hurt. It really hurt!

Rico said, "See, Henri? He can talk. I told you so!"

Trace said, "Yes, I can talk. I have a question. You said I was a bargaining chip. Did you make your deal?"

"I think so, but we won't know 'til later."

" Let me enter the bargaining. I can get you a much better deal."

"Well, maybe if you were Earl, but you ain't. You're just some lousy impostor. You ain't worth nothing, Imp. Goodbye for now; we'll visit again later this evening."

With that, the two hoodlums left the bedroom and went into the den to do some more drinking and celebrating, leaving a helpless Trace tied up on a bed.

Rico and Henri were celebrating too early. Even crooks should know "it ain't over 'til it's over". Henri had made a big mistake. No gold medal for him. Henri did everything right except for spotting a survivor from the fire. It was Earl. Earl managed to revive, but he was at first bewildered and choking from clouds of smoke. Self-preservation kicked in; he was able to gather his senses well enough to escape the burning house out the back door near the boat house. Earl was still dazed but managed to commandeer one of the boats. He drove his boat further away from the house where he saw the arsonist, hands on hips, watching the fire from a boat he had managed to steal hours earlier. Henri was watching from the stolen boat but watching from the front of the house; he never saw Earl.

Earl was wearing nothing but a t-shirt and pajama bottoms. No socks. No shoes. *I have no way of apprehending that guy. The best I can do is wait him out. When he leaves to go ashore, I'll follow him. Maybe I can alert the police or someone else. I can't let him get away with this!*

And, that's what Earl decided. He followed the arsonist, unobserved, to the Horizon Marina at Alexandria Bay. Earl saw him get in a car by the all-night store and then get out. Evidently, he was getting food or maybe cigarettes.

What to do? There's no one else around. I'm sure if I try to apprehend him, he'll kill me and probably the store clerk. I have no car. I'll gamble. I'll try the trunk of his car ... if it's unlocked and if there's nothing in it, I'll hide there. It's a big gamble, but I don't want that guy to get away.

The car trunk was unlocked. The car trunk was not spacious, but it was empty. Earl became a stowaway. Henri concluded his business in the store. He never saw Earl. After all, this was a gold medal performance.

The gold medal performance was by Earl, not Henri. He was able to survive the 5-hour ride to Sleepy Hollow without detection. However, he did experience several episodes of his Vasovagal Syncope fainting spells on the ride from 1000 Islands. It was understandable. The stress. No anti-VS meds. No food. Nothing to drink. Just darkness. Just cramped space.

Actually, unconscious for part of the trip was a blessing, not a problem.

Henri arrived at Sleepy Hollow and immediately went into the cabin. Earl waited a few minutes, then crawled out of the trunk. He saw the car was parked in front of a rustic cabin on the side of a hill, surrounded by trees, lots of trees. He moved away from the parked car and the cabin's front door around to the side of the cabin and peered into a small front room bedroom. It was unoccupied. He continued down the side of the cabin until he could see into the back room bedroom. There were two men standing by a bed hazing a blindfolded man who was tied down on the bed. Earl heard the blindfolded man yell when one of the men hit him on his leg.

That's Trace! I can't help him now. It has to be later. It's still daylight. I have surprise on my side, but nothing else. I need to wait until dark before I try anything. I can't get in the cabin through those windows; it has to be through a door. I'll wait until it's darker, sneak in the cabin and into Trace's bedroom. I'll untie him; we'll go from there. I feel faint now; I don't want to have a VS here. I'm going to head for those trees in back and stay hidden until it gets darker. I wish I had some shoes; this hard ground is killing me!

At dusk, Earl made his move. From his shelter, he had noticed there was a van parked by the back of the cabin near a cabin rear door. Using the parked van as a shield, he reached the cabin's back door. He opened the door quietly and just watched and listened for 20 long seconds. He saw three men in the den: two asleep, the other was watching TV with his back to the back door. *Now or never!* He entered the cabin on his hands and knees, crept through the kitchen area, and on and into the captive's bedroom. The men in the den didn't stir. The man in the bedroom on the bed did.

"What do you want, now?" the man in the bed asked.

"Shhhhh, quiet! I'm gonna untie you. I'm Earl; I figure you're Trace, right?"

"Yes! I am. You're the answer to my prayers."

"We'll talk about that later. I'm loosening your blindfold a bit, but let's leave it on in case they come in before you're free."

"Okay!"

It was five minutes later when Trace heard Earl spout some profanity. "Damn, Trace", he excitedly whispered. "I can't untie some of these knots!"

"What?"

"I can't untie some of these knots!"

" Look, go back in the kitchen, there must be some knives there."

"Will do. I'll be back shortly."

Earl crept back into the kitchen and began opening drawers to locate some knives. He stayed low, shielded for the most part from the three men up front.

Meanwhile, Rico was tired of watching TV. He said, Henri, wake up!"

"Whatcha want, Rico?"

"We need to tidy up the place!"

"How's that, Rico?"

"We have a loose end that needs takin' care of." He nodded in the direction of Patch, asleep on the den couch. Henri nodded back. He prodded Patch until he woke up.

"Patch, get up! Getup!"

"Oh, Henri what's the matter?"

"Patch, you did a lousy job on that grave. You didn't dig it deep enough! Let's go outside; grab a shovel; you need to finish that job!"

"Oh, Henri."

"Move it, Patch!"

The two men moved to the back door of the cabin, where Earl was in the midst of his hunt for a knife.

Sixty-eight

Earl heard the conversation and saw the two men begin their walk to the back door by way of the kitchen. He was dead, he had to run for it. Then he got a break: The man named Henri stopped, looked back, and said, "Rico! Rico! Now you ain't gonna make that telephone call without me, are you?"

The answer came back, "Henri, I'm making that call in about 40 minutes whether you're here or on Mars."

Henri muttered a few words then resumed his walk to the back door.

His ill-fated companion said, "Henri, there's somebody in the kitchen. I saw him!"

Henri said, "Yeah, I know Patch. I saw him, too. He was standing in a bathtub playing a tuba. Shut up and get goin'."

"Oh, Henri!"

"Shut up! Move!"

They walked through an unoccupied kitchen to exit the back door. Earl had been able to scramble to the walled off washer/dryer utility room adjacent to the kitchen. They could only see him if they looked back into the open utility room as they exited from the cabin. They didn't look back. Rico followed his men into the kitchen, but only to get a beer from the fridge. He returned to the den to watch TV until it was time to make his telephone call.

Earl was shaky. He controlled his nerves long enough to continue his search in the kitchen for a knife. He knew he had to hurry; the two guys who left could come back at any time. The next-to-last drawer had a hunting knife. He grabbed it and carefully, again on all-fours, made his way back to Trace's bedroom without being seen or heard. He reached Trace's bedside and told Trace he had a knife. But then, he passed out. The stress, the lack of meds, and lack of food got him again. He passed out before he was able to start freeing Trace.

It didn't take Henri long to take care of Patch. Poor Patch! He became the first occupant of the grave he fashioned. After Henri did what Rico wanted, he returned from outside to continue the celebration party. First, however, he wanted to check on Trace. He barged into Trace's bedroom to see if all was well. It seemed to be.

Henri said, "Just checking, Imp. Don't want you to miss any of the festivities."

Trace said nothing. He knew Earl had passed out but couldn't see anything. Evidently Henri couldn't see him either. He wanted Henri out of there. Good fortune prevailed; Henri left, closing the door behind him.

Henri went back into the den. "I've tidied up, Rico! Now, ain't it time to call?"

Rico responded, "You worry a lot, Henri. You ain't gonna live long! Sit down and wait 15 minutes. I'm calling our client 25 minutes after I said I would. I want the Florida guys to sweat a little and I also want to give them the impression we're not anxious about anything."

Henri sat down. *But I am anxious. I want to listen in. If Rico's deal goes South, I'm taking charge; Rico will be joining Patch outside.*

After the requisite wait time, the two men went to the front bedroom to make the call.

Nickolas answered the call immediately. "Yes," he growled, "start talking. You guys are late!"

"Deal or no deal?"

"You keep me waiting and you're not going to talk about it?"

"Deal or no deal?"

"You guys know you're through working for me or for anybody I know, don't you?"

"Deal or no deal, Nickolas? I got other things to do."

"The money is in your account."

"200k?"

"200k."

"And another 300k when no Earl shows up tomorrow, right?"

"Yes."

"Okay! Henri says the real Earl is dead; didn't survive the fire he set. I'll take care of the fake Earl; he's still tied up."

"Quit talking! Kill him!"

"Don't worry, I'm enjoying his company. He sends his regrets; he won't be able to attend the meeting tomorrow."

"You make sure of that! I'm betting on that. In fact, I'm betting *your* life on that!"

"Bye, Nickolas! Again, my regards to your partners."

After he hung up, Rico and Henri high-fived, grabbed a half-full bottle of whiskey and began celebrating. Life was good!

Sixty-nine

Rico and Henri were really feeling alcoholically good. It was almost 11 o'clock. They'd been drinking since the telephone call to Nickolas.

"Okay," Rico said. "Let's go! Time to tidy the place up again."

"Yeah." Henri replied. "I've been ready since the phone call. I'd like to get outa here. I've been thinkin' how to spend all that money. I'm going to grab a place on the Caribbean for about 6 months; then, I'll come back up for a time in Las Vegas."

"I'm gonna go to Europe somewhere. Haven't decided where yet, but I'll probably stay a couple of years. Stay in touch because when I return, I'm gonna hire a couple of guys and build up my business again."

"Count me in."

"Sure. Now let's go tidy up!"

Rico and Henri got up from their den chairs and made their way to the rear bedroom where Trace was. They opened the door and stood near the entrance to see their fake Earl on the bed, blindfold off, with one free arm and leg thrashing around to free his other arm and leg.

They both started laughing.

Rico said, "Hey, bro! Did we surprise you? Don't sweat it no further. We'll untie you."

Henri chipped in, "Yeah, Imp. We came to give you some fresh air. Must be tough to stay indoors all day long."

Henri moved forward toward the bed. He took one step, then collapsed, unable to say another word or do another thing. From behind a closet door came an athletic man, hobbled on one leg, who grabbed Henri from behind, put one hand over his victim's mouth while he deftly moved a hunting knife across his throat.

Rico was surprised; he tried to recover. He wasn't quick enough. His attempt to get his gun from his belt failed. Henri's killer threw the knife at him and ended Rico's planned trip to Europe. As Rico collapsed, dying, Trace who had dealt out the punishment said, "Rico, you were so confused. That's the real Earl on the bed; I am the Marine Earl from the closet!"

Earl sat upright on the bed and Trace went over to sit by him. Earl had been untied the whole time. After Earl recovered from his earlier fainting spell, he was able to free Trace. Trace had them switch places to surprise the two hoodlums. It worked.

"Marine Earl, that was great!" the Real Earl said. "But I see your leg is bleeding badly. You okay?'

"It hurts, but I'm okay. Oh, Earl, I might mention this. I watched your thrashing around performance. You better stick with your job at Langston Industries; you are not going to make it as an actor!"

Seventy

The next morning, precisely at 10 o'clock the man at the head table in an Essex Hotel conference room, made this announcement: "Ladies and Gentlemen, I declare that this special scheduled Board of Director's Meeting of Langston Industries is now in session. My name is Dr. Gordon T Brewer, Chief Operating Officer of Langston Industries and Vice-Chairman of this board. Per our bylaws, I am acting as chairman this morning in the absence of our chairman, Earl T Langston, the Chief Executive Officer of Langston Industries. If there are any objections, please state them at this time."

Pause. "There are none. Mr. Secretary, for the record, please identify yourself and introduce the other board members who are present."

"Yes, Mr. Chairman. I am Roland Turlington, Chief Corporate Attorney of Langston Industries and Secretary of this Board.

"Mr. Orin Baker, Chief Financial Officer of Langston Industries.

"Dr. Garland T. Olsen retired co-founder of Langston Industries. We are always happy to see and greet Dr. Olsen."

Dr. Olsen nodded his head in appreciation.

"Mr. Nickolas Fontano, investor.

"Mr. Dario Bruno, investor.

"Mr. Marcellus Bruno, investor.

"Seven of eight members are present, Mr. Chairman. We have a quorum."

Gordon replied, "Thank you, Mr. Secretary. Now there are some guests present. I have two: Mr. Martin Wheeler, Operations Director of Langston Industries. And, Mrs. Martha Langston, member of the Langston family. We're happy to see her; she came all the way from Arkansas to visit with us."

"Thank you, Gordon," she said.

"Mr. Fontano, I believe you have a guest?"

"Yes. This is Dr. Larry Axle. Dr. Axle is a retired FBI officer who worked in their Criminal Investigation Unit."

"We are glad to meet you, Dr. Axle."

Gordon continued, "We are happy to have all our guests. As a reminder, each of you signed a confidentiality agreement regarding our proceedings. We also ask you to not indulge in any conversation unless recognized by the chairman or indirectly through a board member.

"This morning we are meeting to resolve a tender offer made by Kesterson Corporation to acquire all the assets and liabilities of Langston Industries. The offer was made 44 days ago and expires in 17 days. My understanding of our bylaws states that because our Chief Executive Officer is under the age of 30 years old, a majority vote by the Board of Directors can render a binding decision. Those are not the precise words in the bylaws, but I believe that is a correct rendition. Mr. Secretary, your opinion."

"You are correct, Mr. Chairman."

"Thank you. Each of you received relevant details of Kesterson's proposal over 30 days ago. I assume you have reviewed it and are ready to vote. However, this is a momentous decision in the life of our company. We should not take our vote lightly. I think it appropriate that each board member should express his opinion for the record before we vote. I propose each person be limited to 10 minutes."

Marcellus said, "We're wasting time, Gordon. Let's vote and get it over with."

"Then you're proposing we vote on a matter this significant to the company and its employees without any further discussion. I suggest we might be subject to lawsuits."

Roland said, "I think discussion is needed and appropriate before we vote."

Nickolas said, "Okay! Okay! I'm ready to vote, but a little more time won't make any difference. I don't need 10 minutes. Some of you other guys don't need it either. But I'm okay with 10."

Gordon said, "Everybody else okay with 10?"

Heads nodded, nothing was said, the 10-minute limit was consensually accepted.

Orin, the CFO, was first. He used all of his time providing numbers showing the offer seemed too low. He said he was not against a buyout per se, but this offer was unacceptable.

Roland, the attorney, used all of his time stating the absence of the founders, particularly Dr. Langston, placed the company in jeopardy as far as attaining meaningful growth. He thought the offer was reasonable.

Garland, the retired co-founder, thought the company's current management were carrying on admirably after Michael's untimely death. He didn't like the raider corporation making the offer. He was opposed to any buyout offers unless Langston's core businesses and employees were well taken care of.

Nickolas used only half the allocated time. He felt the company was a good investment when Michael began the company and as he continued to grow the company. He thought Earl didn't have the capability to run a lemonade stand. He wanted out and the offer was reasonable; in fact, he thought in a year his investment would be worth 20% less than the offer by Kesterson.

Marcellus and Dario took even less time than Nickolas; they were ready to sell.

Gordon was the last board member to share his opinion. As he ended his opinion, which was to reject the buyout offer, there was a knock on the conference door. Before anyone could answer, a small man wearing the attire of a hotel manager, entered the room and said, "I'm Maximilian Keiner, one of the hotel security managers. I'm sorry to interrupt your meeting. There's no reason to panic, but I do need you to leave the premises until we check out a bomb threat made to this floor and the floor above it. Please follow me. Again, do not panic. There is no immediate danger; just follow me to our service elevator."

Seventy-one

There were about twenty or twenty-five people outside the back of the Essex gathered in a parking area who were already serving time outside the hotel because of the alleged bomb threat. All of them were out there another 45 minutes before Mr. Keiner made an all-clear announcement and led the board members and their guests back to their conference room.

They were not the first ones in the conference room; Earl was there! He greeted each one of them as they returned. The Florida guys were not pleased; they had a difficult time holding back their anger.

Gordon gave up his place at the head of the conference table for Earl. After all were seated, Earl said, "For the record, Mr. Secretary. Let's state that this BOD meeting was interrupted almost an hour by an alleged bomb threat. We have reconvened and I have joined the BOD in its deliberations. I am Earl T Langston, the Chief Executive Officer of Langston Industries and Chairman of this board. I apologize for my late arrival; I was unavoidably detained. As you know these proceedings are recorded. While you were out, I had the time and opportunity to see and hear all of the board members' prior discussions. What the board members said about the proposed tender offer just reinforced my views. I am opposed to the tender offer and, as Chief Executive Officer of Langston Industries, I totally reject that offer and reject any further negotiations with Kesterson. I ask for the board's support of my decision. Mr. Secretary, I call for the vote."

The vote was anti-climactic. With the benefit of Earl's extra vote, the tender offer was rejected, 5 to 4. The three Florida investors and Roland, the attorney, were the minority losers.

Earl regained the gavel. He spoke. "A decision has been reached. We have formally rejected Kesterson's offer. Roland, please inform Kesterson and the media of our decision. Now, for those of you who are not an employee of the company and who are not supporting this decision. I would like your resignation from the board immediately. A company so united and profitable as we are cannot long exist if our outside directors are not working as a united team. You wanted a buyout. I suppose you wanted to cash in your otherwise unmarketable shares. Our company will buy all your shares at Kesterson's tender offer less 10%. I think this offer is fair. Mr. Fontano said if we rejected the tender offer, Langston shares would be worth 20% lower in a year. So, our offer to you, Mr. Nickolas Fontano, and to you, Mr. Dario Bruno, and to you, Mr. Marcellus Bruno, is all of your shares for Kesterson's tender offer less 10%. This offer will be reduced by another 10% every 30 days. Orin, would you take care of this, please?"

Orin, the CFO, nodded his head and replied, "Yes, sir."

"Roland, I would like to discuss your future with the company as well. My dad had faith in you, and you have always been a loyal employee. We can do this outside the confines of the board."

Roland replied, "Yes, sir. I'd like to do that."

Earl, then looked directly at Nickolas. "Now I wish to add my personal note before we close this meeting.

"Mr. Fontano, I cannot let the charge you made against me go unanswered. You said I did not have the capabilities to run a lemonade stand. Sir, you are mistaken. I ran a profitable lemonade stand for three years after I was nine years old. My dad never gave me an allowance; he did, however, match my earnings from my lemonade stand, and later my paper route and lawn care business."

Earl picked up the gavel, but before he said anything, Nickolas stood up, pointed his finger at Earl, and said, "Not so fast!"

"Sonny," Nickolas continued, still staring at Earl, "You and your buddies here can make all the edicts you want, but we're not resigning or nothing. You have opened the way for a gigantic lawsuit. We can tie up this company and its miserable management for years."

He looked around at each of the surprised board members, and continued, "The man who's been leading the show here is not Earl Langston. I don't know who he is. He is an impostor. I don't care who he is, but's he's not Earl and he's not the legitimate chair of this board."

Gordon spoke up, "What in the world are you talking about, Nickolas?"

"Yeah, Gordon, so pious, so innocent! You know all about it. You brought in some turkey to be Earl, so you'd get your way in this meeting."

"I agree!" said Marcellus. Dario nodded his head in assent.

Earl said, "Mr. Fontano, you're making some serious charges. I suggest you prove them immediately."

"I intend to. Dr. Axle, my guest today, is an expert fingerprint specialist. Before he retired, he worked many years for the FBI as a specialist. As all of you are aware, each of us had to be fingerprinted before we were appointed board members. That data is among other records that are available to all board members. I have provided Dr. Axle with a copy of Earl's fingerprints. Let's take some fingerprints of our purported chairman and prove who he isn't."

A concerned Dr. Olsen shook his head, and said, "Nickolas, I don't like this. I don't like what's going on. This young man is Earl. I've known Earl before his ... before his lemonade stands. You are greatly mistaken. I want you to stop this sham. It's not becoming to you or our board."

"Be quiet, old man. When did you start believing assumptions over facts? I say let's do the fingerprinting and see."

Earl then made an offer, "Mr. Fontano, I will go through with the fingerprinting, but if you are wrong, you and the Bruno brothers will agree to resign from the board immediately and agree to sell all your shares at the price offered earlier. In addition to your resignations, you will sign a confidentiality agreement, under penalty of a fine and the law, maintaining total silence on what has transpired today."

"You got it, buster!"

"Roland, you heard the deal, take care of the legalities, please."

"Yes, sir, I will."

The ones standing sat down. There was little talk during the fingerprinting, and even less while Dr. Axle was making the comparisons between the fresh prints of today and the printed records from the board. After a short time, he nodded his head to Earl. "I am ready to report, sir."

Earl used the gavel to get attention. "Dr. Axle, please report your findings, sir."

Dr. Axle rose to his feet and succinctly said, "I have compared the fingerprints between the record of Earl Langston's file and the fingerprints of the person claiming to be Earl Langston today. I can say with over 99% certainty the man is, who he says he is. Earl Langston."

Silence reigned in the board room.

Earl used the gavel again and said, "This meeting is adjourned."

Seventy-two

It was difficult to restrain the levity that reigned over what amounted to the final get-together of all the principals involved in the deception Gordon had undertaken and directed. After a splendid dinner, Gordon rose and became the master of ceremonies:

He said, "It is against my nature to be deceitful. I apologize for what we did, but not for the result. I thought the future of Langston Industries was at stake. It looked grim to me. We began something I thought had little chance of succeeding but it did succeed by the man of the hour, an actor named Trace Reinhardt. An actor so good, that a number of attempts were made on his life because his assassins believed he was someone else. Yet, he will never be acknowledged or accredited by the people in his industry. He will have to accept our immense gratitude for a job more than well done. Trace, we missed you at the Board today. Do you have an explanation?"

"Yes. When Earl and I talked to you from Sleepy Hollow last night and told you what went on, you told me to go to ER and have my leg looked after and for Earl to go to the Board meeting. So, that's where I've been. Earl saved my life in Sleepy Hollow, and I owe him an impossible debt of gratitude. I think you've all been told of his and my situations over the last couple of days. I thank you, Gordon and Martin, for being my partners and go-to guys in times of stress. I will miss being the CEO of this company. I will miss all of you, but mostly I will miss the perks. Oh, incidentally but most importantly, I would like to introduce my fiancée, Melody Jones, most recently known as Dawn Young. I'm not going to miss her; I'm taking her with me."

Gordon replied. "Yes, Martin and I helped orchestrate what went on at the Board. We were the only ones who knew that Earl would be coming to the meeting late; we wanted others to say what they wanted to say in Earl's absence. More deceit, I suppose."

Trace had a question for Earl. "You fainted in the room while I was captive. I was blindfolded and couldn't see, but I knew one of my captors looked in the room at that time. How'd he miss seeing you?"

"I was, we were, very fortunate. I fainted between the bed and exterior cabin wall. The bed must have obscured his view. Can you spell 'lucky'?"

"Are those fainting spells permanent?"

"No. The doctor told me they would diminish over time. I am to exercise and stay on the meds. I'm counting on Gordon and Martin to reduce my stress."

"You might look elsewhere," Trace laughingly said.

Everyone laughed.

Trace continued, "One more question, Gordon."

"Shoot."

"How did my kidnapper know about the transmitter? He sure did a lousy job removing it, so the ER guys told me."

"I'm not completely sure, but we think that information got passed to your assailants from an informant in our Utah office. We had added some temps to our kitchen staff when we first took you to Utah. We caught one of them, a ski bum, red-handed in your office rummaging through the desk looking through your files. He must have seen some of the paperwork about Dr. Janssen's surgery. He evidently read it but missed the fact that the surgery was for a change in appearance rather than corrective for the auto accident. So, he knew about the transmitter, but not that you were not Earl, and that Earl was in 1000 Islands. We are also pretty sure he was passing on information as to your whereabouts, like your snowmobile excursion and where you were in Europe. We caught him when our staff was gathering material for Earl that he had requested in 1000 Islands. The Utah police have all we know about him but it's unlikely they will be able to prosecute him. Oh, I guess I should mention we fired him."

Then, in turn, each one of them addressed the group telling them what they intended to do in the days ahead:

Earl, after telling them how he had turned his life around, planned to be the real CEO of Langston under Gordon's guidance and tutelage.

Gordon, at his own request, said he would stay with Langston another two years, then retire to Austria. He was pleased that Earl had made such a big turnabout and had no qualms about Earl's capability to run the company.

Martin said he would stay with Langston Industries until Gordon retired, then he would join Gordon in Austria in the hope Gordon would start a business there so he would have something to do.

Dawn said she was overwhelmed and even scared sometimes with her role at times, but Gordon and Martin helped pull her through. She and Trace hope to get married as soon as they can. "Then it's honeymoon time ... and we're not saying where!"

Grandma said. "I will be in Arkansas. It's way too much excitement here in New York City for an old lady, even with friends. Everybody is sure welcome to come and visit me when they can."

After everyone finished speaking, Gordon stood up and rapped on the table to get everyone's attention. "The waiters will be coming forward to fill your wine glass with champagne. When they are finished, I will make a toast."

He paused until the waiters completed their task; then, he lifted his glass and said, "Here's to our impostor who followed and fulfilled the directive of his mission, ***'Deception without Detection'***."

After all of them had subscribed to Gordon's toast, it was Trace who stood up and spoke next. "Let the waiters come forth again," he said. After the glasses were refilled, Trace lifted his glass and said, "Here's to the watchwords of the mission that were so important to the impostor: ***'Be calm, be cordial, and above all, be careful'***."

After the toasts, the get-together was about to break up; when suddenly the door to their private dining room opened, and a small young man entered and stood before them. He was casually dressed, all the way down to his white tennis shoes.

"Excuse the interruption," he said, " but I wish to apologize to those of you who were in the board room today. My name is Everett Emerson, not Maximilian Keiner as I introduced myself in that meeting. I do not work for the hotel. I am a student at the NYC Film Academy. I was the winner in my class of actors who wanted to portray a hotel manager. You saw and mingled with my actor classmates while you were outside during the alleged bomb threat. I should have introduced my classmates to you. Sorry for the interruption this morning and for this one as well. You may blame Mr. Martin Wheeler for both interruptions."

Martin nodded his head and lifted his wine glass to acknowledge his accountability.

The actor-in-training continued. "Incidentally, in German the name Maximilian means the best of the best and the name Keiner means nobody. I truly can say hotel manager Maximillian Keiner is the best of nobody.

"Before I leave, Mr. Wheeler asked me to present this gift to Mr. Trace Reinhardt as a token of appreciation. He said, 'Wear it proudly!'"

The gift was a brightly colored t-shirt with the phrase "I'M NOT EARL" in big letters emblazoned on front and back.

Everett bowed, Martin nodded his head again in acknowledgement, and Everett left to applause and laughter.

Grandma shook her head and said, "Oh, no, oh no! Not another actor!"

Seventy-three

A week after the disastrous Board of Directors meeting, the FSC members were back in Florida angrily licking their wounds, their self-inflicted wounds, in their lair, the Indian River Ranch.

Nickolas said, "Well, the howdy-doody boys haven't changed the locks on this lodge yet. So, let's enjoy it while we can."

"I'm not enjoying anything now," said Dario. "Gordon and his boy Earl gave it to us. We had no answer, but I'm not going to forget. That's for sure!"

"Me neither," said Marcellus. "We got a public whipping. We need to retaliate ... and, do it soon and in a big way."

"I agree," said Nickolas. "I say bring in the Bangor Brothers. Forget accidental stuff. Give them free reign over their specialty. Accidental don't work."

Dario said, "We wasted a lot of time without any results except to expose ourselves. We can't take legal action; we probably would get criminal actions filed against us. Let's hire the brothers and get on with it."

"How about this?" Marcellus said. "Kill the imposter, Gordon, and Martin. Cripple Earl for life."

"Sounds right to me!" exclaimed Dario.

"Yeah," said Nickolas. He picked up the small blue jar off the coffee table and threw it against the fireplace where it broke into more than 10 blue pieces. "And, we don't need any more bean verdicts. That's over and done with. Let's get a drink and then call the Bangors."

The other two men nodded their agreement as all of them headed to the liquor cabinet.

As Dario walked by the fireplace he said, "Do you guys smell something funny?"

Marcellus asked, "It's not gas, is it?"

Nickolas said, "Well, maybe ..."

His last interrupted sentence was completely drowned out by the sound of the explosion that completely leveled the lodge.

An observer, a lone man, standing more than 50 yards away, turned away from his view of the explosion and began slowly walking away, talking to himself. *Jane, Jane, my lovely daughter, Jane. That's for you. How I miss you. Yes, it's all for you, sweetheart. I'm going home now. My business in Florida took a lot less time than I expected.*

***

Postscript

The Imperiled Impostor is a story that features characters who are doppelgangers. Doppelgangers are people who look-alike but are not biologically related. So, the look-alike twin brothers in Alexander Dumas' *The Man in the Iron Mask* are not doppelgangers. Neither are the two men (distant relatives) in Anthony Hopkins' *The Prisoner of Zenda.* There are not very many books and films featuring look-alike characters who are doppelgangers; however, there are a few. Some well-known literary characters who qualify as true doppelgangers are in the pages of Charles Dickens' *A Tale of Two Cities* and Mark Twain's *The Prince and the Pauper.*

Now, consider this question: Is there someone out there in this world of over 7.4 billion people who would qualify you as being a look-alike ... a doppelganger? Thinking you might be a doppelganger might be a little disconcerting to you, but for some of your family and friends it might be downright scary.

The doppelganger in my story becomes an impostor hired to deceive others deliberately and expertly. That raises a question from a Machiavellian treatise: "*Does the end justify the means?*". In my story, does deceit and deception justify the final "good" result?

Most impostors are not doppelgangers, nor do they portray someone else; they just misrepresent themselves with fake credentials, wealth, etc. For instance, Ferdinand Demara assumed many identities until he got caught. This serial impostor was named *The Great Impostor* by the story and movie of the same name. (The movie lead was played by Tony Curtis.)

Many impostors are just characters played for entertainment. Impostors in operas are not uncommon. For instance, in Gioacchino Rossini's *La Cenerentola:* Alidoro, the prince's advisor poses as a beggar, the prince subs as his own valet and Cinderella's makeover fools everyone (even some of the stagehands). *Evidently everyone else in the opera is too busy singing to notice!*

However, the largest group of deceivers are not impostors; they are the impersonators: people who make their living legally by expertly imitating or acting like others. There are body doubles in movies and there are political decoys ... Soviet Union's Joseph Stalin had a double as did Great Britain's Field Marshal Bernard Montgomery in World War II.

Most impersonators are entertainers. Comedian Tina Fey does a good job looking and talking like Sarah Palin, the Alaskan politician. There are also some entertainers who did multiple impersonations like Rich Little and Phil Hartman. And, we can't leave out Elvis Pressley's vast throng of impersonators. Several internet sites claim there were 170 Elvis impersonators in 1970. One site estimated there were 35,000 in 2019 and there will be 69,500 in 2060. Contrast those conservative estimates with Guinness World Records estimate of 250,000 to 400,000 ETAs (Elvis Tribute Artists) back in year 2010. Yikes! Earthshaking numbers! ... What if all those Elvis impersonators were to gyrate at the same time?

Now let me be personal about being a doppelganger. Surely no one looks like me ... and in that remotest of possibilities that a person might just resemble me ... the stark question would surely be: who would admit it? Consider this poem from *Death Mask* by Edward Reed:

In the mirror now, what I see
reminds me I won't be here forever.
I don't feel like that face at all
Inside it, I protest ... I'm quite different.
It's somebody's grandfather, not me.
Whose grandfather is that? I don't want him.

Finally, I note that April 20 is National Look-Alike Day. It's a day one can celebrate looking like someone else ... hmm?

Mirror, mirror, on the wall ...
Surely no one looks like me at all!

It is what it is; go celebrate. For me, I am secure in the knowledge no one could possibly look like me, so I will just continue to remember and honor April 20 as my mother's birthday.

About the Author

Charles Lake, a native Texan, was a data processing system analyst at Texas Instruments before he retired. He is a 1952 graduate of Texas A&M University with a bachelor's degree in Statistics. After graduation he served as a communication officer in the Army Security Agency on Okinawa during the Korean War.

He and his wife, Joyce, have been happily married for 67 years with four children, eight grandchildren and one great-grandchild. He and Joyce stay busy with activities related to their family, friends, church ministries, and travel. For over 17 years, they have been volunteer workers in *International Friends*, a ministry of First Baptist Church Richardson that teaches English as a Second Language to international adults. At one time they played competitive duplicate bridge attaining the rank of *Silver Life Master*, but several years ago they retired from this pastime. He and Joyce have made their home in Richardson, Texas since 1960.

This is the fourth book Charles has authored and published. His first book, *Grabbing Operas by Their Tales,* flippantly retells the plots of 15 of some of the world's most popular and best-known operas. It is written in the style of Dr. Richard Armour's books, a favorite author of Charles'. His second and third books, *The Mortician and Other Short Stories* and *The Seances and Other Short Stories* are anthologies of short stories. Most of the stories in all of his books originated during summer months in Colorado where Joyce and Charles vacationed for two months each year over an 18-year period. For his family and friends, he has compiled four anthologies: two of favorite poems, one of favorite and familiar Bible verses and one of humorous anecdotes.

Enjoying one of those nice summer days in Colorado.

Charles Lake

cel52@sbcglobal.net

Acknowledgements

I wish to thank my great and creative friend, Jim Hamner. Jim was a source of inspiration on my "Opera" book. Then, he started me on my short story writing journey, and he guided and encouraged me along the way. He was very helpful in the development of this novel and, in particular, the book cover. Jim is an accomplished and talented musician who is active as a church organist, pianist, and performer in the Dallas Metroplex. A number of his entertaining videos are on *YouTube*.

When our country began its unprecedented Covid lockdown in March 2020, Jim began to livestream 30 minutes of his piano music and entertainment twice a week entitled *My Quarantune Happy Hour.* He has continued this entertainment since March 2020; he currently has 329 recorded half hour programs with over 44,600 *Facebook* views ... and counting!

When I read Frances Willis Shaw's poem, *Who Loves the Rain*, I think of my friend Jim:

Who loves the rain,
And loves his home,
And looks on life with quiet eyes,
Him will I follow through the storm;
And at his hearth-fire keep me warm;
Nor hell nor heaven shall that soul surprise,
Who loves the rain,
And loves his home,
And looks on life with quiet eyes.
Frances Willis Shaw

I appreciate my son Paul's help very much. He helped me with file storage, data transmission, and the picture image pages appearing in the interior pages of this book. Thank you, Paul.

My wife Joyce and friend Jim did a great job of proof-reading and editing the manuscript. Both of them also provided me with their thoughts about improving the story itself. Thank you, Joyce and Jim.

I would be negligent if I did not mention the staff of BookLocker who helped me greatly in the many activities it takes to produce a finished book from an author's manuscript. Thank you, BookLocker.

Prior Books

Sound and Vision

authorhouse

BookLocker

Printed in the USA
CPSIA information can be obtained
at www.ICGtesting.com
LVHW040105300723
753822LV00037B/409

9 781958 890004